The
Witch's
Grave

By Phillip DePoy

The Witch's Grave

PHILLIP DEPOY

ST. MARTIN'S MINOTAUR NEW YORK

www.minotaurbooks.com

Library of Congress Cataloging-in-Publication Data

DePoy, Phillip.
   The witch's grave : a Fever Devilin mystery / by Philip
DePoy—1st ed.
      p. cm.
   ISBN 0-312-31537-6
      1. Folklorists—Fiction. 2. Appalachian Region, Southern—
Fiction. 3. Mountain life—Fiction. 4. Georgia—Fiction. I. Title.

PS3554.E624W58 2004
813'.6–dc22
                                                    2003058569

First Edition: February 2004

10 9 8 7 6 5 4 3 2 1

The Witch's Grave is dedicated,
with true thanks,
to these thirteen (a witch's coven):

Keith Kahla for poodle images
Maria Carvainis for garden talk
Frances Kuffel for a walk in Little Italy
Jennifer Weltz for keeping on;

The Edgar committee: Cara Blackó, Nageeba Davis, Dirk Wyle,
Laura Joh Rowland, and John Westermann
for letting *Easy* have the statue;

Lee Nowell for constantly bewitching everything a go go
and twice on Sundays;

Bob and Barbara DePoy for candy corn;

and Monica Starr, the April witch, wherever she may be.

Acknowledgments

Acknowledgment must be made to
the Georgia Council for the Arts,
the Georgia Folklife Program,
and
the Mary Roberts Reinhart Foundation
for grants over the years
that enabled research in the mountains,
the fruits of which are a part of
The Witch's Grave.

Those departed, gone before, sleep in peace, return no more. Some poor souls that peace ignore. The witch's grave is an open door.

—Folk, anonymous

The Witch's Grave

One

No one expected violence at church, or the dead bodies that soon followed it. Services at Blue Mountain Methodist were among the more sedate in our county. No snakes, no rolling, no wild tearful confessionals, only a covered dish dinner the envy of angels. Panfried corn was my favorite. I knew Mrs. Nichols had taken the barbecue grill into her corn patch, started a hickory fire. She always bent the stalks over until the ears were touching the grill, snapped them off, let them roast for twenty minutes before peeling back the husks. Then she cut off the kernels with a butcher knife into a pan on top of the grill, milked the cob within an inch of its life, added sugar water and cumin. The corn was fried until it had absorbed all the water, covered, and left in the field to rest. The result is why God invented corn.

"Andrews," I said between mouthfuls, "you've got to taste this."

He'd made progress of his own: fried chicken livers all but gone, boiled squash disappearing. With Lucinda gone for the week, it had seemed the perfect time for a visit from my favorite Shakespeare scholar. Pale and blond, he stuck out everywhere he went, though as much because of his odd demeanor as his accent. His friendship had grown to mean more since I'd left Burrison University, though he was my closest colleague when I ran the folklore department there. This was his second visit to Blue Mountain, meant to be a peaceful stay in the hills of Habersham.

"I can't say much for the content of the service," he muttered for my ears alone, "but if this is Christian food, sign me up."

Though raised Church of England in Manchester, Dr. Andrews fancied himself a druid. Still, his assessment of the Methodist worship was accurate. Compared to my friend Hezekiah Cotage's lye-drinking Pentecostal performance—the only other religious ritual he'd attended with me in the mountains—the meeting we'd just seen was designed more to cure insomnia than sin.

Regular Wednesday night prayer meeting had been changed to Thursday night in order to dedicate a brand-new addition to the church. I knew about the covered dish dinner and I thought Andrews would enjoy it. The crisp hall in the church basement was too well lit, linoleum floor too shiny, freshly painted cinder block walls bouncing sound everywhere like a bowling ball. Cheap acoustical ceiling tiles were milky, windowless walls bare. The people decorated the place. Though weeknight meetings were more casual than Sunday mornings, most men wore ties; nearly every woman was in a dress. Andrews alone sported a Hawaiian shirt, and I had refused to wear a tie since leaving the university.

I could see Mrs. Nichols, across the room, waving and winking. She knew my weakness for her signature dish, wanted to make certain I acknowledged it. Satisfied with my facial display of ecstasy, she returned to her conversation cornering Pastor Davis.

"What's in the squash?" Andrews asked me, poking it around his plate with a fork. "Onions, I can see that, but what's the sweet? It's like dessert."

"Not *onions*," I began disdainfully. "The Vidalia onion contains more sugar than a Red Delicious apple or a half a cup of honey."

Further lecture on the subject was cut short by an explosion of angry voices from the hallway.

"I don't care if he is your cousin; what he's done is unbelievable!"

"Able," the woman's voice answered softer, "this ain't the place."

"Place! What'd I care where we are? I have a sworn duty."

"You have a pig head is what you have."

"Well, I guess you'd know about that," Able shot back. "You've got four or five lying around your kitchen."

"You leave my brother's work out of it!" Her voice rose.

"You call that work? Stealing hogs?"

The meeting hall had gone silent. Some busied themselves eating or clearing away their covered dish, but most gaped at the closed door hoping to hear more.

"They don't steal," she said, teeth obviously clenched. "They catch wild swine, and it's hard to do."

"We're getting off the track. I'm telling you, my investigation is nearly done, and it don't look good. I swear if he was here at church tonight, I'd ask him about it to his face."

"Investigation." She forced out a laugh. "That ain't your job and you know it."

"Sugar." Able's voice turned softer. "Don't we have enough to worry about with the way folks talk about *you?*"

"That's it." Her voice was muffled; she'd turned away and was leaving.

"Damn it, Truevine!" Able roared.

Footsteps clattered.

"You get away from me, Able!"

"Stand still and listen."

"Take your hands off me."

"Run away, then. I won't chase after you this time!"

A door slammed and the hallway was silent.

"See," Andrews said immediately. "Why can't there be more of that sort of thing in the services here? I'd come every week."

Several around us grinned; the hall slowly returned to a semblance of its former character. Dishes were packed; people began to leave.

"Do you know who they were?" Andrews said, setting down his clean plate on one of the tables nearby.

"The man was Able Carter, Girlinda's brother." I helped myself to the last of Mrs. Nichols's corn. "The woman was Truevine Deveroe, the boys' sister."

"That's right," he remembered. "They had a sister."

Andrews knew about the wild brothers from his previous visit to the mountains, but he was better acquainted with Girlinda, Skidmore

Needle's sturdy wife. He'd visited her in the hospital when she'd been shot, eaten at her red aluminum kitchen table, flirted shamelessly with her seven-year-old daughter.

But he didn't know Truevine or Able.

"Able is the county coroner." I filled my fork. "And Truevine is our local witch."

Andrews glared.

"Seriously." I set my plate down beside his. "She has all the qualities."

"There are qualities?"

"In the twenty-first century," I began, "there is no true folklore left in Appalachia, if our definition remains what it was in the twentieth: anything passed through time and space orally or by direct observation. This owing to the fact that there is no corner of the mountains now untouched by media. This renders all untainted 'true folk' phenomena extinct. Remnants of folk phenomenology linger. Any strange sight after midnight could still be evidence of 'revenants,' kin returned from the grave. Any shy girl with an unusual appearance and a solitary habit may still be called a witch."

Truevine Deveroe was a twenty-three-year-old orphan, raven-haired and dark-eyed, a Pre-Raphaelite madonna in oversize dresses and heavy work boots. Her family lived high up on the dark side of Blue Mountain, in a part of the woods even bats and wild swine avoided. Electricity came late to them, and running water was unimportant. Truevine had discovered two deep wells on their property the old-fashioned way. She found a Y-shaped birch branch, held the two ends, and let the third end lead her to water. She closed her eyes, felt the tug on her *dousing* agent, the simple wooden instrument she'd made, and walked in a trance directly to the site of their first well.

She opened her eyes. "There," she told her three older brothers, and they dug.

She'd also been accused, as I'd heard it, of milking her neighbor's cows by rags.

It's an easy process. Tear an old dress, visit the cows under a full moon, rub their udders with the rags, spit on the cows, say a secret phrase if you like, and go home. The next day you may hang the rags on your clothesline, pull on them, and milk will flow into your pail. The neighbor will be surprised his cows give only viscous saliva with a faint odor of tobacco, which farmers may interpret as a certain sign of witchery. Never mind that the same effect is produced when cows are fed a solitary diet of corn husks, a malady easily cured by any veterinarian.

All she needed was two or three rumors and a shy heart. It didn't take Truevine long to become the witch of Blue Mountain. She and Able made a pair walking down our streets. She took long strides and stood half a head taller; he walked faster, never looking up, shirttail always untucked, hair disheveled, a loosened tie around his neck. They were Gomez and Morticia Addams in small-town garb, a golden glow in their eyes that only appeared when they were together.

"People don't believe it," Andrews said, wiping his hands on the front of his shirt, "that she's actually a witch."

"Not for the most part," I answered, "but it's amusing to talk about."

"Unless you're that girl," he said, looking toward the empty hallway.

At the end of the Thursday night meeting, climbing into my ancient pickup truck at the church, we were stopped by Girlinda Needle. She was toting a huge casserole dish, emptied of its broccoli soufflé. Wearing a flowered print knee-length dress, she looked more zaftig than usual. Her hair was in a bun, but loose strands were everywhere behind her head, like distracting children vying for attention.

She had been married for nearly ten years to my best friend, the town deputy, Skidmore. They were more like relatives to me than my own family ever was. Her face, always flushed, radiated a distress that was rare to her features; unused muscles pulled her mouth in a frown.

"Hey, sweetie," she said, patting my hip, "where's Lucinda at? You better think about marrying that girl one of these days."

"She's out of town," I answered, noting the distraction in Girlinda's eyes. "Be back next week."

Under ordinary circumstances she would not have let the matter drop, continuing to grill me about my feelings for Lucinda as I grew increasingly uncomfortable. That night, something else was on her mind.

"Dev," she managed through tight lips, all her weight on one leg, leaning closer to my ear, "you got to look out for Able. He's been in a stew these past few months, and I think he's got into some kind of trouble."

"You don't mean this argument tonight with Ms. Deveroe."

"Shoot, no," she laughed. "They fight like that all the time." A wink in Andrews's direction. "Young love. Everything's hot."

He looked down.

"I'll admit when they first got together," she digressed, "I wasn't wild about the idea. She's a strange one, and Able's a mess. But they been dating a good while now, and I've come to see she's just what she is: sweet girl, shy—loves my brother, so she's all right by me."

"Something else, then?" I asked her.

"That's right." She got back on track. "Something to do with his work and he won't talk to Skid about it, says he ain't sure yet."

"About what?" Andrews said.

"Won't say," she whispered, glancing up at the bright moon. "But it must be awful. Concerns a great many hereabouts, he said. It sure give me the shakes, what with him being county coroner and all."

"I thought that was like an administrative thing," Andrews said, leaning on the car. "Coroner."

"He is a judicial officer," I agreed, "but responsible for investigating any suspicious circumstances surrounding death in general. Originally a twelfth-century office, it existed primarily to maintain records and, I believe, take custody of royal property."

"Dev," he complained.

"Currently coroners determine the cause of death or, if there's any doubt, hold an inquest."

"Inquest?" Andrews muttered before he could stop himself.

Girlinda shook her head. "Why'd you ask?"

"An inquest," I continued, "is a process to discover the cause of any sudden or violent death. Witnesses are called, but suspects are not permitted to make a defense. It's not a trial. Possible inquest findings include natural death, accidental death, suicide, murder—"

"Can I go home with you?" Andrews begged Girlinda.

"I ain't the one who started him up. You'uns put something in the shoe bin?" She waved in the direction of the church's collection for the needy, then began her way across the crowded parking lot toward her battered blue truck. "Anyway, you'll keep an eye out!" she called over her shoulder.

I assured her with a nod.

"What's she worried about?" Andrews turned to me.

"I don't know, but she has a sense about these things."

"Shoe bin?" He turned in the direction she'd pointed.

"Were you asleep during the sermon?" I whispered, failing in my attempt not to make fun of the title, " 'I cried because I had no shoes until I met a man who had no feet'?"

"My mind did wander," he admitted. "That's what's in the chicken wire bin over there?"

"All new footwear," I confirmed. "You need glasses."

Above our heads bare limbs, silhouetted against a huge moon, were ink spilled across yellow parchment. We listened to the percussion as wind blew across the roof of the church and upward toward the night.

Cars pulled out of the lot and farewells receded into the darkness. I watched the empty hall.

"What are you staring at?" Andrews sidled up to me, following my stare. "Did you see something?"

"I thought so. Probably not."

"Trick of the moon." He headed for the passenger side of my pickup. "The way the shadows move in this wind."

I fished in my jacket pocket for the keys. "I guess so."

A charcoal cloud covered the moon; wind wheezed like an organ bellows. We heard faint laughter. It was impossible to tell where it came from. Down the road some of the parishioners were walking home, but deeper in the woods, where shadows collected waiting to cover everything, something stirred up the leaves like the sound of running feet.

Girlinda called me the next evening.

"Dev," she said, the clamor of her brood in the background, "you heard?"

Andrews and I had spent a gloriously worthless day sleeping late, eschewing the shaving razor, cooking, talking about going fishing, napping, watching a Poe film festival on the old movie channel. He was on vacation, after all, and what sort of a host would I have been if I hadn't joined him in his sloth? We hadn't been out of the house.

"I haven't heard anything."

"Truevine didn't come home last night."

I sat up and motioned for Andrews to mute the television.

"Go on."

"It's the first night in her life she hadn't been in bed by ten," Girlinda said, her voice unusually high-pitched. "Her brothers were worried at five after, started drinking by ten-thirty. When midnight came, they loaded their rifles and went looking."

"How do you know that?"

"Just listen," she insisted. "All Thursday night and into the wee hours of this morning them liquored-up Deveroe boys scoured the mountain between the church and their house. When the sun come up and they still hadn't found her, they did something they generally try to avoid. They come to our house."

"I see."

"Two stood in the yard and one kicked at the front door. He was so drunk he didn't realize he had to set down his rifle to knock. Woke us up. Skidmore went to the door with pistol in hand."

"The boys are generally harmless," I ventured.

"You didn't see them boys, Dev," she whispered. "They were armed and agitated. They said Truvy was gone and wanted Skid's help."

"Did he go with them?"

"He pointed out that all three of them had been looking for her and she might be back at home."

"So he got dressed and drove them back up to their house," I guessed.

"Uh-huh," Girlinda went on, "but Truvy was gone. I wouldn't call you about it except that this afternoon the Deveroes apparently heard the story about Truvy's argument with Able at church last night."

"Now I understand," I told her, sitting back. "Able's missing, too; is that right?"

"The first place Skidmore checked after he found Truevine's empty bed was Able's house in town. Nobody had slept there; Able didn't show up at work this morning. They're both gone."

I could see in my mind's eye each Deveroe brother coming to a different conclusion: (1) she had run off and gotten married; (2) Able had kidnapped her; (3) Able had murdered her in anger and disappeared. Their solution, however, was unanimous. Able Carter was to die.

"The Deveroe brothers are out for blood now," she said, confirming my supposition.

"What do you want me to do?"

"Find Able, honey. And Truevine, of course." She lowered her voice to a whisper again. "I can't have nobody shooting up my kin, Fever."

"I'll do what I can, Linda, but isn't this really a job for your husband?"

"You help him." That was all.

I knew from experience that I could spend hours trying to draw out more facts from her. I took a simpler tack.

"All right," I promised.

"And come over to dinner tomorrow night," she said, her voice returning to normal. "Bring Andrews." She hung up.

I looked over at Andrews. He was staring at the television trying to read Peter Cushing's all-too-thin lips.

"That was Girlinda. We're invited to dinner tomorrow." I picked up the remote and the sound of the movie resumed. "Able and the Deveroe girl are missing. We have to find them."

"So Linda's premonition was on," he said lazily, still glued to the screen.

"I hadn't thought about that," I admitted.

"Maybe they're holed up somewhere apologizing to each other the way I hear some young people do." His eyes drifted my way. "I mean, witchy sex has got to be difficult to pass up."

A woman screamed on the television, backing away from a leering Peter Lorre.

"So do you mind if I do a little looking around tomorrow?" I asked him. "I'd like to help out if I can."

"You mean with my being here and on vacation?" He sat forward. "It'll be fun: tromping through the woods looking for Romeo and Ghouliet."

The television screamed again.

"What *is* this?" My eyes darted to the screen. "There's not a screaming woman in 'The Cask of Amontillado.'"

"Not as such," he agreed, settling back, "but in great literature the woman is always implied. Speaking of same, where is your sometime girlfriend, Lucinda? You told me, I know; I just don't remember."

"Birmingham," I muttered absently, standing. "Hospital thing."

"When are you two getting married?" he teased.

"Shut up; would you mind?"

"You always avoid the subject."

"My parents' union," I said softly, "did little to promote the institution in my eyes, as I believe I've mentioned. What if I had a marriage like theirs?"

"Fair enough," he said, and let it go.

The sun was going down and I thought to open our first bottle of wine for the evening. Out the kitchen window the green of the woods was turning gray, the sky fading into red dusk.

The woods were beginning their sunset transformation from all that was stated by daylight into everything the darkness implied.

Three drunken boys discovered the body next morning. It was broken, dressed only in blood, facedown in a culvert near my home. They stood near the top of the ridge laughing at the naked corpse.

I found myself amazed by the casual cruelty of these boys, puzzled and repelled. Their laughter had drawn me from my bed at seven o'clock on a Saturday morning, barely light in the bite of October sunrise.

We stood on a path as familiar to me as my dreams. I'd walked it daily when I was a boy, nearly as often since I'd returned to the mountains. Rising up from the other side of the ravine was the behemoth of Blue Mountain, a shoulder against which the sky rested. The path ran along the edge, provided the only way around the mountain. On the other side the land sloped downward to the valley and the town. From where we stood we could already see day spreading silver over lakes, gold onto evergreens. A panic of autumnal loss exploded everywhere; leaves of burgundy and pumpkin and cider made a calico covering for the valley deeps.

"Thanks for calling, Dev." Deputy Needle zipped his coat. "God in heaven, what a mess."

"What killed him, can you tell?" I asked.

He shook his head. "Looks like somebody bashed his skull in. Plus he's got a cracked rib—it's all purple; you can see the bone. There's some bits of thread up under his fingernails, like maybe he grabbed somebody. Could be something."

I had been staring at the body for nearly twenty minutes. Andrews stood beside me watching strangers swarm a dead man not sixty yards from where he'd slept. Something on my face must have betrayed my thoughts; he took a step closer to me and spoke in low tones.

"You knew him," he said. "You knew the dead guy."

"When I was six or seven," I began, straining to see the ashen face at the bottom of the slope as the deputies turned over the body, "I was walking along this very ridge. With older boys." My eyes darted to the group of laughing teenagers. "About their age."

The morning was hard and clear. The cathedral of the sky arched into infinity above us; all the stained-glass leaves filtered sunlight over the ground around us. The deep ravine mimicked the sky exactly the way hell mimics heaven: a nearly equal though darker vision. In those cold shadows three other deputies moved and shifted, not entirely certain what to do. Murder was a stranger to Blue Mountain.

"Go on," Andrews prompted me, his accent only slightly out of place against the other voices.

"We'd been squirrel hunting," I said quietly. "One of the boys, a monster by the name of Harding Pinhurst the Third, found a bird's nest in the lower branches of a dogwood tree." I scoured the ravine, then pointed. "That one there, I think. Look how much bigger it is now. At any rate, he pulled it down and found five eggs. For no reason, he took one out and broke it open on a rock. Instead of runny egg, a nearly formed baby bird, slick and blind, came spilling out. He was delighted beyond reason. He began to poke at the thing with a stick, telling it to fly, shrieking with laughter. The other boys, some of the Deveroe clan whom you may remember from your last visit, were watching."

A sudden shock of October breeze sent a shower of red maple leaves toward the ground, raining around the body, echoing the blood.

"I watched the bird's beak open and close, those blind eyes. I couldn't stand it, grabbed the nest, ran into the woods. I think I was crying. No telling how far away from the others I was when I hid the nest under a pile of pine straw, the remaining four eggs."

The policemen finished their work, at least for the moment, and were headed slowly back up the ravine to the path where we stood, finding footholds in ivy and granite. A nod from Deputy Needle and the men standing by the ambulance struggled down the same way, wrestling their stretcher with them as best they could.

I blew out a short breath and was surprised to see that it made a ghost in the air around me. I hadn't thought it that cold.

"I knew I wasn't really saving the eggs," I whispered to Andrews. "Even if they hatched after that, they wouldn't survive. I just didn't want them to be dead with boys standing around laughing. They all called me 'Birdy' after that—for the rest of the school year."

"That's not so bad," Andrews offered.

"You're right." I managed a smile. "When your given name is *Fever*, what nickname can sting?"

Andrews watched the side of my face in the growing morning light.

"Ask the question," I allowed.

"Waiting for you to go on," Andrews said with an indulgent sigh. "But all right, why did you tell me your little *bird man* story?"

"I had completely forgotten the event." I returned my attention to the corpse. "Until I looked at that. Who was he?"

"You're about to say." Andrews knew me too well.

"None other than Harding Pinhurst the Third, dead as I ever wished him."

The group of slack-mouthed monsters erupted in unexplained mirth once more.

"That laughter," I gave one last quick glance in their direction, "is a fitting epitaph for the likes of him."

"Able Carter done this; everybody knows it," one of the boys blurted out to a passing policeman. "He get hung for sure—if Deveroe boys don't get him first." The boy was so drunk he was drooling, delirious from an all-night bout with distilled corn and icy air. "He kill that Truvy Deveroe; now he got her cousin."

"You don't know *she's* dead," another beefy boy chimed in, jabbing a fist at the other's arm.

"She's dead all right. Them Deveroe boys'll kill Able good." He twisted his face in my direction. "What're you staring at, Goliath?"

It always struck me as strange that anyone would make fun of my size. I could have broken him in half—were I the sort. Maybe it was the fact that my hair was prematurely white; they mistook me for an older man.

"That's Dr. Devilin," one of the policemen chided.

"I'n care," he mumbled, softer. "Big albino freak."

"Why is the body naked?" Andrews whispered to me. "And did you know the dead man was the Deveroes' cousin?"

"Of course." I glared at the drunken boys, willing them to silence. "As to why the clothes are gone, I wouldn't have a clue."

"God help Able Carter now," Andrews said, watching the policemen try to muscle the teenagers away from the scene, "especially after what happened Thursday night."

"I think that's a little different from what Girlinda and I talked about," Skid finally allowed. "For one thing, she said Able and Truevine had a lovers' spat. Didn't say it had to do with Harding. Or maybe she did and I wasn't listening."

Andrews shivered. He'd thrown on a T-shirt and his black jeans, wandered barefoot out of the house when he heard all the commotion, two hours earlier. His blond hair was a bird's nest; he was nearly a foot taller than anyone else at the scene. He rubbed his arms, stood next to Skidmore wanting to ask a question. They'd become friendly during Andrews's last visit to the mountains, but the deputy was in no way disposed to idle conversation.

"What is it?" Skid asked, his face drained.

"Why is the body naked?"

"I don't know," he answered, irritated.

"And how did those drunks see it way down at the bottom of this ravine in the middle of the night?" Andrews went on. "Don't you think that's suspicious? Are you holding them?"

Skidmore sighed. "It was a full moon and them kids has crawled all over these woods they whole lives. No, I'm not holding them. In fact, I'd like them as far away from me as possible."

"But—" Andrews protested.

"Skid's right," I interrupted. "Those creatures are as cowardly as they are stupid. If they'd killed a man, they'd have vanished. They wouldn't laugh; they'd hide."

"I guess," Andrews said reluctantly. "But I don't like what this mess does to our investigation."

I had to smile. *Our investigation.*

"This does seem to complicate matters," I agreed with Andrews, moving away from the edge of the path into a spot of early-morning sunlight. "Stand over here; it's a little warmer."

I watched Skidmore as he walked a few feet from us to sit in the front seat of his squad car. He began working on the initial written report. His squad car radio demanded attention; he talked shortly. After he hung up he looked even more tired. He was running for sheriff in the coming November elections; I thought it was taking a toll. His opponent was a local businessman who enjoyed deer hunting and thought it a significant qualification for the job. That candidacy was supported financially by Jackson Pinhurst, uncle of the deceased. Our Sheriff Maddox had died suddenly—dressed only in a red raincoat and saddle oxfords, in the arms of another man's wife. There wasn't much open discussion of it.

Skid deserved to win. No one knew more about Blue Mountain or cared half as much. His spirit was clear and his determination to do *right* belonged in another century, but the politics wore on him, choosing a slogan, campaign colors, making a list of promises.

"Dev!" he called, standing up.

I yawned.

"Linda told me she called you last night," he said, tossing his clipboard onto the seat.

"She wanted me to help find Able."

"I know," he complained. "But the thing is you got to stay out of it for the most part. They say it looks bad for me to have help on a thing like this."

I felt the word *they,* in this particular case, meant one Tommy Tineeta, Skid's campaign manager from Rabun Gap.

"Of course I don't want to get in the way." I smiled. "Tell Tommy I said hello."

"That ain't it," he shot back. "Shut up."

The hospital employees had gotten the body on the stretcher and were making their way back up the slope toward the ambulance.

"I just want you to keep a low profile," he concluded.

"I've come home to do research," I said. "Everyone knows that. They're familiar with the kind of work I'm doing, know it involves talking to everyone. What would be the harm if I asked a few extra questions in the course of my folklore interviews?"

"Something like that," he agreed.

"That way Tommy T. won't make your campaign more miserable than it already is."

"Mr. Tineeta is a smart man, Dev." But Skid hardly sounded convinced.

"He's a transplant from New Orleans, he claims," I explained to Andrews. "Sounds more New Jersey to me. Skidmore's campaign manager." Skid had only hired him in reaction to his opponent's boss. Jackson Pinhurst was our town power broker, Boss Tweed in discount Armani suits, cigar like a smokestack, eyebrows like a hedge.

"Running for sheriff," Skid told Andrews, shy for some reason.

"Not a better man in the state for that job," Andrews said, clutching his own elbows. "I'm freezing. I'm going back to the cabin. Can't stop shivering." He looked down the path to my place.

"This ain't right, Fever," Skid said, watching the paramedics wrangle the body into the ambulance. "I never had to investigate a murder of somebody I knew. Not to mention I have no idea what we'll do with the body after the autopsy."

"Call the Peaker family in Rabun County," I suggested.

"What are you two talking about?" Andrews rubbed his bare arms trying to warm himself, more irritated by the moment. "You have a funeral parlor here in town; I've driven by it."

"That's the problem," Skidmore said as the ambulance door slammed shut.

"Harding Pinhurst," I told Andrews, "was the only mortician we had in this county. The place you're talking about was his."

Two

The rest of Saturday was more typical of October in the mountains: it rained and no one else found a dead body.

It had been a wet year in general; autumn foliage was everything the local businessmen could want. Cool air and fire leaves meant weekend visitors. In cities south of Blue Mountain it could still reach ninety in October, but I lit a fire at night in my cabin, shivered every morning waking up. Strangers from Atlanta filled the streets of town, buying $40 quilts for $200 and marveling at the food in Etta's diner: fried okra, boiled field peas, iced tea one part water to two parts sugar.

The town square had not changed in a hundred years. I left Blue Mountain at age sixteen, went to Burrison University, then Europe, returned to the States to run a folklore department, watched that department fade away. All the while my hometown took little notice, altered less. I found comfort in that, made my troubles less significant, held the center of things together.

Built around an antebellum courthouse and the obligatory Confederate Memorial statue, the town's four streets, each a true direction of the compass, headed away from the center. They would all eventually wind up lost on some shadowy upward slope. Over one mountain southward, drivers might find their way back down to Dahlonega and pan for gold before heading on to Atlanta. Otherwise the roads led into a tangle of dirt and gravel that could keep strangers wandering for hours with no apparent aim or outcome. An open labyrinth, these roads served to protect us from prying tourists. *My grandfather's rocking chair is not your quaint antique.* Strangers in these mountains were treated as coldly as rain in the morning. After dark they might find a warm place by the stove, grudging acceptance, and the most potent alcohol known to humankind. If they were lucky.

Town square was filled with chestnut trees that crazed the air with a yellow too brilliant to see; the eye was forced away by the light. All around them the ground was littered with the dead leaves and the recollection of a hundred autumns past.

Benches were unoccupied in the drizzle but sidewalks clattered and shopkeepers were courteous.

There had already been a brief meeting of these businessmen: tight-lipped agreement to keep the murder quiet. Dying leaves are good for business, dead morticians less so.

I sat in Etta's place talking to Deputy Needle; Andrews had decided to sleep in. The noise of the place was as pungent as the smell. Thirty conversations intertwined, a knot in the air like muscadine vines. Seventeen vegetables, all cooked for three days and nights in half a gallon of fat, steamed the air. Every Formica table was occupied, all booths full. Skid and I sat at the counter on green stools, their chrome stems sprouting like mushrooms from the linoleum floor to the vinyl seats. Sunday dinner after church always packed the place.

"I got to check on some lab work this morning, got some ideas. You'll be going up to talk to Junie." He swallowed the last of his cornbread muffin. "She's always first on your list."

Cornbread was as much an implement as a menu item. Held in the left hand, it pushed errant morsels left on the plate toward the waiting fork. The value was twofold: not even the smallest dot of collard greens could escape the combined efforts of bread and fork, and when the process was done the cornbread had collected the juice and gravy on the plate, and served as a reminder, when eaten, of what the meal had been.

"I will." I wiped my mouth with the folded paper towel. "I have a plan."

I stood, leaving a ten-dollar bill on the counter under my fork.

He stood. "I'd expect no less." He stretched, toothpick in his teeth. Nothing says *fine dining* like a splinter in the mouth.

"I want to record her current version of *'Black-haired Lass,'* if she still sings it."

"Don't know that one," he admitted, waving to Etta, who was nearly asleep by the register.

Etta's white bun lolled on the back of a mule-eared chair, gnarled hands rested in the folds of her rumpled drab apron. She gave no acknowledgment.

"It's about a girl with three brothers," I told him as we made our way between the tables, "who killed her suitor in the twilight of the year."

"Which might lead to more current events," he said, pushing the door open. "I see that."

The rain had stopped; there was a cardinal on my truck. I didn't want to be the one to disturb it. The old Ford held up well. Originally my father's, the '47 pickup had been rebuilt by a student of mine in 1997, its dark green a perfect canvas for the bird's dash of red. I stood on the sidewalk, arms folded, watching the clouds roll across the mountain.

"All these years," I said to Skidmore, "and I'm still surprised when you understand the subtlety of my plans."

He slung open the door to his squad car, wiping water onto his tan uniform pants. "You think a university education and visit to Europe give you an edge, but you fail to realize that I am God's holy instrument when it comes to being subtle." With that he spat his toothpick into the street, sniffed, hawked into the gutter, and tipped his hat. "Dr. Devilin."

The drive to June's house was a matter of ten minutes; the air was delicious after the rain. Skidmore knew June had always been a better mother to me than anyone else alive. I pressed the accelerator unconsciously. Fields flew by; the highway rose upward, aiming me to the sky. The white house was set in black bottom soil between three mountains. Even from a distance, it seemed more cared for than other homes along the same road. The sun shot through a rip in the clouds, gave the edges of new-harvested corn sheaves a gold they could only borrow and would never pay back. Everything about the place had an angel's attention.

I couldn't help thinking about the odd, personal ghost story she often used to tell when she sang "Black-haired Lass." June Cotage, wife of a Pentecostal snake-handling preacher about whom I had written many articles, was among the kindest souls on earth. Her soft singing voice held centuries of unrequited loves, unfair trials, lost travelers; new mornings. But the ghost story was very real to her.

When she was a young girl, the war in Vietnam had just started, but her beau enlisted and didn't come home. She got a government letter that told her he was "Missing in Action." She still thought he would come back and went to visit the veterans hospital in Atlanta once a month, hoping to find someone who knew him. After two years, she met an older man there who was recuperating from his wounds. He'd lost a leg, along with the heart to go home. They got to talking because he was from Bee's Holler, not too far from Blue Mountain. His name was Kenly, and he claimed he'd known her beau. He told June that her boyfriend had died in the same battle that had taken his leg.

He tried to comfort her, said she'd find somebody new by and by, but June was inconsolable.

Kenly got out of the hospital in the autumn of 1967, and through-out the rest of that year he paid regular visits to Blue Mountain. June always asked Kenly to stay and take supper with her family, which he seemed glad to do. He had no family of his own. The talk was always good and the food was fine; they often got into the spirit of trading stories. He was a religious man, a Baptist. He told the old story of Diverus and Lazarus.

Diverus was rich, and he gave a feast and invited all the well-to-do. There was food for a hundred; only thirty were present. Lazarus, the poorest man in town, came begging at the door. And what did Diverus do? He sent out his hungry dogs to bite Lazarus away. But the dogs had better hearts than that and took pity on Lazarus, licked his wounds. Lazarus petted them all and called them by name. So Diverus sent out his bodyguards to beat Lazarus away. They had not taken one step for him when the power to raise their arms left them; they couldn't move. So Diverus himself went to the door and called to Lazarus, "Go away!" So Lazarus left and that night he died. Starved to death. Two angels out of heaven came to guide his soul home. "There is a place prepared in heaven on an angel's knee." The next night, Diverus died from gluttony. Two serpents out of hell came to guide his soul to its reward: "Come with us. Because you turned away a beggar, you have to stay in hell until you find a place to sit on a serpent's knee." Diverus is there to this day, because he hasn't yet found the knee of any snake. So if a stranger comes to the door, don't turn him away. Have him in by the fire, and fill him with food. That wandering stranger may be brother Lazarus, come to our door.

June always told it that just as Kenly finished his story there came a knock on her kitchen door.

A stranger stood there, his hair unkempt, his beard unshorn, clothes barely enough to save modesty. His bones were clear to see in the pale moonlight, his eyes hollow and lifeless.

After Kenly's story, June felt she had to let him in.

The stranger moved over the threshold and into the warmth of the kitchen like a revenant. It was a full quarter of an hour before he stopped shivering. He ate three full plates of food and was slowing on his fourth before he could look up again.

He said, "I have no idea where I am. I don't know my name nor my kin nor life at all. I'm a traveling creature."

June told him, "Get over by the stove."

"What place is this?" the stranger asked.

"Blue Mountain."

At this he seemed disturbed. "What year?"

"It's Nineteen sixty-seven," June answered. "Where've you been? Who are you?"

"I fought in the war. I was wounded and left for dead. Spent time as a prisoner. The Lord was my salvation. More wandering. The mind is cloudy."

He pulled back his hair to show a terrible scar on the side of his head and drew back his thin coat to show another in his side.

"They've all but healed now," he told everyone in the kitchen, "but I'm a ghost. I don't have much memory and scarcely any reasoning. I know I'm looking for someone. I can't find her, but I see her every night in my dreams, and I hear her voice every day. I'm tired to death, but I'm not weary of the search. I want to go home, and I've toiled to get there. I'll never rest until I find her."

With that he took a broken locket from around his neck. "She gave me this on the day I shipped out. I'll know her when I find her; she'll know me no matter how much we've changed. She kept the other half of this locket."

Then, every time she told the story, June would reach up to her throat and show me a silver chain.

"Here it is around my neck," she'd say. "This is the match, the other half. That stranger was Hezekiah Cotage, who is now my husband."

The story never failed to give me a pleasant chill, however much she embellished it over the years. As I pulled my truck beside her white Buick and reached for my ancient Wollenzak tape recorder, I half-hoped she would tell it again.

I got out of the truck, glanced at the little pillows on the porch rockers embroidered by June's hand with medieval scenes from the Book of Revelation: four skeletal horsemen, angels drowning in blood. All with her gentle touch.

June did not attend her husband's services. Hers was a more sedate religion, despite the images from her needlework. True, she often told me, all life was suffering and there would be a terrible judgment in the last days. God would harvest the wheat and burn the chaff, but there was no need being harsh about it.

The instant my foot hit the first step to the porch she was at the screen door.

"Hey, sweetheart," she said, standing on the threshold.

"June."

"You want you a little bite to eat?"

"I've just come from Etta's."

She stepped back into her dark living room. It was small, smelled of wood smoke and fifty years of cooking. The windows had not been opened since 1962; the curtains had been closed most of that time. Family portraits on the mantel stared at me, the door hushed as it closed.

"I see you got your machine." She was already headed for the kitchen.

"I have to send the publisher something by Thanksgiving." I followed her. "I was hoping you'd sing today."

The kitchen was brighter, the surfaces glittering. She moved into the light, I was struck by how much older she looked since I'd come home. I remembered her hair auburn; now it was snow. Her ginger eyes were encased in wrinkles. The long gray dress didn't help; the hard black shoes made matters worse—she was a parody of age.

An ancient percolator was plugged into the wall by the sink and she went to it immediately, poured without asking me, and handed over a cup of hot black water.

"You know this coffee's not strong enough to get itself out of bed," I told her, setting the cup down on the counter.

"What you come to record?" She was always nervous around the tape player, even when it wasn't on.

I plugged the Wollenzak into the wall by the coffeemaker and took the microphone out of my pocket, a Shure Vocalmaster, my favorite. I'd made a cushioned stand so it could sit on the tabletop without picking up stray noise. People would tap the table, bump it; sounded like thunder on the tape.

"I have several versions of 'The Black-haired Lass' from you," I said, hoping to distract her by clicking on and starting without the usual slow build. "Some of them go back ten years. I'd like to get a variant that's more contemporary. For comparison."

"Uh-huh."

I looked up.

Her arms were folded and her face was steel. "You think I don't know this is about the Deveroe girl and Skidmore's brother-in-law?"

So much for the subtlety of my plan.

"Skid asked me not to be too obvious," I told her, turning off the tape recorder. "He's worried about his election."

"No, he ain't." She took a seat at the table, relaxing with a final glance at the Wollenzak. "Long as you two known each other, you don't see. He's afraid you'll show him up."

I'd been told before about the so-called competition between us. I'd never noticed it.

"How exactly would I show him up?" I took a seat across the table from her.

The kitchen light came from everywhere, not just the windows. The perfection of June's cleanliness bordered psychosis.

"You running for sheriff? If you find Mr. Carter and that girl, everybody might want you to. Then what'd he do?"

"Nobody in this town is going to want me to run for dogcatcher. I was a strange one when I left, more so now that I'm back."

"I know it's hard to be a stranger in your own hometown." She leaned her elbows on the table. "That's a fact. But folks take to you more'n you think they do. Look up to you. They wouldn't say it."

"Then how am I supposed to know?"

"You a grown man, Fever. You ought to figure things out." She laughed.

For sixteen years in the mountains I'd heard that kind of laughter, though it was rarely as soft as June's. My parents were traveling performers, my father a magician, his wife the beautiful assistant. They were gone as often as they were around, and I'd fended for myself since I was seven. Skidmore and I had scraped away a world of dirt and pine straw scuttling all over the woods. When I needed comfort, I was fed in June's kitchen. But when I needed explanations, I went hungry. Derision was never in short supply for a huge shy boy from a carnival family. I wasn't comfortable with laughter.

"I'm grown in some ways," I agreed. All it took was the merest suggestion, and images long dead rose up in my mind. I was a child of seven, shivering on the steps of my abandoned house, watching dark shapes move in the wood, the creatures that only came out at night.

"Comes a point, boy," she said sternly, "when you got to let the past go, own up to your part in it, be a person to yourself."

"Could we talk about Able?" I said, shifting in my seat. "Do you have anything to tell me or not?" Even the ghost of subtlety had flown.

"I don't." She folded her arms and locked her body. "Not that I know for certain myself."

I knew there was more. She shot a quick glance at the kitchen door, the place where her husband would shortly enter, coming home from his work. She knew something about him he wouldn't want told or something he'd rather tell me himself.

"All right then," I said, moving the microphone closer to her. "Let's get on with the recording; I know it makes you nervous. We'll get it over with, and I can get on to the next chapter."

"How's it coming?"

"Slowly," I said, pretending to adjust the recorder, "but great work takes time. I'm creating a new definition for an entire academic discipline."

"Okay by me." She sat back, glaring at the microphone. "Tell me this time before you turn that thing on."

"Of course. Etta slept through the lunch crowd today. Is she all right?"

"She ain't been to Wednesday meeting in a month." June shook her head, lowered her voice. "I think she might be drinking again."

"She's a hundred and seventy years old, June, and she has rheumatoid arthritis."

"I'll look in on her."

June's shoulders were slumped back to their normal position; her face was smoother, her breathing less quick, movements more fluid.

"Turning on," I warned her, and snapped the Wollenzak.

"Lord." She began to fidget, clicking her fingernails.

"Now, June," I said absently, making a note in my field log, "your husband is a preacher."

She'd done this a hundred times with me, and it always started the same way: she barely spoke, and it seemed we'd get nowhere.

She nodded in the direction of the microphone.

"He handles snakes in his services," I coaxed.

"I don't take to it, raised a Methodist."

"Yes," I said, avoiding her eyes. "You don't go to his church. But he tells you about it when he comes home."

"I reckon."

"Any good stories lately?"

"No."

"All right." I moved the mike closer to her, still looking down in my log. "Any stories at all?"

"Nothing but foolishness."

"You think your husband's religious ideas are foolish."

"Hezekiah's ways mean something to him, I don't deny that," she cranked up, "but the Bible is clear. Taking up serpents and drinking lye, it's just a show to me. God don't care for a show. He wants it plain."

The perennial enmity between June's quiet faith and her husband's flamboyance had done the trick. She was no longer paying attention to the tape recorder or her suspicions and had launched a campaign of education.

"The Bible says," she explained to me, tapping her index finger into the palm of her other hand, " 'That ancient serpent who is called the Devil and Satan, the deceiver of the whole world.' Why'd I want to mess with that?"

"Where does it say that?"

"Revelations." Her favorite book, Hieronymus Bosch meets Clive Barker.

"You sound angry, June." No angrier than usual on the subject, but goading always worked. "Has something happened recently?"

"That old man," she plowed on, "thinks he can scare me with his talk, and I won't have it." Another flirt with the kitchen door. "I shall fear no evil."

"I see; he's trying to scare you?"

"Come home last night and would not keep shut about that grave-yard."

"Let's clarify," I said to the microphone, my voice steady despite my anticipation, "that your husband goes to his church up on Blue Mountain every evening, close to the public cemetery."

"That's right," she said, elbows on the table, "and every night there's fools up in the church house with him, listening to what he says."

"When he came home last night . . ." I circled my hand.

"Come busting in the house," she went on, "going on about that boneyard, top of the mountain."

"On about what?"

"Oh, usual mess." She dismissed it all with the flick of a hand, sitting back in her chair. "Scary noise, moving shadows. Ain't even a story."

"Maybe he's revving up for Halloween."

"You know better'n that, Fever."

June and her husband, as did many older people in town, eschewed Halloween as a celebration of the demonic.

"You prefer to stick to the truth about revenants," I teased her.

"I do," she answered without a hint of irony.

"Didn't you have some story about your Uncle Hiram?"

"Woke up one night." she confirmed, "shortly after he moved into his new house in Blairsville. Every lamp in the parlor was lit. Come in and found a bouquet of dried flowers on his rug. Doors were bolted from the inside, all the windows locked. Found out an old widow woman died in the house. She was buried with that bouquet, they said, because she had no man to give it to. Hiram reckoned she give it to him because he took such good care of the house and garden. She didn't have a husband in this world but found one in the next."

"And that's a true story."

"People leave behind all sorts of things when they die, son. Some leave furniture, some letters. Once in a while, a body forgets part of the soul. They leave it behind, and it's got to wander for a time."

"But that's different from what Hek's talking about."

"He's trying to scare me." Arms folded. "Thinks it's funny."

"Why would he try to scare you?"

"I got a burial plot up there, belongs to my granddaddy's family. Hek says he can hear me calling him from time to time when he passes by the graveyard." She gnawed on her upper lip a second. "Says he's worried about me. But he wants me to get buried over in the little garden by his church, is all. With him. For some reason he don't like our public cemetery."

She wore no wedding ring. Her belief was that it showed ownership and she was not her husband's possession. But she rubbed the ring on her little finger, one Hek had given her the first Christmas of their marriage, a ruby rose in peach gold.

"'The golden bowl is broken,'" she sighed, "the dust returns to the earth as it was, the spirit returns to God Who gave it.'"

"Revelation."

She shook her head. "Ecclesiastes Twelve Six and Seven. Everything ends."

Her face betrayed a true fear. Dying wouldn't be bad; missing her husband, unendurable.

The silence that followed her quote was snapped in half, a sudden snarl of the doorknob and Hezekiah's step. He was panting.

"Lord, it's a chill out there." Slam. "Hey there, Fever."

"Hek." I smiled at him, but he made no eye contact.

He went immediately to the percolator, took a mug from the cabinet above it, and poured. He was in a black suit, white shirt buttoned at the collar, no tie. His hair was a tangle of wires; he'd been running.

He gulped the coffee, both hands around the mug, then stared down at the table.

"You recording?"

"We can stop." I reached across and shut off the tape player.

"Sorry. Keep a'going if you want."

"What's the matter with you?" June said, looking him up and down. "It ain't near enough cold out for you to carry on. Where's your glasses?" To me: "Left in church again."

He looked at me, shook his head. "You know what's wrong," he said to June quietly.

She rose up out of the chair. "That's enough of that."

"Junie."

"I told Fever about your little story." She went to the oven; it creaked open. "He agrees with me: you're out y'mind."

"We never really discussed my opinion," I said to Hek.

He took a seat a the table, I cleared the Wollenzak and microphone out of the way. June set a warm plate in front of Hek, holding on to it with a blue dish towel. He sat and watched the plate until she brought him a fork and a paper napkin from the drawer beside the sink. His fingers were shaking very slightly, his face flushed, his pupils dilated.

"Ain't nothing wrong with me," he mumbled.

"There's everything wrong with you," she said, taking her seat, chin in hand, watching him eat. "Has been since the day we met."

"If that's true," he said looking up at me, "then what'd she marry me for? Ask her that." The whisper of a smile touched his face.

"Shoot fire." She swatted his shoulder, hard, and blushed, covered her mouth with her hand.

"What did you see in the cemetery, Hek?" I itched to turn the recorder back on.

"I saw what I saw." He lifted a forkful of mashed potatoes to his mouth; it hovered. "Ain't the first time, neither." In went the fork.

"She told me," I said, "you saw or heard something last night."

"I don't mean that," he shot back, irritated. "Happen every so often, you see things up there."

"But this is different."

He stopped eating, eyes blank. "It surely is." He blinked, turned my way. "She called my name. And more."

"Who did?"

"Woman, from across the way. Over the graves and brambles." His shoulders shook a second; then he returned to his plate.

"You saw a woman standing in the graveyard?"

He bobbed his head once.

"Someone you knew?" There was more; I had to wait for it to come out slowly.

"It was not a thing of this earth," he whispered, his eyes shifting between me and his wife. "That's what I think."

"Hek," I coaxed. "You don't really believe that."

"I won't say who or what it was, then." He sniffed. "But it looked like June."

That was an attitude I'd recorded time and again, especially where paranormal events were concerned: skepticism, reluctance to appear foolish, and acknowledgment of the phenomenon—in one sentence. Strange voices from the grave were eerie but perfectly acceptable effects of night wind, a wandering stranger. Or they could just as well be evidence of unearthly revenants. Not saying everything he was thinking kept Hek in command of the situation.

Not saying was, in fact, an art form in my hometown.

"You think you saw June up there?"

He shoveled steaming field peas into his mouth. The scrape of the fork on the porcelain plate was the only sound in the kitchen. June and I sat waiting for him to finish.

"Okay, boy." He sat back, strength returning to his voice. "Great many years I been hearing things from that old graveyard, and I ain't the only one. Mostly amongst the Newcomb graves up there."

The sound of his voice curled back over the name of Newcomb. Our town was called Newcomb Junction until 1925, when Jeribald "Tubby" Newcomb married his half sister and all the resulting progeny bore serious birth defects or an unusual dwarfism. Town meeting in October of that year unanimously agreed to change the name the town, call it after the mountain we loved instead of the family we reviled. Jeribald moved the entire brood to Chattanooga.

His oldest boy, Tristan, was the smallest person ever born in Appalachia. When Jeribald died, Tristan took his inheritance, separated from the family, moved back to Blue Mountain, and embraced his mountain heritage. He billed himself as "The Newcomb Dwarf" and began the fabled *Ten Show,* a traveling entertainment comprised of ten strange acts, which had employed my parents. He died in 1968 and was buried in the graveyard of which Hek was apparently frightened.

"People say the fuss up there is Newcombs restless in the cemetery." He shoved his plate away from him and let out a breath.

Hek was one of the people who said it; I'd heard as much from him on a dozen occasions. Citizens of Blue Mountain were slow to forgive, slower to forget. Traces of the Newcomb name were rare, old records put away in damp basements, older memories, tombstones covered with blackberry brambles. Their mansion sat in disrepair on the other side of the mountain; no one ever went near. People said crickets wouldn't chirp within a hundred feet of the place.

I was one of the people who said that. As boys, Skid and I had taken a dare to camp out in the house. We lived to tell the tale—the ruin of days gone by, our midnight adventures.

"If I turn on the tape player, would you talk about this?" I knew what he'd say. "For the research?"

"Rather not." He had stopped shivering and the food had contented his face.

"Fever's worried about Able Carter," June told her husband. "Thought he could trick me into talking about it with his machine."

"He ought to know better." He rumbled a laugh. "I'm the only man can trick you." A sideways glance.

"Hezekiah." She blushed again.

That rose in her cheeks was a window on their marriage. I was aware of their secret, the true reason for June's schoolgirl flush—and for bounteous crops on their land. They were a traditional couple in many respects; one of those traditions was the uncharacteristically pagan practice of having sex in their fields on every solstice. Four times a year these churchgoing grandparents would wait until midnight and sneak out to the acreage behind their house. They'd spread a quilt and lie together in as passionate an embrace as weather and advancing age would allow. I knew this because their amorous noises had been so ferocious one night I'd heard them halfway up the mountain. I'd been walking late in the summertime, years ago; drawn by the sounds I had made my discovery. I'd never told them, they'd have been mortified, but I'd always admired the concept.

The practice was a well-documented folk custom traced to pre-Christian farming. The more fertile and enthusiastic a husbandman's behavior with his wife, the better the crop yield: sympathetic magic. Giant ears of Cotage Silver Queen corn were the envy of the county, considered proof of the theory.

There was nothing in the academic literature, however, to suggest the vigor, the sheer volume, of Hek and June's magic. The corn spoke for itself, but the true value of the practice was, it had always seemed to me, more domestic than agricultural.

"These noises you heard last night in the graveyard," I began, jotting down a few notes in the spiral pad, "are the continuation of a phenomenon that goes back years, you're saying."

"After a while," he answered, "rumor becomes fact; gossip takes on the shine of history. I know that. I'm ashamed to admit it I've done my share of telling stories. Makes it harder for you to believe me now." His right shoulder twitched again, a memory shiver.

He was right: I'd heard stories about that graveyard my whole life. Every town has its haunted places; I think there must be something in the human spirit that needs darkness, a tangible place for fear's repose. Nightmares have a boundary then, a definition, and are easier to bear. But there was more to Hek's chill.

Time to ask the real question.

"Why rekindle those stories now, Hek? What's got you so scared?"

He sucked in an echoing breath, let it out like a death rattle. "Okay, then." He leaned forward on his elbows, reached into the breast pocket of his coat, and laid a torn bit of peach-colored cloth on the table in front of us. Tiny roses dotted the fabric in a strange pattern; I'd never seen anything quite like it.

June gasped, covered her mouth with both hands, froze, eyes wide.

"Woman in the graveyard held her hand out toward me," Hek rasped, "something in it." He turned to his wife. "I can't find my glasses; you're right. Honestly couldn't make out who or what it was." Back to me, voice hushed. "I headed her way; she ran. This was on the marker when I got there."

The torn swatch lay curled on the tabletop, a petal. They glared at it, June had stopped breathing.

"There's something about this material?" I asked her.

One curt nod, she took her hands away from her bloodless face.

"I've never seen any other like it," she whispered. "Looks to be from the dress I was wearing when Hek and me was wed. It's long since gone to dust."

Three

June was upset enough to excuse herself from the table; Hek made apologies. Within five minutes I was back in my truck, headed for home. It wasn't at all unusual that a sensible couple like the Cotages could find themselves worried about visitors from beyond the grave. Their daily lives were filled with religion; a spirit that might find mansions in the sky could just as easily be lost on earth. In truth I scarcely knew a soul in the mountains who didn't have a strong spiritual appreciation of the occasional event beyond the natural. June and Hek had more proof than most. I didn't believe that he was lying or even exaggerating when he told us about the woman he'd seen. I had my own opinions, of course, but I was as stubborn an adherent to the art of *not saying* as anyone in my town.

The day was growing darker again; steel clouds locked out the sun. Thunder rumbled from the other side of the mountain, and a rush of rain swept across the fields. Roads were suddenly slick black rivers. I was glad traffic was sparse.

If the weather had been nicer, I might have resolved to drive past the cemetery right then, have a look at the stones, scour for patches of cloth in the brambles. I thought I might find answers to one of our mysteries immediately. As it was, a cup of espresso, an early fire, and waking up Andrews held infinitely more appeal.

I turned off the road onto my property and saw the squad car.

Skid was sitting on the porch, still in his slicker, rocking, cup of coffee in hand. Andrews was standing at the rail, blankly gazing at the sheets of rain hung like curtains against the sky.

"Afternoon!" I called, climbing out of the truck and dashing for the relative comfort of the porch.

Andrews rallied.

"Thanks for letting me sleep." He rubbed his eyes. "I guess I needed it. Skidmore woke me up about a half an hour ago. How's June?"

"Fine." I watched Skid chew the inside of his cheek. "I thought you were conducting a murder investigation."

"That's why I'm here." He set his mug aside. "Harding was killed early Thursday night, broke neck and blunt trauma to the head. Plus we got the fiber study back from Atlanta. They found little bits of fiber belonged to Able, matched it with DNA from a shirt in Able's closet."

"That was quick," I said, impressed with his work.

"I don't mind you still looking for Truvy," Skid said firmly, standing, "but I got to ask you to leave off anything concerns Able, and you bring me what you find right quick."

"I understand. How's Linda taking this?"

"We don't talk about it." Skid's face was lined, eyes rimmed red, clothes rumpled. His hands moved too quickly; his voice was hollow.

"Must be rough looking for your wife's brother," Andrews realized, "on a murder charge."

Skid scratched his nose with one upward movement. "I'm serious about this, Dev."

"I know you are." I laid my hand on his shoulder.

"Is that it for our case, then?" Andrews didn't bother to hide his disappointment.

"In fact," I answered, heading into the kitchen for espresso, "I may have some good news about that."

They exchanged glances and followed me in. As had happened often since I'd moved back to the mountains, my house filled me with contentment as I stepped over the threshold. Solid oak beams framed the large room downstairs, galley kitchen to the right as you came in the front door. My parents had set a cast-iron stove into the stone hearth to the left by a large picture window. Gray air was changed to green out that window by the surrounding pine and cedar trees. Behind them hung a more distant Monet of autumn. Quilts on the wall, like church windows, did their best to brighten the room. The staircase in the far corner led up to three bedrooms.

"You found something?" Andrews said, interrupting my domestic reverie. He was pouring himself coffee from the larger coffeemaker.

The house was chilled and dreary; gray light dabbed the corners; the ceilings were musty. I wanted to start that fire, but I knew Skidmore couldn't wait.

"Truevine may be hiding out in the city cemetery," I said over the grinding coffee beans.

"Christ." Andrews turned, sloshing coffee onto the counter. "What makes you think that?"

"Hek saw her, I think," I answered.

"Well, that would be Truvy," Skid admitted, a faint crease at the corner of his lips.

"She might hide out in a graveyard?" Andrews pulled a wad of paper towels from the wall, swiped at his spill. "I've got to know more about this girl."

"Andrews once confessed to me," I told Skid, starting the espresso maker, "that his perfect mate would believe she was a vampire."

"My Goth phase." He shrugged. "It was short."

"Truvy's always been a little off," Skid sighed. "The whole family."

"But the rumors didn't really start about her until she got involved with Rud Pinhurst."

"I guess you're right," Skid considered.

"Didn't you say the mortician Pinhurst was her cousin?" Andrews's eyes grew wider. "Does this mean she was involved with one of her relatives?"

"There's lots of Pinhurst family around," Skid said slowly, not looking back at Andrews.

"He might have been a third or fourth cousin, I suppose," I allowed, "but that's not the point."

"Rud was no good." Skid leaned on the kitchen counter, punctuating the finality of his statement.

"Tell," Andrews insisted.

"The town decided about five years ago to set up a kind of living folk museum," I began, "a tourist attraction, really."

Skid shook his head. "More like seven, wasn't it?"

"Anyway," I went on, "part of it was a working smithy. Rud Pinhurst used some connection to one of the business sponsors to get the job. He'd done ironwork around town anyway: horses needed shoes, tourists wanted fireplace sets for their tract mansions in Marietta. The town set up a weekend business for fall and spring. Truevine fell in love with him then, and not much later they broke up. I got her story on tape shortly after that."

I told Andrews the story.

Rud Pinhurst courted Truevine in private. She was in love with him. His hammer was her church bell. He was her religion. On many afternoons they would take to the hills and meadows among the primroses and the sweet william. Rud swore to marry her if she'd lie down beside him.

They made plans. She would learn his trade and help him at his work. They'd live in the shelter of a tree, sleep on a bed of meadow grass. She'd lie content in his arms through summer's sun and winter's chill.

All that autumn every time some city visitor would say, "Who's that fine boy?" she'd say, "That's my blacksmith." She was happy, thought she was wiser than any woman alive.

When the year turned old, the cold wind blew all around; there was warmth by the fire at his bellows, warmer still by the hearth in her house when no one else was about.

At Christmastime there was a dance everyone attended. It was the only time many people came into town for fun—not for business, not for need, only for want of company. Dancing close to someone was an added enticement, but Truevine had a better plan for that night. She was going to announce her devotion to Rud at that party.

It would be the night she'd show him off; the world would know he was hers.

She arrived early, anxious to share the good tidings, but kept silent. Long hours passed; it was nearly midnight. Many had gone home by the time Rud finally came. He carried strange news. As boldly as he ever struck his anvil, he declared it for all to hear:

"I can only stay a moment. I have a secret to tell." It was clear he had been drinking. "I've come to say to you-all that I'm married."

Everyone thought it was odd that he should marry in secret; the room was hushed.

"Uncle Jackson arranged it; she's Tessy Brannour, fine woman from Rabun County. Some of you know that big house of theirs on South Stonewall. Her daddy and Jackson arranged for me to work in an office, no more sparks and hammers for me. We're married these past two months." He staggered. "Had to wait till she was asleep, slip out of the house." He gave out with a laugh.

The crowd gave quiet congratulations.

All save Truevine.

They were heard to argue moments later

"What's become of the promise you made me when I lay beside you?" she demanded.

His eyes shone from drink. "Promise?"

"You promised you'd marry *me*. We'd live in the fields; I'd work in your smithy."

"Don't be silly, girl. How'd we live in a field? Nobody could."

"I could." She barely spoke up. "With you I could."

"Sh, now." He turned to walk away.

"You promised."

"Who knows that?

"I do." She followed after him.

He looked down at her. "And who'd believe you?"

"God knows the truth," she said to him.

"I'm married, Truevine."

"Then you listen to me." Her words were calm. "I give you the curse of Truvy Deveroe for a wedding present."

Only one or two standing close heard her say it.

Rud laughed, but there was something different in his eyes from that moment on, in his step. She planted a seed of fear in his breast.

Rud went home without another word, home to his rich wife and his big house. There's a strange end to the story. Rud grew more and more bent low as the weeks went by, walking lame and slow through the streets of Blue Mountain. Rumors spread about Truevine's curse, and that began her reputation as a witch.

It seemed more likely to me that bitter remorse, a knowledge of his own hard heart, had made Rud limp, but perhaps mine is too Freudian an explanation.

Not long after, a tourist happened to see Rud hobbling in the street and asked Truevine, of all people, "Who is that poor thing?"

For all to hear she said, "I do not know that man."

"It's been a good while since anyone's seen Rud anywhere," I concluded. "The supposition is that he's left the state for good."

My kitchen was quiet. The house contemplated my telling of Truevine's story. The rain was letting up, only a drizzle from the eaves; the house did its best to resist gloom as it had for a hundred and fifty years.

"I know you tell me these folktales so I can understand what's going on up here," Andrews said softly, "but there are some things about your town I hope I never understand."

"Amen to that," Skid agreed. "This is why I say Rud Pinhurst was no good."

"Let me get this right." Andrews rubbed his eyes, pushing off the kitchen counter and heading for the parlor area. "This poor girl has now lost her parents, survived a horrible love affair, and taken care of three feral brothers." He took the overstuffed chair that faced the window. "Her reward is to be called a witch. In the twenty-first century."

"It's not all bad." I finished my espresso and joined him in the parlor.

"Nobody bothers her much," Skid agreed, teasing Andrews, "when she's in town."

"I mean," I told Andrews, staring out the window with him, "those ideas help her through some tough times. Doesn't matter that it's nonsense; what matters is that she gets relief. She misses her parents, her mother in particular: she's told me on several occasions that she can summon her mother any time she cares to. Fingernail clippings were saved from the old funeral parlor when the body was cleaned up."

"Fingernail clippings." He wouldn't look at me.

"Or hair from a brush works equally well." I sat on the sofa. "Any part of the person you hope to affect with your spell, you have to take something, a part of the sympathetic magic. Truevine burns spices, mostly sage, breathes in the smoke, drawing the dead fingernails, tied in one of her mother's old handkerchiefs, toward her face. She won't tell me the spell, but she says it brings her mother near. They talk. When all the smoke is gone, so is the spirit."

"She's never done this for you." Andrews shifted to face me.

"No, of course not, and it doesn't matter what the truth is; she finds comfort in talking to her mother, real or imagined. That's the power of magic."

"So if she's angry with someone," Andrews grumbled, "she can stick pins in a doll and the victim gets a headache; she feels triumph. Passive aggression, I call it. How long were she and Rud together?"

"Not more than a year."

"And then she took up with Able," Andrews said roundly, partly to goad Skidmore, who would surely not care to have his brother-in-law date a witch. Not in an election year.

"They didn't start up right away," I told Andrews. "And their relationship was a secret for the first year of so, but they've been together nearly—is it three years now?"

I turned to Skidmore for an answer. His eyes were far away.

"DNA evidence," he said slowly, "that's some amazing stuff, you know it? Did it ever occur to Dr. Devilin, I wonder, about the similarities between a bit of witchcraft hair or fingernails and the science of fiber evidence."

"Interesting," Andrews allowed.

"What are you thinking?" I wanted to know.

Skidmore chewed on his lower lip. "I have to get me something out of Ms. Deveroe's closet, check and see is there anything from her stuck on the person of the deceased."

"Is that the scientific term?" Andrews said. *"Stuck on?"*

"Didn't occur to me she might be involved."

"Skid," I demanded, "what are you thinking?"

"I'd rather not say."

"Tell us what's going on in your head," I said, leaning forward. "Or am I going to have to get Andrews to beat it out of you?"

They both grinned.

"I know you're reticent," I went on, "because you have to do this yourself, or at least Tommy said you had to. But what's the harm in talking to us in the privacy of my home?"

He sighed, leaned on the beam by the kitchen counter.

"Okay, I had it figured that the argument everybody heard Thursday night was about Harding. Able was carrying on some secret investigation about something and he said to Truvy, 'I don't care if he is your cousin,' which, I know we just said there's a lots of cousins in the Pinhurst brood, but I think Harding and Able had words."

"You think they fought and Able killed him accidentally," I said slowly, "and now it occurs to you that Truevine might have been present."

"That would account for their disappearance better than some lovers' quarrel gone bad." Andrews sat up.

"She left church; Able went after her. Harding followed because he heard the argument like the rest of us did."

"Harding wasn't at the services," I said.

"Hang on; doesn't it bother people in that church," Andrews digressed, "to think one of their members is a witch? They let her come to services and all?"

Skidmore lifted a shoulder. "Don't see why not."

"The two are separate," I explained. "Doesn't matter what you think of a person around here; you'd never dream of keeping them out of worship."

"Church is for everybody," Skid agreed. "But what I'm saying is

Harding Pinhurst was outside, heard, followed them to get Able to leave off his investigation; words were spoke."

"And the town's only mortician ended up dead," Andrews concluded. "What did you do with his body, by the way? You were worried about that."

"Ain't done nothing yet, still at the hospital." Skid sniffed. "Good thing, too. I got more lab work to do. Damn. I might get the sheriffing business right if I keep at it."

"How long have you been a deputy?" Andrews asked.

"Eleven years."

"Can't say I was sorry to hear about Sheriff Maddox." Andrews laughed a little like a boy.

We'd both had uncomfortable business with the town's foremost officer of the law before his untimely and—try as I might to think otherwise—amusing demise.

"Well, you ought to know the ropes by now," Andrews said, calming.

"Wish I could take more of your help, Dev," he said hoarsely. "I got to go."

He leaned toward the door; I stood; Andrews returned his eyes to the woods outside the window.

"I am helping," I said, coming to see him out the door. "It's more roundabout than usual."

"I guess."

The rain had completely stopped, but the sky was still covered. Midafternoon seemed twilight.

"I hope you're wrong about Able," I said as we stepped off the porch.

"Me, too." He tapped the top of his car, thinking. "You might go up and talk to the Deveroe boys, see if they tell you anything they won't say to me."

"I was going to check out the cemetery anyway," I agreed, "see what there is to Hek's story. Their house isn't that much farther."

"Don't go up the boys' place at night, you hear?" He swung into his car. "They might shoot you."

"You look tired."

"I am. Worried."

"Do you want me to talk to Tommy?" I asked. "He might let me help more if he knew how unobtrusive I can be."

Skid started the car. "You're near seven feet tall, your hair's white as snow, you're loud, you're a know-it-all, and your name is *Fever*. You're as 'inconspicuous as a tarantula on an angel food cake,' or however that goes."

"Isn't it a wedding cake?"

He backed out slowly.

A rattle of stones and a spray of mud, the squad car was gone.

"Andrews?" I called, heading back into the house. "How would you like to go sit in a graveyard tonight?"

"There's a Raymond Chandler on cable," he whined.

"When I was two," I began, settling into the sofa, "my father thought he was teaching me to speak by pointing at things and saying what they were. 'Chair.' Point. 'Cow.' Point. A hundred things. He never bothered to look at me. I was staring at his index finger the whole time, not at the thing he wanted me to look at."

"I hate these little memory digressions of yours, you know," Andrews sighed.

"I couldn't for the life of me figure out how that finger could have so many names."

"What's your point?" he said, slumping in the chair. He knew there was one.

"The nature of observation."

"I am *not* getting into the phenomenological vortex with you again." He started out of his chair.

"I'm saying we have to consider that our perceptions can always be misdirected."

"You think too much about misdirection," he began in his best university professor's voice, "because your father was a magician. You really could benefit from serious analysis."

"It always helps to turn things around, try to see them from another perspective. That's what Skidmore was doing just now. He realized that he had focused so much on his brother-in-law that he didn't see the bigger picture."

"He was overcompensating." Andrews continued his intellectual pretension. "He didn't want people to think he was going easy on Carter, so he went double hard."

"The bigger picture," I continued, "includes all sorts of things we can't even imagine, completely unlikely, random scenarios."

"Chaos."

"Not exactly, but nature certainly isn't required to follow human order."

"We're not dealing with nature," he insisted. " 'Murder most foul, strange, and unnatural.' "

"Hamlet," I guessed. Even away from university, our Shakespeare scholar's mind was rarely far from his obsession.

"Correct. Ghost of Hamlet's Father, Act I, scene v." He stretched. "I don't want to sit in a graveyard with you tonight. I know you're going to try and convince me that it'll be all weird and Halloweeny, but in fact it will be primarily boring, with a side of soggy cold."

"I'll bring some of my apple brandy."

"See," he said, sitting up, "that should have been your lead sentence. *That* catches the attention. And PS: Why haven't you dragged it out before now?"

"Because I know your fondness for it," I answered, "and I was saving it to bribe you, in a situation like this one."

"Good answer." He stood. "It worked."

"Where are you going?"

"Take a long hot shower, get the bones warm." He grabbed the stair rail. "Prep work for the brandy and tombstones. I'll be having a bottle all to myself, you realize."

"Should we go over to the Deveroe cabin before?"

"We're not going afterward." He started up the stairs. "Didn't you just hear Skidmore say not to go there after dark?"

"I mean should we try to get that visit in today before we go out to the cemetery or should we wait until tomorrow?"

"I think my shower is going to take well on toward sunset. Answer your question?" He disappeared upstairs.

One of the many reasons I enjoyed Andrews's visits was not having to sit in my house alone. Like Truevine's craft, it didn't matter to me that I had no genuine belief in ghosts; they came to me nevertheless. My mother sat on the stairs, head in hands, straggled hair brushing the hem of her black dress at the knee. My father banged pots in the kitchen, answering her snarling questions with vague, hollow repetition. Mother's infidelities, father's mental absence, money problems all haunted the cabin, hung in the rafters like smoke, waiting for a quiet moment to seep into my skin.

I turned on the lamp beside the sofa, went to the stereo. Sometimes music dispels the spirits. I put on an older record, Hazel Dickens and Mike Seeger's Strange Creek Singers. I'd first heard of them at Antioch College in Ohio, where I'd taken a summer semester before starting at Burrison University. There I had the odd fortune of meeting a woman called Mama Jaambo. No sooner had her name come into my mind than I realized music had not dispelled but called forth other spirits.

Mama Jaambo was from New Jersey. Her gift was reading auras; her session began the second night I was there, at moonrise, in a room with big windows on all sides and two dirty skylights.

"Leave the lights off," Mama intoned. "It's easier to see auras by the moon."

Her assistant, a slender young woman in a floor-length dress, said, "Now when you want your aura read, just say, 'Here, Mama,' and she'll look."

Mama was a large woman in a soft blue dress. Her voice was like an iris petal. Students would sing out, she would turn in her chair. "Your aura is light blue. You are a musician of great tenacity; you are kind, have loving friends."

That was the evening for nearly two hours. All were amazed at Mama's power of insight. I felt above the proceedings, given my knowledge of carnival tricks, but at last other students prevailed upon me to speak the magic words: "Over here, Mama."

She turned as she had done every other time, settled her eyes on me, smiled, and said, "Your aura is oh my God!"

The assistant rushed to Mama's side. After a flurry of whispering, an ascendancy of larks, the assistant turned to the assembled.

"You'll all need to leave now, except that boy. He will to come talk with Mama. Thank you for having us; it's been a wonderful night." She instantly began ushering people out.

Obviously I'd done something wrong. Maybe Mama knew I held her tricks in contempt. I stood, looking down, while everyone else filed out, glaring at me.

Mama beckoned; I approached.

"Have a seat. You got an aura could knock down a horse."

"Is that bad?"

"It's not good or bad, just the way it is."

"Are you mad at me?" I wondered.

"No. I got news. Sometime between now and Christmas you'll most likely die. Ice or cold water is what I see. That's it."

She stood. The assistant rushed to her and was helping her to the door before I found my voice.

"Excuse me?"

"I tell you this as a warning; maybe it'll help." She didn't turn around. "If not, they won't find your body till next spring."

I left Antioch at the end of August, forgot most of what I learned there.

That winter a group of friends was crossing Clear Lake, near my house, and it cracked underneath us. Seven drowned. I survived because at the last minute I hesitated closer to the bank than the others, yelled at Skid to stay behind me, a premonition or a memory. I still fell through the ice, submerged. Skid pulled me out, pushed the water out of my lungs. I started breathing seven minutes later—a minute for every dead friend—and stayed in the hospital for a week. My mother didn't visit once, but the seven who drowned stood around me every day, close to my bed. Sometimes they told me to get better; sometimes they invited me to come away. It was a difficult decision.

Voices on the stereo mixed with childhood memories, ancient deceptions, nameless guilts, waking nightmares, old words that ought to have been buried but would not die. I turned up the volume.

A half an hour later Andrews called down, "Kind of loud, isn't it?"

The record was blasting; bass made books next to the speakers jump and twitch.

"Andrews," I answered, "I've been thinking."

"Oh God." His voice was muffled from his room, but I could hear the tone.

"About this perspective shift."

"What about it?" He appeared at the top of the stairs in his robe, drying his hair.

"What if the events of Thursday night didn't transpire the way we think they did, the way Skid outlined?"

He stopped rubbing his hair, his voice weary. "In what way?"

I turned the stereo down. "What if Harding Pinhurst wasn't the victim?"

Four

"Christ, he's the dead one," Andrews insisted incredulously, lumbering down the stairs. "Of course he was the victim!"

"We don't know he's the only one dead." I lifted the needle, turned off the stereo. "Truevine's missing; no one knows where Able is."

"But in this case the definition of *victim*—"

"You know," I said, "a hot shower does sound good. I hope you didn't use all the water."

An expletive exploded from Andrews that made the house creak. He returned to his room.

"Why couldn't you look at it another way?" I said, climbing the stairs after him. "Harding was angry enough to attack Able, Able defended himself, Harding fell down the hill, hit his head, Able panicked, now the Deveroes are out for blood, so *Able's* the victim."

"You'd panic, too," he shouted from his room, "if the Deveroe boys were after you!"

"They saved my life last year on the Devil's Hearth."

"They didn't mean to," he corrected, showing his face in the doorway to his room as I hit the top of the stairs. "It was a coincidence they happened to be up there looking for snakes to sell Hek. And it still doesn't make Able a victim. Yet."

"You're right about the Deveroes," I admitted. "I'd be nervous if they were after me."

"I shudder to think." He disappeared again. "But Harding's the victim here. *And* he was stripped naked. Damn."

A shower, a sweater, and a swig of apple brandy launched Andrews and me into my truck, on our way to the city graveyard.

Our cemetery was a fair resort for the many members of the community who chose not to be buried in their own gardens. The city yard had begun as an attempt at respectability. The town would no longer be a crass colonial settlement; we would have a proper park for repose of our departed.

The notion allowed larger families to purchase grand multiple plots, hoping to lead the way out of our dark past as superstitious hill people and into a shining future of sophisticated citizenship. Eighteenth-century Newcombs led the way buying acres of terraced solitude. June's family, prominent in dry goods, had bought some of the last available parcels near the beginning of the twentieth century. The idea lost its luster after that, when so many families gave sons to world wars. A child lost so far from home was better buried near the house.

Some of the older families clung to their plots, but the place was kept in business at the beginning of the twenty-first century primarily by people without families: orphans, childless spinsters, lost souls, criminals, non–church members, strangers, or blackbirds. Huge bats were the rumor, but aggressive ravens were more likely to swoop a visitor.

The entrance was easy to miss. A once-impressive granite arch had been rendered invisible by poison ivy. The road past it, less traveled than any other in the county, was little more than tire ruts in wandering weeds. I had visited many times as a boy walking over the mountain and coming in the back way, but I couldn't ever remember approaching it correctly and almost missed the gate.

The sun was setting on the other side of the mountain; black shadows spread across the narrow road through the yard. Truck headlights did nothing to dispel the darkness, only disoriented the eyes. Low branches of ancient juniper swept the truck's doors as we drove past, grasping at the handles, whispering to the windows.

Wind clacked bare limbs of a dead oak ten feet from the road; a shudder of wings shook the air.

"You're certain those aren't bats?" Andrews rolled up his window all the way.

"Crows." I watched them take to the higher branches of pine.

"Whatever they are," he muttered, taking a sip from his personal bottle of apple brandy, "they're big enough to carry the truck off if they wanted to."

It was difficult to see tombstones; I thought there must be more deeper into the cemetery. Hek would have walked by the northern edge going home; I headed in that direction.

"Keep an eye out," I reminded Andrews, already a little lax from drink.

Remembering his duty, he reared his head up, cast a sullied glance around. Without warning he grabbed my arm, sloshing his drink everywhere.

"What the hell is that?" he gasped.

High on the slope to our right was a flying woman. I hit the brakes; the truck skidded to a halt, slightly sideways.

A second later, realizing she was frozen in the air, I let out my breath. "The Angel of Death. Biggest statue in the park."

"They don't really call it that," he whispered, shaking his head.

"Ours is a happy little community, don't you think?" I resumed driving north.

"Seriously, that's the name?"

"The Angel of Death," I assured him. "It was ordered from a company called Revelation Statuary, in South Carolina. A reminder God's harvest is continuous; today you're here on a visit; tomorrow you'll be back as a resident. Now if you could manage to be a little more alert and a little less arm-grabbing, we might not end up in a ditch. Like to spend the night here?"

"Christ." He put the stopper back in the bottle and scoured the area with his eyes. "Don't tell me anything more about this cemetery, all right?"

We rolled past the statue, the road all but vanished. Only an ancient memory of sunlight lit the higher rises of the yard. Bending gnarled branches made the way more treacherous, and at last I was forced to surrender, stopping the truck.

"What are you doing?" Andrews locked his door.

"There's no more road. I want to see the place where Hek passed by." I opened my door, reached under my seat for the flashlight I always kept there. "I think it's a short walk over that way."

"Why don't we come back tomorrow?"

"Because tomorrow," I reminded him, "we visit the Deveroes."

He offered an unrepeatable remark, leaned against his door, sloshed out his side.

The grass was tough despite the recent rain; my flashlight was no more successful illuminating our way than the truck's headlights had been. Twilight in a cemetery will not be ruled. Artificial light is made for more defined darkness, not the vagaries of time between sunset and night.

Blackberry brambles tore at our ankles. *Fairy beggars,* I had heard them called: they feel like thorns snagging the cuffs of your pants, but they could just as well be nature folk tugging, asking for a handout. Without the slightest genuine belief in such an idea, some old-timers still tossed a penny into a thorn thicket. Giving money to the fairies was not, they clearly advised, done for reward. The only benefit was that the fairies would consider leaving you alone. As much to impress Andrews as to indulge my heritage, I reached into my pocket and tossed a penny into the blackberry canes.

"What was that?" He jumped.

I explained; he drank; the wind picked up.

We made our way up a small rise, pine filling the air.

Night came on.

A curtain dropped over the sky, it happened in an instant, and the flashlight bit into the blackness in front of us. The world was transformed. Every sound was amplified: crickets were deafening;

tree frogs tore the fabric of night; shaking limbs above us rattled thunder. Every sound in darkness is more important than a prayer.

The occasional white tombstone leered as we shuffled past, but that part of our graveyard was populated chiefly by night noise, drying weeds, a canopy of bare oak. As swiftly as the sun had gone, the moon came up over the mountain. The landscape was dusted silver, separated from its previous mien by time, not distance—the exact amount of time it took for day to exhale its last breath and die past the western horizon.

Moonlight ran like water over the slope; we waded through it to the top. Below us on the other side of the slope was a dark valley scar, a place where nothing grew. Rocks and dead clay, a gash across the face of the earth, lay splayed in lunar autumn.

"Christ." Andrews stared down at the desolate patch. "Why is it so bare down there?"

"Combination of red Georgia dirt and erosion," I answered, shining light across the crags. "Some places get ruined, never come back to life."

"No wonder this spot was chosen for a graveyard."

"This was all Newcomb land," I said. "Jeribald sold most of it when he moved his family away."

"The incest Newcombs? with The Newcomb Dwarf?" Andrews picked up his pace. "This keeps getting better. You don't live in Blue Mountain; you live in Amityville."

"On the other side of those rocks is the far edge of the cemetery, where Hek saw his ghost."

"Truvy Deveroe."

"I believe so, yes."

We made our way over the boulders and the slipping gravel. A barbed wire fence ran the ridge, a worn path the other side of it. I moved the flashlight slowly over the undulating land: more boulders, moss, brown sticks once wildflowers. A corner of fencing bent where the property ended, cradled a number of grave markers, green in gray, the most we'd seen.

Unknown Vagrant, died of hunger, 1858

Eloise and Davy Deveroe, together once more

My wife Sarah, gone to angels without me, 1803

Russell Pike, good patriot, better father, killed a wild boar and seven Britash [sic] who meant to ruin this country. Died in bed, 1793

Sally Pike, seven, lost 1818

None had known care in the current century, possibly in the previous. Many were toppled and unreadable. In spring, under a certain sun, it might have been a pleasant spot, picking blackberries, looking down the mountain, smelling pine and cedar. After dark in the older part of the year, only melancholy existed, recollections of lives forgotten, thorns without fruit.

"Who were they?" Andrews whispered. "What was it like to be them?"

"I know," I answered. "Gives you an intimation of what's in store."

He swigged from his bottle. "Not to worry. I won't forget you when you're buried here."

"I see." I switched off the flashlight; our eyes adjusted to the moonlight. "And what happens to my good name when you go?"

"Not in my plans."

"You're not dying."

"Don't think so," he said, offering me the bottle. "What's your idea here? Wander about hoping to catch a glimpse of a girl who's so adept at hiding that even her own brothers can't find her?"

"Good point," I admitted, refusing the brandy. "But I thought we might find evidence of her."

"A rag, a bone," he drawled, "a hank of hair."

"Shut up."

"Would you like to know what I think of your little excursion to this place tonight?" He waved his drink grandly.

"Not even a little bit."

"I think," he forged on, "that you are trying to give me what is commonly called *the willies*."

"Why would that be of the slightest interest to me?"

"Because you're bored, you have nothing to do up here, you long for your little mysteries so you can feel useful. Also, you have a genetic need to feel superior and you think I'm easily frightened, so it's a bit of fun for you in the bargain."

"Aside from the fact that you look a little like Icabod Crane," I began, "why would I imagine you're easily frightened?"

He was prevented from answering by a scream.

It came from the woods beyond the fence. I snapped the flashlight back on, stabbed it in the direction of the sound.

There was a blur of motion in the trees, a frantic rash of leaves, more shouting.

"Help me!" Then a muffled groan.

"That's not a woman," Andrews said, heading toward the noise without thinking.

"Who's there?" another voice shouted from inside the chaos.

"Come on, then," I told Andrews, headed for the fence.

I used one of the posts to vault over the wire; Andrews got a better head of steam and cleared it with a light hurdle. We ran in the direction of the voices, now clearly several, flashlight leading the way as if it might protect us.

A shot rang out, hit a tree yards away from us. Andrews splayed on the ground. I stopped running and turned off the light.

"Sh," I told him.

We froze.

"They're over yonder, ignor'nt." It was the voice of Donny Deveroe, I was certain.

"Boys?" I called out. "Is that the Deveroes?"

"What the hell are you doing?" Andrews rasped at me. Stage whisper.

"Who is it?" another voice shouted.

"Is that Dover?" I yelled back. "Stop shooting at us. It's Fever Devilin."

There was a flurry of conversation we couldn't make out.

Silence.

"Dr. Devilin?" Donny called innocently. "Is that you?"

"Didn't mean to startle you," I said, walking their way, light still off. "I wanted to show Andrews the graveyard. You remember my friend Professor Andrews from—"

Another shot spattered the clay inches from my right foot.

"Sorry, Dr. Devilin," Donny said, genuinely apologetic. "We're kind of in the middle of something here and we would rather have our privacy."

"I understand." I looked back at Andrews.

He sat up, trying to make out who else was in the grove.

"We heard someone yell for help," he ventured from the ground.

Another rustle of whispers.

"Dover. He fell in a muskrat hole."

Silence. Cricket, frog, crow, wind, breath—all kept still.

"Is he all right?" Andrews managed, coming to a stand.

"Oh. Absolutely. Say something, Dover."

A thin, clear cloud slit the moon, moved on.

"Ow."

Andrews came to my side.

"We'll go on back to the cemetery, then," I said. "I was thinking of paying you a visit tomorrow; would that be okay?" I aimed the flashlight in the direction of the voices and switched it on.

Bodies exploded in motion; I counted four before the next shot was fired, wrecking pine straw a foot to our left. Andrews did his best not to jump right.

"Turn off that damn torch!"

I did.

"Sorry," I told them. "I don't know this part of the mountain very well and it's hard to see." I handed Andrews the flashlight. "Catching snakes?"

Silence.

"Yes."

I leaned close to Andrews's ear. "Take the flashlight, shine it toward the cemetery, head back to the truck."

"What are you doing?" he whispered back harshly.

"I'm going to find out what they're up to. How many did you see?"

"Four."

"And there are only three Deveroe brothers."

Before he could object I crouched low, lumbered to a nearby stump, waving him on his way.

He took a second to consider his predicament, then turned away, switched on the light, and moved carefully back over the fence, into the knot of trees that hid my truck.

Satisfied I had waited long enough, I moved, still low, toward the boys. They weren't talking, but they made sufficient fuss cracking twigs, thudding the ground, tossing leaves, grunting. If I hadn't known better, I might have considered they were wrestling swine.

Their noise covered my movements; their activity distracted them. I was able to get within twenty yards, hiding behind the branches of a wild holly.

The moon had difficulty breaking apart the shadows in the grove, but here and there a shaft of silver cut the night and I could make out all three brothers, rifles in hand, surrounding a fourth man. He had a gunnysack over his head pulled to his mouth, where the edge of it had been made into a gag. His clothes were in shambles, torn, rubbed with mud. His hands were tied loosely behind his back. He staggered, trying to get away, muttering through the cloth.

It wasn't until they put the noose around his neck that I realized what they were doing. Dover held one end of a length of heavy twisted hemp and Donny put the other end over their captive's head.

My heart doubled, I took a step past the holly before I could consider the consequences. They didn't see me.

Dover hauled the rope over the lowest limb of an older pine; Donny tightened the knot. All three brothers set their guns against the trunk, grabbed high, and hauled their victim into the air.

"No!" I crashed through the undergrowth, the whipping twigs, bent on tackling the Deveroes.

They were startled, turned my way, but kept hold of the rope.

The man in the air kicked and twisted like a fish on a hook, flailing almost sideways in the air.

"Stop!" I huffed, five feet from them, diving to tackle.

As Dover reached for his rifle there came a thunderous wooden crash like a house falling down. The limb cracked and fell on the boys.

Some unseen part of it managed to catch the side of my skull. The victim, miraculously thrown to one side of the fallen branch, only took a heartbeat to realize what had happened. Adrenaline burst him free from his fetters. He got to his feet, ripped the bag from his head, took a single look around, and shot like a bullet into the night.

When I saw who it was, I wanted to sprint after him, but my legs wouldn't work and my temples were exploding.

"Damn damn damn!" Dover struggled, swatting at the immovable limb, gasping for air.

I touched my head. There was blood, but the cut wasn't deep.

I managed to stand, cracking smaller twigs away.

"Who's hurt?" I croaked.

"*You* don't sound too good, Doc!" Dover sang out, obviously smiling.

"So." I came to stand beside the branch, looked down at him. "You're not angry with me?"

"Not hardly," Donny said, straining against the part of the tree that held his leg. "You ain't the one that broke this damn tree."

"I told you it ain't hold him," Dover said plainly, looked up at me. " 'Sbeen too wet these past days."

"Well, it's holding you down right good."

The third brother was silent, unconscious.

I couldn't figure why they were being so cordial to me when I'd just foiled their hanging and let the quarry escape. It was stranger than the rest of the event, but I was grateful for whatever angel watched over me, and set to the matter at hand.

"I'll see what I can do about the branch," I told them. I prepared. "I'm going to push it back, if I can. If I make things worse, like it starts rolling over you, sing out. Right?"

I leaned my back against the branch, dug my heels in, took a deep breath, got my palms underneath the thickest part. Arching my back, I strained my legs. The wood creaked, moved. Donny and Dover pressed the branch away from them hard, gasping. The limb rolled away enough for them to drag themselves out, retrieve the third silent family member.

"Is he hurt?" I said, moving slowly out of the way, making certain the limb wasn't coming back my way. "He's unconscious."

He moaned, opened his eyes, blinked, belched, grinned.

Clearly the boys had been drinking more than copiously.

"What did you think you were doing?" I had to ask, breathing hard, leaning against the fallen pine.

"We wasn't gonna kill him or nothing, if that's what you're thinking," Donny said slowly. "But we surely did scare him a good sight."

"Shut up," Dover said, swatting at his brother. "We were only messing around." He stared up at me. "Did you see who it was?"

"Did you see where he went?" the one on the ground said, rallying.

"I wouldn't tell you where he went," I assured them calmly, "and he had a bag over his head. Honestly, what's the matter with you boys?"

"I miss Truvy," the one on the ground said softy. "That's what's a matter with me anyway."

His sentiment silenced his brothers.

Moonlight brushed away a small portion of darkness in the grove; crickets took up their communion once more; night resumed. I peered into the woods where the hanged man had run, but he was long gone, no movement there at all.

"Lucky you was here, Doc," Donny said finally, reaching out his hand. "No telling how long we'd a had to lay out under this here tree."

I helped him up.

"I'm glad you see it that way." I couldn't help a quick glance at their rifles.

Dover noticed. "You know you'd already be gone if I'd a wanted you dead."

I knew. They were perfect shots; the night was clear; I was a big target.

"I'm still coming to visit tomorrow, if that's all right."

They looked at one another.

"Problem?" I folded my arms, legs apart.

"It's just that since Truvy's gone," Donny said, eyes to the ground, "the place is kind of a mess."

"It's a train wreck is what," Dover agreed.

"I don't care about that," I started.

"Maybe not," Donny interrupted, "but Tru, she'd be mortified for you to see her house in such a state. Could we meet out on the road?"

"Or we could come to your house," the nameless brother offered.

"Hush!" Dover commanded.

"How about ten tomorrow morning?" I relaxed. "I'll pull up and honk the horn."

"Good enough," Dover said quickly.

An owl called, an arrow sound through the air.

All four of us jumped.

"I'm going back to the cemetery now," I said. "Andrews is in my truck drinking apple brandy and I'm afraid he might try to drive."

"You don't want that," Donny said, retrieving his rifle. "When you have a lot to drink, it's better to walk."

"Good night, then." I turned without another word, my back to three armed men. I heard the shuffling boots, clacking barrels, sniffing.

As their sounds receded behind me, I let out a breath, realized my fingers were shaking. The image of the dangling man, barely real, batted inside my head.

Up toward the path, moonlight spilled an abundance over the open field. Moths and night birds zagged the air; a rabbit, roused by our noise, was looping around white rocks by the fence.

Aching a little from the strain of moving the tree, I held the top wire down and managed to step over the fence. I stood a moment, calming. The tombstones seemed cleaner in moonbeams than in flashlight. I stared at the oldest, the war hero's grave. Part of the engraving was covered over by dead honeysuckle; I pulled the vines aside.

Cursed be him that moves my bones.

I knew Andrews would be amused to hear that a phrase written on Shakespeare's tombstone was to be found in our graveyard as well.

A short drift of autumn breeze lifted my hair; a spiderweb fluttered in the brambles that topped the stone. Woven into the new edge of the web were three frayed strands of artificial thread from a cloth or a dress, the color of roses. I pulled one; the web shuddered but held, collapsed when I removed all three.

I pocketed the thread, took a last look about. The Deveroes were gone, as far as I could tell. The night had closed around the place where they'd tried to hang a man. The rest was fall: crisp breeze, flurry of brown leaves, white beams brushed across a dying landscape.

Once, walking the last few hundred yards back to the truck, I saw a figure move out of the corner of my eye, but when I turned, it was a billowing pine bough, beyond it the Angel of Death.

Andrews had locked the truck from the inside and it took a little doing to get him to open my door.

"God, if you had been one minute longer," he said waving his empty bottle in my face, "I swear I'd have started this truck and gone home without you."

"I told them I was afraid you might," I said, sliding in behind the wheel.

I told him what had happened; he listened with growing attention, widening eyes. It had all gone so quickly. I realized as I was talking how stunned I was. The retelling of the events assumed a dreamlike vapor in my mind.

"I don't know where to begin," he said, slumping at the end of my report. "They weren't angry with you for breaking up their lynching. They were grateful to you for taking the tree limb off, which I'm not sure why you did. And you let them go to catch the poor man again? Do we go to Skid's house or call him or what?"

"I thought you said there was a Raymond Chandler on television tonight." I started the truck.

"Are you out of your mind? We have to find the man they were trying to hang. We have to call the police!"

"Look." The truck's headlights blasted the way in front of us. "The boys aren't quite as stupid as they seem. They know I saw what they were doing tonight, so they know better than to go on with the plan now. They realize I'll tell Skidmore what I saw. If anyone ends up hanging from a tree, they'll be the only suspects. Also, they didn't want me to come in their house tomorrow. It could be they're actually embarrassed about the state of the place, or it could be they're hiding something. I don't want the police up there messing with things before I get a look." I pressed the accelerator. "I haven't told you the worst of it, the main thing."

"There's more?"

"I saw who it was they were murdering." I found the way; the granite gateway came into the high beams.

"You said he had a burlap sack over his head."

"After he got his hands untied, he ripped it off."

We pulled through the front entrance, out of the graveyard, and both let out a breath. The truck turned right and picked up speed, on toward home.

"Are you going to tell me?" Andrews asked, realizing at last his bottle was empty, setting it at his feet.

"You'd know," I said, "if you could clear your head."

He only took a second.

"Holy Christ, they were trying to hang Able Carter."

"That's right," I confirmed.

Five

"But he got *away*." Andrews wanted confirmation.

"He did," I assured him, "but you can't imagine the look on his face."

The way was bumpy; Andrews clutched the armrest on his door. "I would have lost my mind," he said, mostly to himself.

The shock was wearing off for me as well. The realization of what it must have been like to be dangling in the air was prying its way into my mind. I was having second thoughts about calling the police.

"Luck, that branch breaking when it did." But my voice was shaky.

"You don't think it was luck," Andrews said suspiciously. "You think it was some Jungian bit of Universal Synchronicity."

"I think the recent rain made everything soggy," I told him, "and the boys were in too much of a hurry or too drunk to realize that low pine limbs always break off and fall."

"Despite the fact that they're smarter than I think."

"Shut up."

The rest of the ride home was silent. The moon that had been bone white in the graveyard was a more reassuring snow color on the open fields. The racket of night was soothing as the road made a gentle sweep around the mountain to my home.

Once safely in my driveway, I turned off the engine, reached into my pocket.

"Look."

Andrews opened his door and the overhead light showed him the threads in my hand.

"You found those in the graveyard."

"More fiber evidence."

"I need coffee." He swung out of the cab and lumbered toward the house.

We'd started a fire, watching it instead of television. Andrews cleared his head; I tried to focus my thoughts. The orange light from the iron stove twisted around all the darker places in the room.

"Those graves we saw," he said lazily, slouched down low on the sofa, feet up, shoes off. "Were they the loneliest things in the world or what?"

" 'Sarah, seven, lost' was the worst," I agreed.

"Sally." He folded his arms. "That one's name was Sally; the wife gone to angels was Sarah. Does it mean that little girl Sally was lost in the mountains or something and never found?"

"Probably," I said, scraping one of the last kernels of popped corn from the bowl between us. "Happens every now and again. There are all kinds of stories about people lost on the mountain."

"Stories you've collected, you mean?"

"Right."

"You've been doing it, what? Ten years, I mean officially?" He closed his eyes.

"All my life, really," I nodded, "but about twelve academically."

"Which is eighty-four in dog years." He reached into the bowl, found it empty, growled.

"Did I ever tell you about Truevine's parents?"

"Did you ever tell me you were going to eat all the popped corn?"

"Apparently the whole clan was much calmer," I said, "when the parents were alive. More like other mountain families at the time. Davy and Eloise were fine people."

Andrews demonstrated his interest by swinging open cabinet doors in search of something more to eat. "I can't find the popcorn."

"There isn't any more."

"Well, I'm starting to get a headache from that brandy and I need food."

"Whose fault is that?" I slumped down, staring at the flames.

"Who gave me that evil crap to drink in the first place?" he said, rubbing his temples.

"How did the Deveroes find Able?" I wondered, ignoring him.

"You mean when we couldn't." He poured himself some water from the pitcher in the refrigerator and came back to sit by the fire. "Especially when the brothers were, you said, twice as drunk as I was."

"They found him near the graveyard," I tried to continue my line of thought.

"Why do you say that?"

"Why would they take him any farther than they needed to?"

"Why didn't they do it in the cemetery, then?" He put his feet up on the newspaper-strewn coffee table in front of us.

"Superstitious," I answered, "especially about that place." I sat back. "You know, there is a strange feeling up there, don't you think?"

"I do."

"Like someone is watching. Like someone is there."

"Besides the Angel of Death," he laughed. Stopped, sat straighter. "Hold on. Davy and Eloise. The Deveroe parents. Were they the ones on the grave we saw up in the cemetery?"

"That's what I was assuming," I said, watching the glow of the coals.

"You'd think that family would be the kind to bury Ma and Pa in the backyard."

"You'd think," I agreed. "But if there *is* a Deveroe family plot there, I think it's more fuel for my theory that Able and Truevine were hiding out up there. The girl likes to consult her mother on nearly everything."

"No, that doesn't make sense," he said. "Where was Truevine while all this was happening to her swain? She wouldn't just stand by."

"Good point." I glanced at the envelope on the kitchen counter that held the strands of cloth I'd found on the tombstone. "I can't wait to find out if that thread belongs to her dress."

"You like the theory," Andrews said slowly, "that Able and Harding had words, Harding was accidentally killed, and the two lovers beat it into the greenwood, hiding out in a cemetery waiting for everything to blow over."

"When you blurt it out like that," I told him, "it doesn't sound like much of a theory." I closed my eyes, sighing. "But it's something to do with all three; I mean Harding's death and the couple's disappearance are linked."

"Sure," he agreed, "but I think it's as possible that the Deveroe boys saw Harding, thought it was Able, jumped him in the dark, realized their mistake, and left him. And we've seen evidence of that behavior tonight."

"They can see better at night than you and I can at noon," I argued. "And Harding's their cousin."

"It's all guessing," he whined, "and my headache is worse. You're positive we shouldn't call Deputy Needle and tell him what we saw?"

"In the morning."

"But," Andrews objected, "why are we waiting? We saw a crime and we should report it, not to mention the fact that you have evidence in a murder case sitting in your kitchen."

"We don't really know anything. I have no idea what the threads are, could be nothing. And I'm sure the boys are home in bed by now. They looked exhausted and they miss their sister. They want to be home tonight."

"Guessing."

"Educated."

He gave up.

The fire popped; the glow dimmed. Eyelids were heavy; heads were light. Somewhere between waking and dreams, I saw my mother climbing the stairs.

She turned twice in a full circle, dancing in slow motion, in a black slip and no shoes. She was young, smiling. Her hair like a raven's wing fanned out as she spun, and she called out a man's name, not my father's.

I sat up; she vanished.

Andrews was out, snoring. I rubbed my eyes and stood. I tried to make as little noise as possible as I made my way out the door, onto the porch, braced by the cooler air.

Everything was damp from the rain earlier, and the smell was fresh and ancient at once. On the left side of the house, where the largest patch of sunlight stays most of the day, the spice bed filled the air with a war of smells. I stepped off the porch; the moon was high, bright as dusk. Two full sage plants, one variegated, one blue-green, edged the northern curve of the bed. I pulled one long stalk from each, fanned them in the air shaking off the rain. Drying them further with the sleeve of my shirt, I went back inside. Burning sage can banish any spirit.

Kitchen matches by the stove filled the air with sulfur; it took five to ignite the wet sage. Once both stems were smoking, I waved their incense around the kitchen, moving slowly toward the stairs, smoking the air where my mother's ghost had danced.

Satisfied with my work, I tossed the rest of the sage into the flame, and the room filled with its scent.

Andrews roused then. "Something's on fire." He didn't open his eyes.

I glanced once at the old trunk in the corner. The fire was nearly dead, I closed the stove doors. In the silence I knew I wouldn't sleep. Too many ghosts.

"Andrews," I asked him, "do you think you could listen to something, just for a second?"

"Listen to what?" he mumbled.

Why would my mother haunt me when I was thinking about Truevine Deveroe? And why bring me the dancing taunt of her infidelities?

"I have to read you something."

"Why?" He opened his eyes. "Is it about our case?"

"Not so much," I admitted. "It's more about *my* case, I think."

I went to the trunk in a darker corner of the room, sat, opened it as I had done a thousand times, a boy alone in the house. What's sadder than memorabilia of the long dead? Why this preoccupation engaged me time and again I have no idea, except that I wanted some reassurance that the past was dead, the ghosts weren't real, the bodies were buried.

"When my great-grandfather died at the age of seventy-one," I tried to explain to Andrews, "all of his things were sold at auction except for this trunk. It contained papers and some personal valuables which he sent to my father, his favorite grandchild. My great-grandfather had been born in Wales but apprenticed to a silversmith in Ireland. The auction of his things brought a sizable bit of money. Some of it came to me for my university education. I'll never forget the first lonely rainy afternoon, nothing better to do, opening this trunk."

I raised the lid; the yellowed paper crackled; the story sat waiting to be read once more. I picked up one stack. There were perhaps a hundred others like it in the trunk, written in my great-grandfather's arcane hand, all the same story written over and over again, all with the same title.

"It's called 'The Lily.' May I read it to you?"

He didn't understand and he was sleepy, but Andrews nodded, settled back in his chair, and indulged me. "Read away."

I turned on the lamp beside me, closed the trunk and sat on it, and began to read aloud:

" 'I wake from troubled sleep to write these lines. I can find but little rest. To and fro in my dreams I see her walking now, and I cannot keep to my bed. God in Heaven, there must be some release in the telling of my situation, else why would I be compelled to write it down over and over again in ink as black as night?

" 'There am I, in Ireland, with Mr. Jamison.

" 'My father had sent me from a lonely, motherless seaside village as apprentice to a man he barely knew. Still, I was glad to go and find my way in this world. Down the sunny path I passed through the garden gate without a care in this world. I had not yet stepped foot into the Jamison household when I first heard her voice.

" 'She was stirring peat in the fireplace to ready the evening meal, as I could see through the open kitchen window. Her face was white and fragile as the porcelain teacup in her tiny hand. She took no notice of me.

" 'I'm come from bold stock. I straightway cut a lily from the garden walk and went into the kitchen.

" 'She turned. I offered her my lily and she took it without a word.

" 'She locked me eye to eye. "What's your name, then—and what's your business here in this house?"

" ' It's Conner Briarwood, and I'm expected."

" 'Her smile was wider. "It's a rough name."

" ' I come from a wild place, but I've manners enough to offer a flower to the finest woman in this world."

" 'Now she was teasing. "What if I'm the daughter of this house and you've set yourself off on the wrong foot, too bold with the only child of your new master?"

" ' He'll find me likewise bold in all manner of things and he may as well learn it now as later."

" ' But what if I'm only the serving girl and he thinks me beneath your degree?"

" ' Then Mr. Jamison will do just as well to learn I have no patience with the notion of high or low degree when it's God's made us all. I can't be other than I am."

" 'With my eyes so locked on hers, I had not seen Mr. Jamison himself enter the room by the other door. There he was and spoke up strongly, a twinkle in his eye: "Well said, boy. You've got the Devil in you."

" 'I was startled out of myself; she dropped the lily on the floor.

" 'Mr. Jamison smiled, a kindly man. It was in that moment I knew why my father had so trusted him. That smile would win the dead—it won me all the more, being especially full of life that day.

" ' Back to work now, Molly," he spoke as gently as if it had been his own daughter. "Master Conner's been walking all day and he'll be hungry. Go on clean up, then. Your lodging's out by the smith house, a fine set of rooms. I've often kept myself there when

I was late working. Off now, and we'll catch up over dinner." He started out of the room, then turned. "But don't leave without first fetching the lily you've cut from my lady wife's garden walk, give it again to our Molly. Once a lily's cut, its savor wanes."

" 'And he was gone.

" 'So it was I came into the house of a good man, into my time of apprenticeship. I learned to spin silver into teapots and fine plates and loving rings and ornate buttons. The nights were filled with longing for sweet Molly, a stolen moment in the kitchen or garden before falling to fitful sleep. When the day came at last that Mr. Jamison let me take on a project of my own, I fashioned a silver lily. It took the better part of five nights. The old man could see I'd not slept for working, and he praised the silver lily.

" 'What'll it be, son? A pin, an ear piece, a ring?"

" 'It's a gift, sir." I could not look him in the eye. "Useful for nothing else save a token of affection."

" 'That night after dinner I found excuse to wander in the garden, moon the color of the little lily folded in my right hand. Molly came out into the moonlight when she was done with chores.

" 'Look how fine this night is, Mol."

" 'She laid her head upon my shoulder as sweetly as autumn leaf falls to the ground. I could barely breathe.

" 'She looked up into my eyes. "You're the dearest man ever I knew, Conner Briarwood—and I love you till the seas go dry."

" 'Look here, Molly. I've made you a lily that'll never fade. It's a token of my regard for you. This silver lily would sooner turn to clay before my affection for you is cold. I love you till the day I die."

" 'And then we kissed.

" 'Straightway I went to Mr. Jamison and told him of my intention to wed Molly. While his gladness seemed a little short, he was happy for me, offered to pay for the church on All Saints' Day. But his final word was strange. "This world is filled with the bitter as well as the sweet." He'd say no more.

" 'The next day was clear and golden; all the leaves were turning.

I heard Molly's laughter down by the brook at the farther field, under the hazel.

" 'The sight that stabbed my eye when she came into view still cuts my brain.

" 'Molly was entrapped in another man's arms. I could see he was a lord by his fine clothes. I could see he was kissing her neck. I could see he would not let her go. She hadn't been laughing at all but crying for help. I ran to her aid.

" 'Out came the dagger and rapier to my hand.

" 'You there!" I shouted. "Leave off with that girl or I'll break open your breastbone. You're a dog and I mean to kill you."

" 'Molly broke free from his grasp. Her face was flush with fear and she came running for me.

" ' No, Conner! Don't fight him!"

" 'But she need not fear for me. I grew up wild and brawling with tougher men than this rich pastry, and I told her so.

" ' Quit this place, Molly. I have something to do with your malefactor."

" ' Hold, boy," he said calmly. "You don't have the understanding of this situation."

" ' Will you take out your sword?" I spit back at him.

" ' Here it is then." He drew. "But I only mean to relieve you of those weapons and calm you down. You don't rightly know what's at work here."

" 'There was a rage in me; the Devil had my throat. I threw myself at him and beat down his resistance at once. He fell backward puffing and stumbling and trying to shake off his cape. Molly was screaming, but the rage in my head would allow me nothing save the object of my blade. I took my dagger to his chest without a word, cracked his breastbone, spilled his blood, cleft his heart in twain. He fell to the earth, dead.

" 'Molly was crying like a madwoman. Others from over fields and houses were running to see. She flung herself on me, beating my chest with her tiny hands.

" ' What in God's name have you done? Don't you know you've

killed a lord who was going to take care of me with gold and silver and a house of my own? You've ruined me, you stupid boy."

" 'On her hand was a ring of gold as wide as a beam of sunset.

" ' What are you saying?" I dropped the rapier, took a step back from her, drenched in rich man's blood. "You're to be married to *me* this week."

" ' What girl would marry an apprentice," she rasped, "when she had a fine lord? There's to be no wedding; there never was to be no wedding. And now you've murdered the only man who could have saved me from a life of serving and fetching. You'll hang, boyo. You'll hang!"

" 'She reached in her bodice and pulled out my silver lily, threw it in my face.

" 'On All Saints' Day I fed myself on a jailer's soup in place of wedding cake and watched the sun pass through prison bars.

" 'The day of my trial was in cold December, when all the birds had fled. Mr. Jamison found me a lawyer from Belfast who assured me there was a flaw in my indictment which could have me free. I had little hope. I'd killed a man of high degree, and my only love was witness against me. What good would freedom do me anyway?

" 'The trial began with legal talk; lawyers and judges speak a language all their own. The lawyers met up at the judge's bench and jabbered again in Latin for the space of half an hour.

" 'I could make out but little: ". . . third page of the indictment no mention of the word *fiancé* . . . page seven *Briarwood* misspelled . . . page eleven a blacksmith, far cry from a silversmith . . . shoddy work, flaw after flaw . . ." until at last the judge cried, "Enough. Step back!"

" 'The silence of the tomb was on the courthouse that day. The judge cast his eye about the place, slowly took in every face. At last he spoke.

" ' This indictment is riddled with flaws; I must release the prisoner until a new one may be filed."

" 'He banged the gavel down; the room exploded. I scarcely heard a sound of it. I watched as Molly rose and departed the place with never one look back at me at all. Not one. I soon left Ireland the same way.

" 'My name is Conner Devilin now, and I live in America. I've a fine wife and grown children and still more money in the banks than I know what to do with.

" 'It might have been that my fate would be to write these lines from a prison cell after killing a man in wild anger. But God devises various prisons—some are not made of stone and bars. For I wake from troubled sleep nearly every night of my life, can find but little rest. In my dreams I see her walking, setting fire to my heart, and cannot keep to my bed.

" 'So I write it down again in ink as black as night, but it is no use. The ending is always the same: I love her still, her voice like an angel, her tiny hands.

" 'There's the proof on my table: the lily—still silver, not clay— bright as the moon, the only true pain, and the only real light, I will ever know.' "

I looked up. Andrews snored softly in his chair; I had no way of knowing how much of the story he'd heard. I put it back in the trunk.

I suppose I had always considered the story, my obsession with it, an influential factor in my becoming a folklorist. It was not only the fact that its story explained derivation of the Devilin name or that it was impossible to tell what of it was truth and what fiction. There was something more emotional and immediate for me. In stacks and stacks of curling paper there were a hundred versions or more of my great-grandfather's story, varying only slightly in length and dia- logue. His obsession with the past is what spoke to me most.

Although I searched the trunk quite thoroughly in my younger years, there was no trace of the silver lily. I asked my father about it. All he could remember was something odd about the funeral, some trouble with the widow, my great-grandmother Adele. She didn't like the fact that the old man had insisted on being buried with a lit- tle silver lily in his right hand. He was, they say, laid to rest with his right hand closed at his heart. No one at the time knew why, except perhaps my great-grandmother. She wandered off from her nurse less than a year later and was never found, died alone somewhere in the mountains. Her body was never recovered.

Her ghost sat beside me, staring silently at the pages I held, brushing gray hair with bone-white fingertips, resting her head on my shoulder. Some ghosts, so cold, cannot be dispelled by smoldering sage; they need a blazing fire.

Six

The next morning I awoke downstairs on the sofa with no memory of getting there or falling asleep. Andrews was slouched in his chair. Sun shouted through the windows. To make matters worse, the phone would not stop ringing no matter how hard I stared at it.

Somehow I got to a standing position but failed to move any closer to the phone. Andrews shot up angrily, scowled, stomped over, and grabbed it.

"Devilin residence," he said calmly. "Oh, Skidmore, we were just going to call you."

He held out the receiver in my direction.

I took a deep breath, came to the phone. "Skid. We had an adventure last night."

I told him the story. He got angry; we argued; he told me not to touch the thread from the gravestone, he'd be over in twenty minutes. I hung up.

"Okay, you were right." I gave Andrews a glance. "We should have called him last night."

"Sometimes I don't know what's the matter with you," he growled.

I saw no point in going over the long list of things the matter with me, including why I'd slept on the sofa. Instead, I made breakfast: omelets with fresh basil from the spice garden and the last of the tomatoes on the leggy vines outside the door. I was making the second round of espresso when Skidmore knocked.

"Come in." I didn't turn around.

He entered silently; I knew he was glaring at my back.

"Damn it." He stood just inside the doorway.

"Here's the envelope," Andrews offered from his seat at the kitchen table, pointing to the countertop.

"We're having a little espresso before we head up to the Deveroe place," I said, my back still to him. "Want some?"

Skid and I had found over the years that ignoring a problem, in combination with the right amount of humor, could make the problem go away. Or at least it went unspoken, which was as good in my book. That would be the oft-mentioned Book of *Not Saying*, perfected in Blue Mountain generations before I was born.

"Okay then." He moved to pick up the envelope, sighed. "I reckon I could use a little of that engine sludge."

"You insult it," I said, facing him, handing him a cup, "but you drink it."

"I tolerate it for the sake of our friendship," he answered pointedly. "What's left of it."

"I told him to call you last night." Andrews shifted in his seat. His hair was a blond squirrel's nest, and his sweatshirt looked as if he'd slept in it.

"Maybe it should just be you and me working on this thing," Skid said to Andrews. "Leave out the middleman."

"Factory-direct crime solving." Andrews nodded. "We pass the savings on to you."

"You get what you pay for," I said, pouring.

"No kidding, Dev," Skidmore said softly, "I need you to tell me when something like that happens. Not sit on it all night. What if them boys had found Able again? And now all that trail's nine hours cold. I mean, *damn*."

"I told him all that," Andrews put in.

"Now you're just getting annoying," I informed Andrews. "I've changed my mind about taking you with me up to the Deveroe house."

"I didn't want to go in the first place." He leaned back. "I'm on vacation."

"There you go," Skid said, sipping.

"Fine," I told them both. "I'll take care of our little problem myself, then, shall I?"

"Which problem would that be?" Skidmore said, casting a side-long glance at Andrews.

"I'd be leaving the murder to you, of course," I answered innocently. "I'm simply trying to do your wife a favor and find her brother." I finished my espresso in one gulp. "And since the Deveroe brothers were the last to see him, I think I'll head up to their place."

I turned, set my cup in the sink, and bounded upstairs.

I could hear Skidmore and Dr. Andrews discussing matters, most notably yours truly. Odd hearing my best friend from the mountains and my closest university chum talking without me: country mouse, city mouse conspiring. Most of what they said was lost when I got in the shower, but I was certain I heard Skidmore tell Andrews to meet him in an hour. What they were planning was anyone's guess.

I was back downstairs, khakis and dark green sweater on, within minutes. Skid had gone.

"What were you two talking about?" I asked Andrews.

"You mostly."

"He left?"

"Without saying good-bye," he said, mocking.

"Are you going with me or not?" I pulled my keys out of my pocket.

"Not," he said firmly. "I'm taking a nice shower, a stroll through the grandeurs of nature, then a run at some cheap paperback that has nothing to do with Shakespeare, because, I may have forgotten to mention, *I'm on vacation*."

"Well, there you are," I said, heading for the door.

No need to confront him with the fact that I knew he was lying.

The Deveroe cabin sat on a harsh slant near the top of a craggy rise, the dark side of Blue Mountain. Many generations had called the place home. What caught the eye in the morning's light was a lush verdance that seemed to grow from the house itself. Cardinal climber, purple hyacinth bean, morning glory, pumpkin vines all twined as one around *six front* porch columns. The roof was covered with sod and growing moss, a green roof that cooled in summer and warmed in winter. The wood was gray with age, unpainted but looked solid. Windows were spotless and hung with white lace. The front yard rivaled Monet's: nasturtiums, mums, cleome, begonias mixed in with butternut squash, chard with purple stalks, and the perfume of giant rosemary guarded the steps. It was easy to see why people might think more than simple agriculture was at work in such abundance—nature had been aided by the supernatural.

I honked the truck horn as a formality: the boys knew I was there; the curtains at the window shivered.

Donny appeared in the doorway grinning. He hadn't changed clothes since the previous night, and his hair was wilder. He waved, stepped off the porch. I kept my eye on the windows, hoping for a glimpse inside, but the house was dark, impossible to see anything past the lace.

"Hey, Doc!" he called.

"Morning," I answered, suspicious of his tone, his grin.

"Sorry to make you pull up and honk like that," he went on, coming slowly toward me, his voice too loud. "Like I said, place is a mess."

In a flash he was standing by the car. His overalls were grimy, flannel shirt ripe. Hair unwashed for decades obscured his forehead. Suddenly his hand shot into the cab and turned off the engine. My keys were in his pocket before I knew what he was doing.

"Don't want you to run off." His smile was gone.

I was trying to think what weapon I might have in the car, a tire iron, even the flashlight under the seat. He jerked the door open.

"Dixon don't want you to know this," he whispered, "we had a fight about it, so I got to talk fast."

I struggled to remember which of the brothers was named Dixon—the silent one?

"Our house is *sealed.*"

I twisted in my seat. "I need you to give me my keys back, Donny."

"I will," he whispered, his eyes imploring me to silence. "But you got to help us."

"I can't help you if you keep my keys."

"No, I mean you got to *help* us." He grabbed my arm, flung me out of the truck, nearly facedown in the dirt. He was dragging me toward the house. I panicked, flailed.

"Hold still!" he growled.

I had barely gotten my feet under me when the silent brother, Dixon, appeared, blocking the way in front of us, wordless and scowling.

"He's the only one can do it, Dix," Donny said, his face red, fists full of my sweater. "I know your feelings on the subject, but damn. We can't have it like this."

Dixon stood his ground, still as granite.

I don't know where Dover came from, not from the house, but he appeared, tackled Dixon; they rolled over the nasturtiums. Donny used the moment to haul me closer to the cabin door. Struggling was useless; his forearms were the size of a cow's head and he was used to wrestling wild swine.

I tried sitting; he dragged. I grabbed a smooth black rock set in the garden path and swung it at his head. He ducked and ignored.

I was on the steps, hit my shin, winced. He pulled once and I went sprawling onto the porch, the rock tumbled from my hand toward a pile of garbage that lay in the sunniest corner.

"There." He stood on the steps, blocking my way back to the truck, and everything was still.

"Christ." I got my breath, rubbed my leg. "What the hell are you doing?"

The other two were standing behind him in the yard, resigned to whatever Donny wanted from me.

"Fix it." He lifted his chin in the direction of the cabin door.

I turned. Nothing looked broken, I had no idea what he was asking me to do. I stood. No one moved. The frame was old but steady, the door solid, the hinges clean.

I stood, reached to test the doorknob.

With no warning a shock so hot it seemed electric stunned my hand; I stumbled backward. Donny caught me, kept me upright.

"It's sealed," he said again. "Us boys can get in and out, but it ain't comfortable. Happened before when we was little, we just went out the window. We can't figure why Truvy did it this time, and since she ain't here . . ." He didn't finish.

I looked at the doorway again, trying to focus, find a bare wire or anything that would explain the buzzing pain in my hand.

"You mean," I said, took a step closer to the dark door, "you think your sister put a sealing spell on your house."

"What did you think I mean?" He clearly felt I was an idiot. "Plus that's how we know she ain't dead: her binding spell's still working. Otherwise, you know, we might have killed that Able Carter."

A sealing spell could put a field of energy around anything—a book, a shed, a whole house. Its intent was to keep out unwanted visitors. It took effort on the part of the sealer and usually wore off after time or if anything happened to the person who set the spell. I'd heard about such spells for twenty years, first from people like June and then in my research, but I'd certainly never experienced one.

I took a step forward, raised my hand slowly to the door. My fingers tingled, burned the second I reached for the frame.

I turned. The brothers were gathered behind me on the porch, watching me. I couldn't help but grin, astonished as I was at the phenomenon.

"It feels like an electric current," I said, aware of the wonder in my voice, "or a hot blade."

"We feel it." Donny said plainly. "Tried to drag a pig in last night, after we saw you? Damn thing near did a flip in the door and landed on Dixon's foot. Would not come in the house for love nor money."

Dixon held out the foot to show me.

"Let me think," I said slowly, turning back to the door.

I stood for ten minutes or more, shifting weight from one leg to the other, examining every molecule of the frame before my eye caught an upward drift of dust from the bottom of the doorsill. A puff of gray, nothing more, distracted my eye; dust motes shot upward like a rocket. I got down on my hands and knees, still a good six inches back from the door, examined the paper-thin crack between the porch floor and the doorjamb. A razor of burning air was blasting up through it with a near constant intensity. I stood.

"Excuse me." I muscled through the trio, jumped the steps to the ground, crawled up under the porch.

The boys were behind me again, this time bent over and peering in after me, still silent.

Jagged rocks directly under the door, most the size of a crouching man, were arranged in a careful, thought-out pattern. There wasn't quite enough light under the porch to see clearly. The dirt was wet; the boards were dripping but thankfully free of spiderwebs, other creatures. I inched as close to the pile of rocks as I could. I felt the heat. I touched one of the rocks, pulled my hand back. It was scalding. The pile was arranged, as far as I could tell, around a small hole in the ground to direct a furnace blast of heat in a thin sheet upward through the crack in the baseboard of the door frame. The crack further defined the stream of burning air. I slithered back out from under the porch, got to my feet, brushed myself off.

"Boys," I said quietly, "you know there's a hole under your porch."

They all looked past me, bending, and stared into the darkness there.

"That pile of rocks is around it."

They straightened.

Donny grinned. "We don't usually go crawling up under the house, Dr. Devilin."

The other two snorted.

"But your sister does."

That shut them up.

"She did seal the house," I agreed, "after a fashion."

They glared, unblinking.

"Didn't your sister find wells once, water on your property?"

"Uh-huh," Donny said slowly. "Good while back; she was little bitty."

"And several of them were dry, or you didn't find water in them, I mean."

"That's right." Donny folded his arms. "How'd you know that?"

"One of the dry holes you dug was close to the house," I went on, "and recently Truevine asked you to make a tunnel. Is that true?"

They looked at one another. Dixon took a barely perceptible step back.

"No," Donny said slowly. "But a good time ago Momma asked us to do something like that. How you come to know a thing like that?"

"I'm guessing."

"She didn't say what it was for," Dover whispered. "Was it the house-sealing spell?"

"It was," I confirmed. "One of the wells you dug hit on a geothermal pocket. It's unusual but not unheard of. Truevine remembered that and used it, arranged the rocks."

Not twenty miles to our west there was a hot springs in the side of a mountain roughly the size of ours, a moneymaking tourist attraction.

"What is it?" Dover asked, still nearly inaudible.

"Very hot air or steam trapped in the earth, under the mountain." I glanced at the door. "Your sister figured out how to direct it to your house. She's a genius, you know. Do you realize how impressive this is? I had no idea she was capable . . ." I trailed off, shaking my head.

"Our sister," Donny told me in no uncertain terms, "is the best person there is."

"So you understand that she's arranged those rocks down there to send a blast of hot air up to your door."

"If that's the spell," Donny said calmly, "then I understand."

I had in my head about a half hour's worth of explanation, and then I heard the voice of my old teacher, now discredited, also dead, Dr. Bishop. He turned out to be a less than perfect human being, but that didn't mean all his ideas were wrong. Ideas can be perfect even when their inventors are not.

"Folk explanation of any phenomenon," he had told me a hundred times, "creates its own phenomenological dasein, a gestalt that supports itself. Who are you to say a scientific explanation is better, especially in the folk context? A woman says rubbing sage on her pillow keeps a ghost from waking her at midnight. You say it makes her believe she's safe, so she sleeps better. The result is the same. Let the explanation be a part of phenomenon. Let the observer be a part of the observation. Don't obscure the phenomenon with what you perceive to be the facts."

I nodded to Donny. "That's the spell. If you want to keep it up, leave the stones alone. If you want it to stop, move the stones."

All three heads turned as one once again in the direction of the dark underside of the porch.

"If Truvy's done all that work," Dixon announced firmly, "I still say we leave it be."

"I thought you wanted me to fix it," I said, exasperated.

"Dixon been saying Tru put it there for a reason," Dover said. "If she went to all the trouble to crawl up under the house, I reckon we ought to respect that."

Everyone had calmed. I surmised that the boys had really only needed outside confirmation of their sister's work. Fixing the situation had not been, after all, what they'd wanted. There are occasions upon which faith must be confirmed by the facts.

"All right, then," I said, sitting on the first step of the porch, "let's move on. I want to find your sister almost as much as you do. Also, I promised Girlinda Needle I'd find Able, and I think he's with Truevine. I'd like to find him alive. If you all keep catching him and stringing him up, that makes my job a whole lot harder."

They pondered.

"Ms. Needle's a good woman," Donny allowed. "But her brother." He shook his head.

Time for psychology.

"Would you like *any* man who was interested in your sister?" I asked. "Honestly."

I gave it a moment to sink in. Puzzled faces contorted.

"What if I liked her?" I went on.

They tensed.

"You *got* a good woman, Doc," Donny said, clench-jawed. "You ought to get married to that'un."

"My point is: you don't think any man would be good enough for your sister." I leaned back. "And from what I know about her, you might be right. But she's got to find her own way. She falls in love, you have to let her. She wants a husband and children, that's her business. If you chase off every man who comes around, by and by she'll stop trying. What then?"

Donny started to speak three times, stopping each time before words would come out. Finally he managed, "Where is she, Dr. Devilin? Where's our sister?"

"My theory," I answered, "is that she and Carter are hiding out in the old cemetery. But you probably scared them off last night."

"You think she's up there," Dover rasped, "in that boneyard?"

"That don't make sense," Donny agreed. "Why don't she just come on home?"

"I think she had something to do with your cousin's death. She's afraid."

"Harding?" Dover could barely say it.

"That moron." Donny shook his head. "I know he's family, but he's as worthless as a teat on a tree."

"Not to speak ill of the dead," Dover said quickly.

Doing so could merit a visit from them. Deceased spirits are quite irritable, especially immediately after their death, prone to visit anyone who doesn't speak glowingly of them.

"She didn't have nothing to do with that," Donny said after a moment, "and even if she did she'd still come home."

"Unless she was worried about bringing the police to you," I returned. "I'm not interested in your nefarious activities, but I know you've run afoul of Deputy Needle, and now that he's running for sheriff, he's apt to be even more stern about the appearance of illegality. Especially since you nearly hung his brother-in-law."

"He can be a stickler," Donny admitted. "So Tru is staying away to keep the police off us."

"Just an idea," I admitted.

"All right," Donny said strongly, "I get it. You came up here to make a point, Doctor. You want us to help you find Able and Truvy. You think you're a whole lot smarter than us, and you are in a lots of ways, but we know things you never heard of."

"I agree," I answered, brushing the dirt from my pants. "That's why we'd make the perfect team. Between us, we know everything."

I grinned, hoping it would put my proposition over.

They exchanged silent communications.

"Okay then," Donny said finally, "you'd best come on in the house, if you think you can get past the spell, have you a sit-down. We got some information about Harding you need to know."

"About what?" I said.

"I believe we might know why he was killed." He took the steps.

The kitchen was a sty, smelled worse than a slaughterhouse. Despite the jolt of extreme discomfort crossing the threshold, I made it in, along with hundreds of flies who seemed perfectly at home. Blessed shadows obscured the details of what lay on the dining table, but the word *entrails* was on my mind.

There was one large room in the cabin, and a ladder that rose to a sleeping loft. The downstairs room boasted the huge table, a kitchen, a sitting area, and a stone fireplace. The ceiling was hung with dozens of dried spices, long twigs of rosemary tied together, thick braids of garlic, bundles of thyme, cress, hyssop, sage, lavender. They battled valiantly but lost the war of smells.

"You boys made a mess in pretty quick order," I observed, trying not to inhale. "This looks like a week's work. Did you kill a hog in here?"

They looked at one another accusingly.

"Dixon said not to open any windows," Donny tried to explain, "might break the seal."

"I won't be able to take this for long," I confessed, hand over nose and mouth.

Dixon sighed, began gathering hog limbs and jowls, scooping them off the table into his arms, clutching them to his chest. Flies gathered about him. He shook his head once in my direction and exited through the front door. Dover followed behind with what seemed to be a collection of fish spines. Donny opened the window in the kitchen area.

"Not so bad over here," he invited.

All things being relative, he was right, but I still found it difficult to breathe. As the sweet air from the side of the house poured in, I leaned and closed my eyes.

Behind me Donny said, "Dr. Devilin, I want you to understand a few things. You went to college; I didn't. You read books; I don't. You think one way; I do another. In the realm of God's world it's all equal, I believe." He leaned against the counter next to the sink, inches from me. "My point is: I want you to understand that I read some parts of this world the way you read a book. I know the alphabets of the air and the leaves. My sister is better at it than I am; otherwise I'm the best there is. Now, I realize you don't have no idea what I'm saying, but you need to know I'm a whole lots more observant than you might give me credit for. That's my say. I'm going to make some coffee. You need some?"

"Coffee's good," I managed.

He wasn't menacing in the way he'd been before, but I still felt threatened, maybe by his proximity, maybe the strangeness of what he was trying to say. I knew he wasn't a stupid man, that what he was saying about our different kinds of knowledge was true. There are kinds of education that don't take place in a university. He put a kettle on the stove.

"I wonder if we could stick to finding your sister," I said.

"That's what I'm trying to do!" He pounded the edge of the sink with such force it rattled the dishes sitting in it and sent me scrambling backward. "You don't see the circle in the wheel. You don't see the way things are. You're making a mistake and it's a mistake that's been made before, with dire consequences."

Dire consequences seemed a bizarre phrase coming from his mouth. I felt dizzy from the stench and disoriented by the darkness of the house and the sound of Donny's voice.

The kettle's whistle startled me. He reached up to the cabinets beside him and got an old press coffeemaker. He dug into a ceramic pot next to the sink and pulled out a handful of black whole coffee beans. He put them in a pestle, ground them by hand, then dumped them into the bottom of the coffeepot, poured the hot water on top, put the lid in place. The sounds of the day picked up, and a rush of autumn air flushed the kitchen area.

"I love my sister and I need for her to be happy. I don't want that to happen to her, what you said about her giving up on marriage. We need to leave her be. She was right about you: you're a good man. Reckon that's why she told us to look after you."

Truevine told them to watch over me, I thought. *That's why they let me go last night. Remember to thank her when I see her.*

"Okay, Donny," I said calmly. "What's this about knowing why Harding was murdered?"

He cast his eye about the cabin. "Quite a smell in here, ain't it?"

"I can barely stand it."

"Smells like a slaughterhouse," he agreed. He took out blue coffee mugs, poured the contents of the pot through a sieve, and handed me one. "Or a mortuary."

"No," I corrected him, sipping, "mortuaries don't smell like this; they smell of formaldehyde and rubbing alcohol—"

"That's right," he interrupted, avoiding my eyes, "if the bodies have been taken care of proper. Of course, if they ain't been treated right, like if a mortician don't do his job . . ." He wanted me to finish his thought.

"A mortician." I set the mug down. "Harding was killed because of something he did wrong at his funeral home."

Seven

The Deveroe boys were reluctant to let me leave. They wanted me to stay, find their sister. A few minutes of arguing and a well-chosen phrase about law enforcement convinced them I had to go. I needed to clear my head, rid my memory of the stench of their place, collect my thoughts.

I was pretty sure Andrews hadn't left the house. If I hurried, I'd be able to catch him before he ran off with Skidmore on their secret mission.

I pulled away from the witch's cabin, sped home as quickly as I could.

When I got there, Andrews's car was gone. I switched off the truck, sat in silence a moment, trying to imagine where he'd gone, what he and Skidmore were doing. Without me.

I reached for pad and pencil in the glove compartment, made random notes:

Able Carter discovered something about Harding's mortuary. That's what they were arguing about the night Harding was murdered. Why was the body naked? Visit the mortuary today. Truevine and Able won't come home because Able killed Harding, Truevine's hiding him. Where are they now? Why were they in the graveyard? Find out more about Truevine; is she the key element?

I felt I was writing from pure instinct, one of the tools I had used for years investigating folk material. These collection talents were the exact techniques required for solving Harding's murder. Folklorists *are* detectives. Dr. Bishop once told me, when I was frustrated by university politics, that I should never try to acquire new skills for new tasks if I could apply old talents I already possessed. "Fix academic problems in the department the way you would collect a folktale or song. Use those abilities you already have; make them metaphorical; translate." Genius. I knew I could only solve the murder the way I would ordinarily investigate a folk phenomenon.

I stared at the empty house. Our day had ripened nicely, though the air was slightly chilled. Sun the color of snow glazed the roof, made me squint. What were Andrews and Skidmore up to? I climbed out of the car, deciding not to let their little play distract me from larger questions. What attributes did Andrews have to contribute to my work after all? A Shakespeare scholar's perspective: decidedly useless. Best to operate alone. I always had.

The problem, and I knew it, was that my mind could run from ignorance to paranoia with lightning speed. Skid and Andrews were working together. They were plotting. They were doing something behind my back. They were working against me. They were deliberately trying to subvert me. Not just me, my entire way of life. That's the path my thinking could take without the slightest provocation, that fast.

I felt an itch on my leg. Surely it was a hive. A hive would grow to cover my leg. My leg would swell and become useless. I wouldn't be able to walk. The hives would get into my throat. My throat would close up. I wouldn't be able to breathe. Because of my swollen leg I'd never make it to the truck, couldn't drive to the emergency room. I would die on the front steps, as far as I could crawl before my esophagus closed entirely.

That's the way fear grows: from nothing to death in ten sentences. I'd taken that course of thinking a thousand times. The only way to avoid it was to concentrate on something else with such ferocity that everything was blocked out. For decades I'd used a fear of my own thinking process to focus my mind, the secret of my success in the field. Sometimes I had to use my mind to trick my mind, a dangerous Möbius path.

Onward, then. Go to the mortuary, see if I could discover what Donny was trying to tell me. On the way, stop by June's house. Find out more about Truevine Deveroe, if she was to be my focus. I pulled the truck back onto the road.

The slant of sun was blinding down the mountain, and the black shade on the other side of it seemed night. The sky was endless above me; curling leaves in the wind sighed upward, last gasping of the old year. October's story is always regret: the things May might have done. It's a time for ghosts, my mother's voice leaving, my father's shallow breath—all the things I should already have told Lucinda.

As I pulled up to June and Hek's home I promised myself, a prayer, to speak more honestly with Lucinda when she came home. Tell her secrets my father never told my mother, talk things out. If the sins of the father are visited upon the son, how much more is that son haunted by the father's regrets?

I honked the horn getting out of the truck, then sang out.

"June!" Hello the house.

A gust of wind, the leaning of wheat in the field behind the barn, and, at last, her voice answered.

"Come on in, then."

The creak of the screen door was a final announcement. I knew to head for the kitchen; I could smell the cornbread.

"This is a treat, seeing you two days so close," she said before I was through the doorway.

"I'm here on business."

"Of course." She nodded. "Truevine."

Even though I knew that news traveled fast in our town and had also long suspected June's unacknowledged psychic abilities, I still managed to stumble over the threshold, surprised by her perception.

"Careful, boy," she said, still stirring something on the stove.

She stood in her apron and dark dress, ancient shoes, in what little light the northern kitchen window allowed. Her hair was pulled back so tightly the skin at her temples pinched, but she had not put it in a bun, as was her usual style. A gray ponytail dangled at the back of her head, an oddly young afterthought to the gently aged face.

"New hairstyle?" I took a seat at the kitchen table.

"I got up quick today." Her words were uncharacteristically clipped.

"Well, the truth is," I confessed, "I am looking for something more about Truevine. I don't know what, though."

Leave it open. Suggest, then be silent. The open-ended query is a bigger net than any specific question.

She stopped stirring. "You know I don't like to gossip."

"That's right." My eyes shot downward.

She took a seat at the table. "You don't want no coffee."

I shook my head.

"Truevine's real power took a hold when her parents passed. She needed something, and that's what she got. Some of these so-called churchgoers call it devil's work, but there's nothing wrong with the way that girl does, and I don't care who knows it."

"You don't care who knows you feel that way," I clarified.

"Right. Some call her bad names. I don't. We used to have several of these women back when I was young, and we depended on them many a time for having babies, curing livestock, helping out one way or another." She folded her hands in front of her and wouldn't look me in the eye.

"Truevine's a good witch," I goaded.

"Don't call her that," she shot back. Then she slumped. "You don't know."

"I'd like to."

"No." She licked her lips. "You wouldn't."

Typical of June, of most of my friends in Blue Mountain. Suggest something mammoth, then demur in the telling. Maddening.

"Well, she put a sealing spell on her cabin before she disappeared," I began.

"Hogwash," June spat. "No such of a thing. Her charm is for animals."

There it was, the first hint.

"Animals?" I tried to make it sound as innocent as possible.

June sighed a familiar sound, the one she made after she had successfully convinced herself that I had dragged the story out of her. She wasn't gossiping, the sigh said. I'd forced her to tell.

"You don't know about the wild dog?"

"No." Careful. Too many words would scare away the story.

"I guess it was when you were at the university." She sat back and closed her eyes, the way she began the real tale. "They say she was in the wood up there by the graveyard, gathering evening primrose to set on her mother's grave, when it come up on her. Black dog size of a calf. Growling. Hungry. You could see his ribs show. Truevine just smiled, fixed her eye on the dog. She says, 'Are you hungry? I've got some spice cake and some dried fish I was to have for supper, and you're more than welcome to it, if that's to your liking.' Dog nods once. She invited him to eat."

Invited: a key point in the tradition.

"She took out all that was left of her food, laid it on her kerchief, spread like a table for a guest, put her flowers to the corner, stepped back. Dog nods his head again. Tru says, 'There. God's table, here in the woods.' Which if that don't prove she ain't a witch I don't know what. Dog nods his head the third time."

"I see," I said, smiling.

It had to be three times, too.

"They say," she went on, "he ate very delicately for a wild animal. Then he turns around like a house dog and lays down right next to Tru."

"She was lucky," I said.

Wild dogs in the woods all over these mountains had attacked livestock, small children, sometimes grown hunters, often killed. They were not pets.

"No luck to it. Girl's got a way. She says, 'You like my company. Come on.' They went all over the graveyard that day. After that the wild dog took up with her every time she went out in the woods by herself. Dog was never seen when she was with her brothers, but alone the dog always found her, kept her company."

"They say."

"They do. So one day she had to go over to Clinch Taylor's dry goods store in Pine City. It's a long walk, and she'd no longer set out than the dog took up with her."

"That *is* a long walk," I agreed. Fourteen miles over rough terrain, a two- or three-hour trek each way, even for a healthy young person.

"She likes that Owen Mill stone-ground flour they sell; she goes over there every now and again. Now you know how they are over in Pine City. Slothful, that's my opinion. They always blame floods or bugs or bad luck, but they're just plain lazy and no good, Pine City is. They'd had a poor harvest that year, I reckon, but the way some of these boys do, they said it wasn't their own fault. They saw Truevine and dog come up over the hill, they commence to teasing her: 'Witch girl. She got her a devil dog!' "

"Her reputation preceded her." I sat back. "Now which boys were these?"

"Some that had to go to work in Clinch's store because their crop failed. I believe they'd been drinking. They kept up teasing, said she was the cause of the bad harvest. They blamed her. Trouble was, others thereabout joined in, and teasing turned mean."

"That can't be good."

"It was terrible," June answered. "They started saying they were going to make her change her spell. She paid for her goods, left right quick, but they started after her."

"How many?"

"Five or six. Drunk boys. She was scared; she ran, which made the boys mad. They chased her all the way to the Little Sancrow River—"

"Between here and there," I interrupted. "It's white water."

"And it started to rain," she agreed, "but those boys were right behind, so Tru and the dog jumped in. She might have drowned except the dog fetched her in his teeth to the other side."

"Amazing." I nodded, prompting.

"Wet to the bone," she went on, her voice full of the power of the story, "no strength left, they cast themselves on the far bank. Those mean boys stood on the other side cursing and shouting how they'd get her still. Tru and the dog were too tuckered to move, and they might have been got, except that God didn't want that. Lightning hit a tree right next to the dog, scared the boys silly. They left off, ran away. Ignorant."

"But Tru was all right?" I asked.

June nodded. "She managed to drag several of those burning branches into the shelter of a covering rock near the riverbank. In very short order she and the dog was both warm as a summer day, dry as parson's throat."

"Nice phrase." Evidence she'd told the story a dozen times or more to others.

"Now the last part is hard to swallow, I don't know if it's true or not, but it's good. They say that dog went back in the water and caught a fish. Tru cooked it there on the lightning fire, and even though it was most likely a trout, that fish was entirely free of bones."

"The dog caught a fish that had no bones."

She stood. "God delights in little miracles as well large."

"The point is . . ." I coaxed.

"The point is that Truevine has a power over animals and sometimes she gets blamed for things which have got nothing to do with her."

I watched her return to her pots on the stove. One was brimming with fresh field peas.

"She can survive in the woods better than most," I said slowly. "She's out there because she's afraid someone will blame her for Harding's death, something she didn't do."

"That college education don't get in the way of your good sense. Much." She was proud of me. "Right to this day you see that black dog up in the cemetery sometimes."

"But that's exactly what I think Able's afraid of. Not the dog. I mean they're both hiding because someone will blame them for Harding's murder. I think they're in the graveyard."

"I wondered how long it would take you to get to that." She stirred serenely. "Hek laid down enough hints."

"Why didn't you let me know that the last time I was here?" No point in telling her I'd already thought it.

"Not my business." She exhibited the whisper of a smile. "You know your Great-grandfather Devilin from the old country, he was one of them to start that graveyard. Along with the Newcombs."

I was well aware of June's propensity for bending the truth if it made for a better story, for further crafting facts to fit ancient songs and tales. Her story about her husband's adventures traveling from town to town looking for her after he was wounded in Vietnam was a nearly word-for-word parallel of the song "Dark-eyed Sailor"— and about a hundred other variants of the same plot. I knew it, she knew it, and still she insisted on embellishing reality. Truth, lies, and a human propensity for hyperbole weave the fabric of folklore—and life, I suppose.

"No. My great-grandfather is buried up there, but he had nothing to do with the graveyard."

"Built part of it himself. Out of guilt for marrying a woman he didn't love," she went right on, as if the story of old Conner Devilin were recent news. June had heard my great-grandfather's history a hundred times.

"What do you think you're doing, Junie, bringing up that old trouble now?"

"Not my business," she said, holding up one hand. "Get you a plate and I'll let you have a taste of these peas."

"I'm not hungry." I stood. Changing the subject to food meant she was done talking about Truevine and nothing I could do would change that. "I might want to come back and talk to Hek about all this."

"He don't know a thing."

"Still."

"You miss Lucinda?"

"I do," I said quietly, unsettled by her sudden change of subject.

"Tell her that when she gets back." June stared out the window. "You don't have much of woman's ways in your life; you could use a little more. You know you ought to marry that girl."

"I don't know, June." I pushed the chair in. "You're aware of my feelings about being married in general, my parents' disaster. I'm not sure I'm cut out for the institution."

"That's a laugh," she responded without the hint of a smile. "You need marrying more than any man I ever knew."

"I'll be back later," I sighed, exasperated.

She nodded. I left. No point in dredging up all the doubts I'd buried deep. They needed their rest.

The air had refused to warm, even though the sun was doing its best. A wind down the rocks of the mountain was ice water, the crack of cold apples. I was glad to climb into the truck.

Harding Pinhurst the Third was killed, I thought driving downward, *because he wasn't doing his job at the mortuary. His work was shoddy, and someone found out. Families take death seriously here. That's what Donny was telling me. I have to find out. How am I going to get into the building?*

Pinhurst Funeral Parlor and Crematorium was an imposing pre-Victorian mansion on the edge of three hundred acres of protected land. The large acreage had been bought by the state during World War II and set aside to extend the Appalachian Trail park system, but work had never been completed. Ancient oaks and odd blue conifers surrounded the place, except for spots in front. Ivy did its duty over most of the front yard, decorating what it obscured.

The house itself, redesigned when Harding took over as director not five years earlier, sat off our town's main road about a hundred yards. It stood three stories, white with ornate ginger trim, a wrap-around front porch guarding it, tall slanting clay-tiled roof, a dozen gables covered. Oversize rockers sat empty on the porch. No drive-way, the yard was always a wreck, cars parked everywhere with no pattern; grass didn't stand a chance. The windows of the house were all beveled lead glass, wavy and clouded, like cataracts. Paint curled away from the wooden exterior like dry skin; the eaves sagged; the columns on the porch were canes supporting a hazardous overhang. Still, it was a grand old structure and in the right light was a set piece straight from *Arsenic and Old Lace.*

No cars. Good. No sign of anyone around. I pulled the truck to the side of the house. Behind the shelter of low branches it wouldn't be seen by anyone driving by.

I hadn't been there since Ida Shumps's funeral six months before. The place was deserted. Steps creaked when I peered into the small window in the back door. I checked the lock. Solid. I tried the window next to it. No luck. I was cold in the shade; wind found the bare skin of my face and slapped it. I worked my way around the back of the house checking windows with no success. On the far side of the house I came across the root cellar. It had no lock.

Gray-wood doors revealed stone steps that led down into darkness. I thought for a second that I ought to go back to the truck for my flashlight, but it seemed ridiculous in the middle of the day.

The steps were hard, a little damp. The cellar was pitch-black. I moved very slowly out of the daylight and into the dungeon, waited at the bottom of the stairs for my eyes to adjust. The ceiling was too low for me; the smell was already nauseating: mildew, stagnant water, formaldehyde—the waiting room for hell's doctor.

As my vision adjusted, I half-expected to see evidence of Donny's suspicions there under the house. All I could make out were buckets and shovels, tarps, bottles, a few long-unused tools, typical cellar inhabitants. To my right were the old root bins for cold storage. To the left an ancient coal furnace sat silent. A black overturned coal bucket stood to one side, a silent sentinel. Behind it were other bins of some sort and stacks of large burlap bags for feed or seed. Just beyond there was a flight of wooden stairs that led up, I guessed, to the kitchen.

The dirt floor of the cellar was not entirely dry, silty, and I slipped a little on my way to the steps, but the handrail steadied me. I made it up; the door opened into the kitchen.

It complained loudly and I stopped in my tracks, certain the noise had alerted inhabitants. I thought it best then to confess my trespass.

"Hello?" My voice offended the silence.

I pushed into the room. Dirty dishes were in the sink; the faucet dripped. The floor was filthy. The kitchen table was a mess, cluttered with paper plates, plastic ware, tissue napkins.

"Harding?" That was stupid. I knew he wouldn't be there. But I somehow thought it was the right thing to yell in case anyone else heard me.

I made my way slowly through the kitchen to the other back rooms, the mortuarial lab, embalming chambers, whatever they were called. I followed my nose.

The first room was locked with a hook and eye from the inside. The one beside it was open and sterling. Spotless. It looked as if it had never been used. Chrome was polished; surfaces dazzled; everything gleamed, far from being the butcher Donny had suggested, the room seemed to prove Harding the cleanest mortician in the state.

I turned back to the other room, knew I had to get in. A combination of fear and determination supplied the adrenaline; a kitchen knife did the rest. I slipped the knife into the door frame and managed, after a few attempts, to simply push the hook up. The door swung open.

Chaos. What struck my eye like a fist was the utter disarray of the room, darker than the other. Tables were shoved against the far wall; stacks and stacks of papers were everywhere, empty medicine bottles, industrial-sized drums of cleaning fluid, and more large seed sacks. The room was a janitorial closet. I realized after a moment that there were several opened bottles of formaldehyde on the counter, completely full, perfuming the room.

It didn't make sense. One room was a showplace, the other a storage room.

And, it suddenly occurred to me, *how did this one come to be locked from the inside?*

I checked the single window: locked as well. That made the room more important. Someone had bothered to secure it from the inside. *Why? To make it look as if someone were in the room? Working?*

I would find the secret exit.

I started at the door and took in every inch of the room, slowly, letting the details sink in. Took nearly ten minutes. Then I started a more physical examination, checking for disguised doors in the wall, trapdoors in the floor, something in the ceiling. Another twenty meticulous minutes later, I found it. Surrounded by the heavy stacks of seed there was a blank space of floor where the boards gapped a quarter of an inch more than in any other place in the room. I moved a few of the sacks aside, finding they weighed more than expected, gazed down at the floor. On my knees, really looking at the floorboards in that corner, it was clearly different from the rest of the wood. I used the knife, worked it into the extra quarter-inch gap, and, sure enough, found I could pry up a section of the floor about three feet square.

I looked down onto the cellar floor where the rest of the sacks were laid. For a man of my size it was a little tight, easing myself down into the darkness. The black coal pail was directly under my feet, a convenient step stool.

Back in the cellar I was at a loss. *Why would there be a trapdoor?*

Clearly Donny had been wrong about Harding; there was no evidence of botched embalming. But the trapdoor phenomenon was eerie, no denying.

After a few moments' pondering, remaining confused, I thought it best to put everything back the way it had been. I stood on the pail, hoisted myself into the workroom to lock the hook from the inside, then crawled back down the hole, moved the sacks as best I could to hide the trapdoor, replaced the false piece of flooring. I smoothed the cellar dirt where my feet had left impressions and was out, the old wooden doors creaking shut.

I don't know what caught my eye first, a glint of something in the woods behind the house, a black blur. Maybe a squirrel moved, but this time I saw dozens more seed sacks laid against a red wheelbarrow about sixty yards from where I was standing.

Harding was never a farmer, and there's not usable land anywhere near this place; what's he doing with all these seeds?

I peered around the side of the house, still no cars anywhere; my truck was fine. I headed for the woods to check things out.

Past the shadow of the house, the sun flickered patterns against the bare limbs in the wind. The woods were in constant motion, and I thought how van Gogh's sense of movement must have been inspired by this sort of autumn afternoon.

The sacks were jumbled everywhere, sixty, maybe a hundred of them. Some had been partly rotted by exposure, and it took me a second look to realize what was odd about them: they were filled with dirt, not seeds.

I stooped down, wind flinging leaves up from the ground all around me; ruby, chestnut, hazel colors floated for a moment like slow birds in the air. The bags were filled with red Georgia clay, heavy good-for-nothing soil. A wet bag that size might weigh a hundred pounds; dry it would turn to concrete, hard as brick. Bag after bag was packed with the stuff and tied loosely at the top.

What the hell is this? I stood.

I could see more stacks farther into the woods, down the slope where the area was guarded with barbed wire, decorated with NO TRESPASSING signs. Everyone talked about the wild dogs and feral swine in that part of the government's property. No one ever went near it. Harding himself had a history of taking shots at high school kids trying to get into the area on a dare or hunters looking for protected game. Though it was unlikely that he'd fire at me that day.

I made my way down the slope, skidding on wet leaves, grabbing what handholds I could. The fence was easy enough to crawl under. The sun still found its way past the trees. The leaves were cathedral windows. I found the wind wasn't so stern down in the hollow; if I'd been set for a hike in the woods, the place would have made for a good starting point, I thought.

Until I saw the rotted human hand.

I didn't respond the way I'd seen people in films react. Disbelief allowed me to be more curious than horrified. I thought my eyes deceived me. I took a step closer to where it lay on top of a pile of leaves beside a tall pine. By the time I realized that my perception was accurate, I confess to being fascinated.

Bone from the ring finger showed through gray flesh; long milky nails clung precariously to the tips. The thumb stuck up stiffly. It was not, as I had first thought, a dismembered body part, simply a portion of a larger body that had been mostly covered by leaves.

I stood, head cocked, trying to make my legs move me closer, when a gust of wind rolled down the slope, scattered more leaves, and revealed the nightmare. There were three bodies stacked one on top of the other against the pine tree. Piled like the seed sacks, partially covered with red clay.

I backed away, unable to comprehend—the shock of seeing the hand was wearing off; I shivered.

Find a phone, I told myself calmly. *Call Skidmore.*

I continued backing up the hill for a moment, stumbling, slipping on wet leaves, then turned and sprinted up the rest of the slope as best I could. Strange noises seemed everywhere; I was very conscious of my own breathing, like a trapped animal. By the time I reached the barbed wire I realized I was making little noises every time I exhaled. There was a ring of fire around my hairline and a torrent of white noise pounding in my ears. When I made it to the truck, I was drenched in sweat.

Trade at Gil's Filling Station was slow, as usual, and Gil himself had gone hunting. A teenage boy whose name I could not remember had handed me the phone. I'd made five calls before finding the deputy. Luckily Skidmore knew me well enough to read the sound of my voice and he was a good enough friend to come quickly without asking any questions.

"You want a co-cola, Dr. Deverling?"

I suddenly didn't feel so bad about not remembering the boy's name. "No, thanks. I think I'll go wait outside."

"You been sick?"

"No. Why do you ask?"

"Sorry, you're breathing funny is all, like you had a cold. My mother she has a cold." He sniffed. "A cold, it can be bad. In the head. That's where she's got it." He blew out a breath. "Right there in her head."

"I ran to get here, use the phone," I said distractedly. "I'm a little out of breath is all."

"You ought to get you a cell phone," he advised me. "Everybody's got one."

"I'm just going . . ." I started for the door.

"You find that Truvy Deveroe yet?"

I stopped.

"Who?" I had no intention of revealing anything to him.

"Everybody at school is talking about it," he assured me.

Easier for a camel to pass through the eye of a needle than a secret to hide in Blue Mountain.

Still, I felt I should try. "What makes you think I'm looking . . ."

"Ms. Needle told you to do it at the church meeting." He was matter-of-fact, confident in his knowledge.

"I see." I folded my arms.

Gil's station was a comfortable place for me, the smell of gasoline and Old Spice, cigarettes, the gas heater. I'd played music in the garage with older men since I was ten. The sound of those tunes clung to the splinters in the walls, stuck in the rainbows of oil by the car lift.

"Do you have an opinion?" I asked the boy.

"Sir?"

"Do you have a feeling about Truevine Deveroe?"

"You mean do I think she's what people say?" He grinned. "I got a lots better sense than that." He straightened. "I'm college prep."

"That's great," I said, glad to change the subject. "What do you want to study?"

"In college? Well, I build Web sites, you know. I did one for school; then I just sort of took to it, I reckon. I'm going to Georgia Tech. Be a computer technologist."

The fact that he worked a little too hard in pronouncing the last two words in his sentence was only slightly less heartbreaking than the fact that his aspiration was eight years behind the times. But what hurt more was the idea that not many years ago this boy's aspiration would have been to work at Gil's, stay in Blue Mountain, marry his sweetheart, play mandolin, have a nice kitchen garden. How long would it be before there were no young people left in town? And how much longer after that would Blue Mountain be another ghost?

"Georgia Tech," I said, smiling. "Very impressive."

His grin covered his face. "Thanks, Dr. Deverling; that means a lot coming from you."

Skidmore's squad car screeched into the lot at the front of the station.

"That's for me," I told the boy.

"Take care," he said, turning his attention back to a bag of potato chips.

I was barely out the door when Skid and Andrews flung their doors open and rushed me.

"What is it?" Skid said softly.

Andrews saw my face, registered concern.

"You're not going to believe," I began, my stomach burning, "what I found at the Pinhurst mortuary."

By sunset the deputies had counted seventy-three bodies and it was getting too dark to continue.

"We need more people, Skid," one of the deputies said, wiping his forehead. He was as shaken as the rest of us, face white, eyes bleary.

"I know," Skid answered. "I just . . ." he trailed off, watching the last bit of red at the horizon. He turned to me slowly. "By the time I realized the magnitude of the situation . . ."

". . . it was too late to call anyone," I finished, trying to reassure him. "You're doing fine. You need to leave a couple of people here tonight, get away from this. We'll all keep quiet until you've had a chance to get your thoughts together, calm down."

Though how any of us would get our minds around the enormity of the problem was another matter. Bodies stacked, three, five, sometimes more, littered everywhere in these woods. As close to the house as forty yards, as far away as half a mile, and every time a deputy reported in over the walkie-talkie in Skid's hand more had been found. Amazement had long since turned to dull sickness.

"I've never even heard of anything like this," Andrews whispered for the third time. "Anywhere."

The bodies were in no order we could determine: some were fresh; some were skeletons; the rest were in every imaginable stage in between. Men, women, children, dressed, naked, wealthy, poor— unknown and all too familiar.

The deputy who had requested more people suddenly sat down on the ground sobbing uncontrollably, grinding his palms into his temples. He had come across the body of his aunt, only recently deceased. He hid his eyes from us; we were too tired to look away.

"I don't even know what it means, Dev," Skid said softly.

"At first I thought it was some mass murder scene," Andrews agreed. "Now I have no idea what this could mean."

We hadn't talked much during the course of the afternoon. As the scope of the phenomenon grew, we talked less. Minds were numb. Eyes were sore. Everyone was shivering and hot at the same time.

I had kept silent, though I was certain I knew what was transpiring. Both men read my silence.

The air was amber, the wind had picked up, and the chill of it stung. All leaves were rust-colored in the last light of the day; all trees were black; all men were shadows. The gentle slopes around us seemed menacing and harsh, crouched, alive. The night sky was an anvil in the east; stars were sparks struck there, burning holes in the air. Nothing was right.

"What is it, Dev?" Skidmore said.

"In the cellar of the house," I began mechanically, "and in the house itself, you'll find more of these sacks packed with fill dirt. I think that's what Harding put in caskets instead of bodies, and the rest he's used to cover up the corpses out here."

The full import of what I was saying was lost on my two friends. They stared blankly.

"Harding has been hauling the remains of his customers out here to these woods, through a trapdoor in one of his workrooms. It leads to his cellar. It would appear he's been doing it for most of the time he's worked there. The cemeteries, as it turns out, might be more empty than we might have imagined." I cast my eye over the Poe landscape. "But these woods are quite full."

"That's not possible." Andrews would not close his mouth.

"Why would he do it?" Skidmore's eyes bored into mine.

"I have no idea," I answered. "But I think Able Carter found out."

That began to register with them.

"Believe it or not," I confessed, "Donny Deveroe hinted at this. Just this morning." Seemed a month ago.

"Somebody found out about this," Skidmore agreed slowly. "That's why Harding was murdered."

"Able wouldn't murder him for this," Andrews managed. "He'd want to prosecute, wouldn't he?"

"Maybe they got in a fight about it," Skid said.

"That's not murder," Andrews argued.

Debate was interrupted by the crackle of Skidmore's walkie-talkie.

"Skid?" the scratchy voice said.

"Joseph," Skidmore answered. ·

"We found another . . ." but the rest of the sentence was scrambled.

"Say again," Skid said, monotone, into the speaker. "You found another body?"

"No, sir," said the voice at the other end. "We found another . . . whole section." Black silence. "Looks like fifty or sixty more bodies." *Crackle.* "Can I come in now? I don't believe I can do this anymore tonight."

The sobbing deputy lay back against the ground, exhaled roughly, stared up at the waning moon. Night was coming on.

Eight

The next morning, Andrews and I were Skidmore's only help. Two deputies called in sick; the others simply hadn't shown up. We stood at the edge of the barbed wire, warming our hands on cups of coffee, watching the woods.

"I called the state patrol," Skid finally said. "They're sending some. Not till later, though."

We nodded.

The sun was barely up, reluctant to shed light on the scene. I hadn't slept well. Neither had Andrews from the look of him.

"Hey. What were you two cooking up yesterday?" I said, scanning the deeper woods, mostly to delay our task.

"Yesterday?" Andrews gave it some thought, as if trying to remember his childhood.

"You spent part of the day together." I had to work to keep a needle point of paranoia at bay.

"That's right. I was mad at you," Skidmore confessed. "I wanted to teach you a lesson. Andrews and me, we did some paperwork. Got more report from Dahlonega. Said the wound on Harding's head was 'consistent with the pathology of being struck a blow by a blunt instrument.'"

"But they wouldn't rule out the possibility," Andrews chimed in solemnly, "that he hit his head on a rock when he fell down the hill."

"In other words . . ." I offered.

"Inconclusive," Skidmore affirmed.

"What about the threads I found in the graveyard?" I ventured. "Truevine's?"

"Nope," Skid answered blankly. "Far as they could tell, just random threads."

"Damn." I rubbed my eyes. "I was sure they had something to do with all this. You didn't do anything else, the two of you?"

"We had a nice lunch," Andrews said.

"So you were mostly just messing with me, then," I said.

"Exactly," Skid agreed. "It was fun."

"Well, it worked; I was messed with."

"Job well done." But Skidmore didn't smile the way he might have the day before.

We knew we were stalling; the subject of the conversation didn't matter the way it might have any other day.

"But we're still considering the whole mess," Andrews said, gazing down the slope into the shadows, "as motive for what happened to Harding."

I had to smile at Andrews. "We are, are we?"

"Don't you think?" He turned to me, ignoring the tone of irony in my statement.

"How far does this state property go, Skid?" I asked.

"All the way up to the cemetery. That's where it stops."

"This land goes all the way to that graveyard?" I couldn't believe it.

"Not so far as the crow flies," he told me. "You're thinking of how it was when we were kids. The graveyard expanded a little, and the new roads weave all over the mountain from here, but straight shot? It ain't but a mile, I reckon."

"Why did Harding do this?" Andrews whispered. He'd borrowed one of my old overcoats, knowing we'd be out in the cold all day. It was a long navy blue monstrosity, too big for him, natty, torn at one sleeve. He'd stuffed his hair into a stocking cap and looked like a derelict sailor. Skidmore was in tight official regalia. I'd layered sweatshirts and sweaters, black hunting jeans with big pockets, heavy wool socks, and hiking boots. We were men from three separate realities.

"What's the Wallace Stevens poem, Andrews," I asked, pulling on my black gloves, "that goes: 'Thirty men crossing a bridge into a town are actually thirty men crossing thirty bridges into thirty towns'?"

" 'Or one man crossing one bridge,' " he finished. "It's called 'Metaphors of a Magnifico,' I think. And I'm not sure you've got the quote exactly right. Why do you ask?"

"That's us. The three of us."

He nodded. "I'm going into the woods for an adventure; you're going for a cause; Detective Needle's on the job."

"But we're all going to do the same thing," Skidmore chimed in. "Let's get to it."

He was right. We'd wasted enough time. He handed me a small bundle of numbered red tags, Andrews a bunch of blue.

"Start with your lowest number; tag every body you come across." Skidmore kept his voice dry, businesslike, hollow. "If you run out of tags, call me." He gave me a walkie-talkie, Andrews had already picked his up. "If you have tags left over, we do the math at noon. Check in with me every so often. Questions?"

A thousand questions assaulted my brain, but none that anyone could answer.

"I take the east, Andrews the west; Dev, you go straight down. It would be better if we kept in eye contact, but the area's too big." He blew out a breath we could see in the morning air. "Cold for October." He headed off without another word.

I looked over at Andrews. "Are you okay?"

"Christ," he said softly. "I'm not nearly *okay.*"

I nodded, reached into my pocket. "Here, I brought this for you. Don't tell Skid."

He focused his eyes on the bottle in my hand.

"Is that your apple brandy?" Hushed reverence hung his voice in the air around us.

"The same."

"I think I'm going to cry." He took the bottle from me quickly. "Don't you want some?"

I pulled a small thermos out of the other pocket. "What do you think is fortifying this coffee?"

"You know you're a genius, right?" he said, pocketing his bottle in the greatcoat.

I headed down the slope.

An hour later Skidmore called. He was the first to find another group of bodies. Seven, including a child.

"What's that make the total?" Andrews's voice scratched over the walkie-talkie.

"We're over a hundred," Skid answered coldly.

I had done my best to keep a more or less straight path from where I'd started. It was slow going because I felt I had to scour every inch of the woods within my vision. I took ten steps, swept everything in a ninety-degree angle from my extreme right to a parallel point at my extreme left. Then ten more steps. Focus was intense, and there was little on my mind. The wind and cold swept away any clinging distractions, and since I had not found anything, the exercise might have been a pleasant meditation—but for the ever-present worry that my eye would come across a pile of rotting corpses.

"How are you holding up?" I asked Skid over the airwaves.

"I'm all right."

"Signing off, then," I said. I didn't like hearing his voice so cold.

I thought I must be nearing the lower edge of the cemetery if it was only as far from the mortuary as Skid had said. I scanned the woods in front of me for the line of state barbed wire.

The woods were a perfect autumn world. A few leaves still pinched the branches of the chestnut and sycamore; their kin carpeted the ground. The air was crisp, the sun dodged clouds, and the sky, when it broke through, was hard blue.

I was a little surprised I hadn't seen much animal life. The occasional squirrel, a darting bird, but nothing else. Considering that the land had not been hunted, I'd half-expected to see deer. The terrain sloped grandly up and down twice before trending steadily upward, ascending the gentler side of the mountain toward the cemetery. The trees, never too close, were thinning as the incline grew.

Just as I was thinking how glad I was that I hadn't found any bodies, I saw something black dart past my peripheral vision, to the left. I jerked my head in the direction of the movement, but there was nothing there. Then a rustle of leaves disturbed the silence behind a large fallen tree. Pines toppled regularly in the autumn, and this one had been old. It had fallen recently; the roots still dangled upward in the air.

Bears sometimes found food in fallen trees of that size, a final bite before lumbering off for the winter's nap. I stood very still, my breathing a little too loud, waiting. I hadn't fired a gun since I was a boy, but I wished then I'd brought one of my father's hunting rifles. I was standing in a relatively clear patch of ground, nothing around me, nothing to dive behind or climb up. No big sticks or heavy rocks were anywhere near.

"Dev?"

The walkie-talkie scraped the air all around me, twice as loud as it had been a moment before. I jumped, gasping.

The thing behind the tree did the same. It scrambled, growled, and sprinted away. I heard it more than saw it, but it was large and black.

"Dev?" the walkie-talkie said again. It was Andrews.

I grabbed it out of my pocket.

"What?"

"I'm running low on fuel. Do you have any 'coffee' left?"

"Christ."

"What?" he said innocently.

"I was just . . ." but I didn't finish.

"Just what?"

"I saw something, an animal, but it ran off."

"What was it?"

"Could have been a bear," I answered. "But it was a small one."

"A bear?" His voice was higher. "Are there bears out here?"

"Probably not."

"But you just said." His pitch grew.

"Could have been a wild dog, I guess, but . . ." I stopped. "Oh my God."

"Do you see it?" He'd jumped an octave.

"It could have been a big black wild dog."

"Well, be careful," he mused, calming. "In some ways I'd rather run into a bear than a wild dog." He hesitated. "So your coffee . . ."

"It's gone," I lied. "Sorry."

"Okay. When's lunch?"

"Andrews," I shot back.

"Fine," he said quickly, "I'm going back to work." His walkie-talkie clicked off.

I tried to see where the dog had gone. It was too much a coincidence, June's telling me about the witch's animal companion, then seeing its twin in the woods. Darting up the final slope winded me, but it brought me to the end of the government property and the barbed wire fencing.

Slipping under it was harder than it had been on the other side. Rocks had been piled on the ground and had to be moved. I still managed to catch my sweater and it took me a few minutes to get loose, all the while convinced that the wild dog would return, find me helpless, and eat my esophagus.

Finally freed, I got to my feet quickly, scanning the edge of the graveyard, trying to get my bearings. I didn't recognize anything.

Find the Angel of Death, I thought.

Grim as it was, the statue was the perfect landmark, tall enough to be seen from most of the yard and clearly appropriate for the day.

After wandering and skirting impossible bramble thickets, I saw it and headed toward its dark wings.

The statue was weathered, covered with lichens, beautiful in the autumn light. It had been purchased by the Newcomb family to be placed at the tallest point in the cemetery, atop the largest communal crypt. The crypt itself was at least twice the size of my house. It was made mostly of granite; the iron gates guarding the entrance were highly stylized art deco monstrosities, the fashion of the decade in which they were commissioned.

The Angel soared over the building, arms reaching out, gown blowing behind, on its way to gather souls. The substantial wings seemed quite capable of carrying angel and company away. The angel's face had always been, to me, the most disturbing aspect of the thing. It was smiling. Mona Lisa had learned from this angel. The smile was grim if I stood on one side of the statue, serene from another angle, ominous straight ahead. Deeply troubling.

I thought it best to try and stand beside it to survey the entire yard. It took some doing to scramble up on top of the crypt, but once I was there I could see that others had come before me: beer bottles, cigarette butts, chicken bones decorated the roof. Fine place for a midnight tryst among the ghoulish high school set.

I stood, arm on the statue, and took in as much of the place as I could. Once again I thought the quiet concentration would have been pleasant under other circumstances. I lost myself in the exercise, and time passed in silence.

The meditation was brought to an abrupt end by the sound of something moving in the crypt.

Impossible for me to get off the roof without making noise, all sound from within the crypt ceased when I moved.

My heart was thumping, my eyes burning. I was trying not to blink. *Could be an animal,* I thought. *A rat would be right.* My breathing was uncontrollably loud from the effort of quitting the roof.

A closer inspection of the iron gates at the front of the crypt revealed that they had been opened recently; the hinges showed signs of disturbed rust and moss. Something had gone into the tomb— and closed the door behind it.

Fear could easily have prevented me from moving had it not been for the curse of curiosity. I had to know what was inside. Still, precautions had to be taken. I pulled out the walkie-talkie and made a loud noise, clearing my throat, then called in.

"Deputy Needle?" I said loudly into the thing. "I'm here at the Public Crypt as you instructed. How close behind me are you? Over."

There was a pause. The thing in the crypt was deliberately still.

"Dev?" Skidmore's voice was uncertain, but he knew better than to ask questions. He'd heard the tone in my voice.

"Yes," I answered more loudly, "I can see you now; the rest of the men are on their way to meet us here."

"Good," he said hesitantly. Then, an afterthought, "Don't go shooting off your gun, all right? I don't want any more disturbance up there."

"Yes, sir," I told him, "I won't shoot my rifle again. Sorry."

"Good. Be right there." Pause. "Andrews, you copy all this?"

Silence reigned.

Then: "Copy?" Andrews had clearly finished all the apple brandy. "Sure. I guess."

"Bring the rest of the men and meet us up at the big crypt."

"Under the Angel of Death," I inserted quickly.

"Oh." Utter bafflement filled Andrews's voice. "Okay."

I thought there might be a back exit out of the crypt and I was half-hoping whatever was inside would find one and take it. Moving away from the gates, I took a vantage point slightly behind a nearby grave marker.

The sun dodged behind a fast-moving cloud; without warning it was twilight. A cold shot of wind speared through the yard; everything was animated for a moment. I looked down at the tear in my sweater. When I looked up, there was more noise from inside the crypt.

I ducked down behind the tombstone, trying to hold my breath. Then scraping sounds, like someone moving furniture, sang out. A human moan, I thought, rolled out from between the bars of the gate. Could have been creaking tree limbs in the wind.

I reached into my pocket and turned off the walkie-talkie. I had no intention of its scaring me or the thing inside. I squinted into the place, willing my sight to pierce the darkness. I thought I saw something, but it moved too quickly.

Suddenly there was a clatter from deep inside. I stood.

There is a back door, I thought.

I shot around the side of the place before I could think.

The ground was level all around the crypt. When I got to the back side I could see two high windows, thick stained glass. One was broken. And it was moving.

There was a hand at the edge of the window, clearing away the broken bits of glass. Then a voice sounded.

"Damn," it said quietly.

The face appeared, and I burst out laughing.

Inappropriate laughter is often the result of released tension. In this particular case, enormous relief was involved.

I stared up at the face. "Able!"

He hadn't seen me and I frightened him. He jerked, startle response, and fell backward into the crypt.

Able Carter lay on the floor of the crypt, barely conscious. Skidmore was kneeling beside him, making certain he hadn't broken anything. Andrews and I stood staring.

Though they'd met, Andrews had not recognized Able's face. It was haggard, covered with stubble, grim-eyed.

"I can't believe that's the same person I saw at the church just the other night," Andrews said again. "He's aged ten years."

"Let's just get him on his feet," Skid said. "Don't appear he's got any broken bones." He looked down. "You stand up, Able?"

Able managed a feeble nod.

On his feet he was still dazed, not quite understanding who we were, even his brother-in-law.

"Girlinda's been worried sick about you, boy," Skid said gently, trying to revive him.

"Worried?" He looked around, trying to imagine where he was.

"Did he hit his head?" Andrews whispered.

"Got the breath knocked out of him," Skid answered. "He'll come around in a minute."

Able looked Skidmore up and down. "Am I under arrest?"

Skidmore started to say something, took in a breath, remained silent, darting his eyes to me for a second.

"We've been looking for you, Able," I said calmly. "Your sister was scared something happened to you."

"Sister?" He was still dazed.

I reached into my pocket for the small thermos. "This might help." I handed it to Able.

"Hey," Andrews objected, "you said that was gone."

Able looked down at it.

"Coffee," I told him.

He nodded slowly. I unscrewed the top for him. He sipped. He sighed. He finished the coffee in one or two more gulps.

I took the thermos back from him and watched his eyes gradually return to the present moment.

"Wow," he said, "I fell."

"You did," Skid agreed, looking up at the high broken window.

"Am I under arrest?" Able repeated.

"Yes," Skidmore said evenly.

Andrews and I kept still.

"Let me explain," Able said, looking down; his hands began to tremble. "It wasn't my fault. I didn't do it on purpose. But I can see how it looks. And I almost got lynched by the Deveroe boys too, so I understand what everyone's got to be thinking." He looked up, locked eyes with Skidmore. "I'm scared, boy. I'm really, really scared." He was starting to shake all over.

"It's okay," Skid said plainly.

"You have to take me into the jail, I get that, but you got to promise me the Deveroes can't get at me. Not until we straighten all this out." Tears were in his eyes. "I loved her, Skid. You know that. Everybody knows that. We were going to be married. I swear to God. You have to believe me." He closed his eyes.

"Able?" I took a step closer to him.

"It was an *accident,*" he snapped at me fiercely; a violent shaking overcame his body. "I could never murder Truevine. I loved her."

Skidmore wouldn't allow Able to speak another word until we were all back down the mountain, seated in his office. He'd called his wife, sent out for food, and warned Able of his rights before any of us were allowed to speak.

"All right, now," Skid began, pencil in hand. "Tell me what happened."

The walk back down the mountain had been a trot. Andrews kept starting sentences that were cut off by sharp looks from the deputy.

Skid placed Able, unhandcuffed, in the backseat. Andrews and I followed in my truck. Skid had tried to send us home, but he could see what a fight he'd have had on his hands, so he gave up and let us sit in a corner watching the strange scene.

Skidmore's office was colorless: off-white walls, acoustical-tile drop ceiling, Kmart window blinds. He sat behind his desk; five ancient office chairs surrounded it, the hollow-core door never completely closed. It was the office of a man who spent little time in an office. Papers were piled randomly, the floor was a little unkempt, but there was a clear space on the desk in front of him and the room did not seem entirely chaotic.

"Go on," he urged Able.

"We had a fight, me and Tru," Able began. "At the church Wednesday night meeting." He looked around. "I don't even know what day it is now."

"We all heard the fight; it was Thursday night last week, remember? They changed it."

"That's right," he answered vaguely, "in the new hall."

"So that night," Skid insisted, "after your argument?"

"She stormed off." His voice grew distant, and he stared out the window. "I grabbed her arm. We were both pretty mad." He shifted in his seat. "Tell you why in a minute, I reckon."

"We think we know why," Skid said, more gently than he had been speaking. "Harding appears to have—"

"Harding Pinhurst is a monster right out of a book," Able interrupted with such force that Skidmore's head jerked back a half an inch.

"But we'll get to that in a minute," Skid said soothingly.

"Okay," Able agreed. "In a minute. So. She run off; I chased her. Lost her in the woods. Moon wasn't up yet." He turned in my direction. "She run in the direction of your place, Dev. I thought I'd find her there, maybe even talking to you. She likes to do that, did you know?"

"Please talk to me, Able," Skid insisted.

Able's clothes were a wreck, torn, dirty. His face was thin; he had lost weight in the days he'd been gone. But he didn't seem to be suffering from the kind of deprivation or hypothermia he might have, especially considering he was still wearing only his church meeting jacket and slacks, brown and tan, no tie. Had he found food? Started a fire?

"She was out of her head. I finally caught up with her. I was out of breath, and still mad as a rooster. She saw me coming; her face was white as a sheet. Like she didn't even recognize me." He lowered his voice. "She gets that way sometimes, out of her head. It don't happen that often." He sighed. "Anyway, I could see she was scared, so I tried to calm myself. Calling her *honey* and all, but she just kept staring, eyes big as saucers. When I got right up close to her she just kept saying, 'I'm sorry; I didn't mean it,' which I thought she was talking about our little fight, but she was way more upset than that, I could tell after a second or two. She just kept backing away from me. I tried to stop her. I didn't touch her, I swear to God."

His body was more agitated; his voice was shaking.

"What happened then?" Skid asked methodically.

"She whomped me good with a big old tree branch. I don't even know where she got it from; it just kind of appeared in her hands." Beginning tears came to his eyes. "I was out for a second or two, I reckon. When I got back up, I looked around for her; my vision was all blurry. I didn't see her at first." His eyes brimmed. "Then I did. Still as a corpse. Down at the bottom of the ravine."

Andrews jumped. I think he had suddenly realized what was also dawning on me.

Skid came to the same conclusion. "Truevine fell into the ravine up there close to Dr. Devilin's house?"

"Reckon she's still there," Able answered; he could barely speak. "I started down to help her; she wasn't moving a muscle. And then I heard them coming."

"Who?" Skid stopped writing.

"I reckoned it was the Deveroe brothers," he said, barely audibly, tears brimming.

"You saw them?"

"Who else is out in those woods that late? I knew what they'd think. They don't like me one bit. I'm scared of them *all* the time, but that night, it was something else." He squirmed again, searching for words. "Since then, Skid . . . they caught up with me once." He seemed unable to believe what he was saying. "They tried to *hang* me. I don't even know what happened; it's all like a dream. I just got away." He shook his head violently, trying to clear it. "I reckon I been out of my head. Maybe I still am. I seen things."

His breathing was labored and I was afraid he might have a heart attack.

"You think Truevine Deveroe fell into that ravine up there last Thursday night when she hit you," Skidmore said carefully, "and before you could go help her, you ran away from her brothers?"

All Able could do was nod, unable to control his facial muscles.

"You have to tell him," I whispered to Skid.

He drew in a long breath, nodded once, set down his pencil.

"Look, Able." He let the breath out. "Truevine's missing, that's all. At the bottom of that ravine we did find a body. It was Harding Pinhurst. He's real dead. That's what you're under arrest for: his murder."

Able's head rose slowly. "Harding's dead?"

Our next stop was the emergency room, where Able was pronounced safe for incarceration, a formality Skid would not have entertained had he not been running an election campaign. It took over an hour after that for Skidmore to fill Able in on what had happened while he'd been hiding, including my bizarre attempt to save him from being hanged. He listened to it all, shivering in a blanket Skid had given him, holding on to a shaky Styrofoam cup half-filled with coffee.

When our story was done, Able finished the cup. "I have no idea what to say." He rubbed his eyes.

It didn't appear to me that Able was lying. Few people in our little town get so emotional; no one I knew from Blue Mountain would have been able to pull off an act of that magnitude. He was telling the truth.

He lifted his head. "But you saw what Harding was doing, what he'd done." His face contorted.

"We saw it," Skid said quietly.

Andrews had opened and closed his mouth ten times, dying to put in his two cents. Each time he'd thought better of it, but the silence in the room proved too much for him in the end.

"Someone else saw it too," he declared.

"Sh!" Skid spat sharply.

"But isn't it obvious—" Andrews protested.

"This is a police matter," I said calmly, touching Andrews lightly on the forearm.

He fell silent, nodding his apology.

"What seems clear," Skid began patiently, "is that Harding Pinhurst is dead and, Able, you've been in hiding for days. You can see it don't look good for you."

"Where's Tru?" he asked, ignoring what Skid had said.

"Dev believes she's hid out in the cemetery." Skidmore shot me a quick glance. "That's how we found you."

Skidmore's eyes spoke volumes. When we were kids, Skid and I spent endless hours in the woods not speaking, exchanging looks, just this side of telepathic. Both of us knew what those looks meant. We'd had decades of mutual experience since that day. I knew the meaning of the glance in his office as if it were a detailed paragraph.

I stood. "Well, this isn't as interesting as I thought it would be." I stretched. "And I'm ready for a bite. Andrews?"

"I could eat," he answered, not understanding.

I started out the door. "We'll be at Etta's," I told Skid.

Andrews picked up the pace. "Etta's diner?" His voice filled with joy.

A memory of black-eyed peas panfried with bacon and fresh sage filled his mind, it was obvious from the transfigured look on his face.

Few things gave Andrews a sense of transcendence more than Etta's cooking.

Out on the street, I headed for my truck.

"We're going to drive there?" Andrews asked, confused. "It's just down the block."

"We're going back into the woods." I pulled out my keys.

Andrews froze in his tracks.

"*You're* going," he said firmly. "I'm eating."

He turned in the direction of Etta's diner. I knew that walk. It would take a baseball bat and two other men to stop him from getting lunch. I pocketed my keys.

"I could eat," I said, falling in beside him.

"What were you thinking?" he asked irritably.

"What do you mean?"

"You know you had a hundred questions to ask Able. He looks terrible, but he doesn't look like he hasn't eaten or drunk anything in nearly a week."

I nodded agreement.

"Then you jump up," he went on, "run out of the office. What is it?"

"Face code," I said. "Skid wants us back up there looking for Truevine."

"*Face code?*" He shook his head.

The diner was crowded even though the lunch rush was over. We managed to find two stools at the counter.

Etta shuffled over, acknowledging us with drooping eyes. She set down a package of silverware wrapped in three paper napkins and indestructible plastic plates big enough for two men. Mine was pale green, Andrews had acquired one of vaguely beige hue. Etta was dressed in her usual dark print calf-length dress, ancient blue slippers, a man's brown cardigan, disheveled white bun for a crown.

We knew what to do. Strangers were sometimes served by Etta, but most everyone else was simply given the tools with which to feed themselves. We took our plates into the kitchen, surveyed the vegetables simmering on the oversize stovetop. The smell of fried chicken came from a large warm oven to the left of the stove.

Black-eyed peas, crisp fried okra, cut-off corn cooked in butter and sugar filled my plate. A square of jalepeño cornbread rested precariously on top of the peas. A golden chicken breast crowned the center.

There was little talk for the next twelve minutes. I hadn't realized how famished I was. The food was gone in short order.

"Banana pudding, I think," Andrews declared, pushing his empty plate away from him on the countertop.

I was still scraping my plate with the last square of cornbread in an attempt to get every last drop of nectar from the black-eyed peas.

Though it didn't appear Etta had heard us, she disappeared into the kitchen and returned seconds later with two bowls of pudding.

That particular dessert, ordinarily a somewhat plebeian affair, had been made glorious by several of Etta's modifications. First, the crust was made from Oreo chocolate cookies. The bananas had been sautéed in Etta's own berry brandy. The meringue contained flecks from at least three vanilla bean pods. A bowl of the pudding cost nearly twice as much as the rest of the meal, and she ran out of it every day.

"That's the last of it," she croaked, sliding the dessert our way. "Had to give you smaller size to make two."

That was all. She turned and went back to her chair at the table closest to the kitchen. There would be no discount, no economic adjustment of any sort. She was only explaining the scant portions. I smiled down at the brimming bowl, large as half a loaf of bread.

We dug in, still silent.

The place began to clear out, Andrews wiped his mouth with a third napkin, I leaned on the counter.

"This was a good idea," I admitted. "My head is clearer. Calmer anyway."

"It might hold me till nightfall," he conceded. "Now what's all this about going back into the woods?"

"Skidmore wants us out there looking for her," I said, "before it gets dark. He's worried."

"You got that from a single look?"

"We've known each other forever," I said. "There's more."

"I'm listening," Andrews said with irritated patience.

"She's in the cemetery."

"We think."

"No," I said, reaching for my wallet, "she's there. Skidmore's face: he saw her this morning."

Nine

The last afternoon sun had reached the peculiar moment when amber and golden hues seem to come from everything everywhere, the sky least of all. In that unreal light, Andrews and I sat down close to the Angel of Death.

"I'm in," he said, leaning his back against a tombstone. "She's not here. You misunderstood Skidmore's face code. I can't do any more of this."

"Been a long day," I agreed. I tried to remember the last time I'd spent all day tromping through the woods. "Let's check her parents' grave once more before we head home."

"Christ," he complained. "We've been there five times."

"Three, and it's on the way to the truck."

We managed our way to a standing position; I took off in the direction of *Eloise and Davy, together once more.* Andrews trudged behind.

The light was dimming quickly. There was no path to follow, just weeds and the last brown leaves drifting down around us from an oak twenty yards away. No order organized these markers. Some were grand, some anonymous. None had been attended to in years. Is there a sadder place than an untended grave?

I was the first to see it, and froze.

Andrews, in his usual daze, ran into me.

"What?" he said, irritated.

I nodded my head in the direction of the nearest stone.

A black dog, like the shadow of a tomb, sat on the grassy grave we were looking for, its coal eyes locked on us.

"Don't move," I whispered to Andrews.

The dog's hair bristled.

"Stop talking," Andrews shot back urgently. "It doesn't like talking."

The dog came to all fours, standing ready.

We played our tableau for perhaps thirty long seconds before sweet whistling turned all our heads.

Two notes. A human sound.

The dog gave us a final glance, leapt like a demon over a high stone wall, and was gone in the direction of the musical noise.

"Did you see that thing jump?" Andrews said, releasing his breath. "Did you see the *look* it gave us?"

"I think it speaks English." It was the most intelligent look I'd ever seen in a dog's eyes.

"At least," Andrews topped.

The whistle came once more on the wind.

"So, there's someone over there." I tried to see where it had gone.

"I stand by my earlier complaint," Andrews said softly. "Why don't you take me home so I won't be in your way?"

I was tempted to go home myself. It's one thing to hike around a quaint old graveyard in late October looking for a strange young girl. It's quite another experience if you've spent the day counting decayed bodies stacked everywhere in the surrounding woods. And you come across a black dog. And you're not alone in the cemetery. And it's nearly dark.

"We have to see who that was," I heard myself say. "They know we're here."

"What do you mean: 'who that was'?" He followed my gaze. "You don't think it's Truevine?"

"I don't know." I turned to her parents' tombstone. "Is there anything over on the grave?"

We both examined it as best we could—nothing new.

"The dog was waiting for us," Andrews said. A sudden shiver took his shoulders. "Damn. Did the temperature just drop ten degrees?"

"It gets cold fast once the sun's gone," I affirmed. "Let's go."

I started off after the dog. Andrews, at a loss for what else to do, followed. The downward slope revealed an area that seemed familiar to me. I assumed it was one of the sections we'd explored earlier, but when we rounded a granite boulder I realized I had visited the site many years before.

I came to a sudden halt; Andrews nearly ran into me again.

"When I was seven or so," I began.

"Memory Digression Alert," he interrupted wearily.

"My great-grandfather died and left some money for me to attend college," I continued. "It was the only way I could have gone; he knew it. It made me the first in my family to get a higher education."

"Thanks." His voice burned red with irony. "I'd always wondered how you managed it."

"That's his grave." I pointed.

Andrews saw it, fell silent, held his breath.

The black dog sat perfectly still, tongue out to one side, on the bare dirt of my grandfather's grave.

"All right. That's enough." A strange voice, low and rough, addressed the dog. It came from behind a sarcophagus ten or twelve feet to our right.

The dog yawned.

A figure appeared where we'd heard the voice. Its features were impossible to make out in the near-darkness. It was a tattered coat, a walking stick, banshee hair blown backward by the wind.

"You are Dr. Devilin?" it continued.

"I am." My voice was an imitation of calm confidence.

"Okay," it sighed.

It headed our way.

The dog stood.

I could feel Andrews behind me readying for a fight. His breathing intensified, weight shifted. I'd seen him play rugby. His fear-pumped aggression coupled with my size were more than a match for the scarecrow.

The dog worried me.

I thought about the thermos in my pocket, wondered if it would be strong enough to bash the animal in the head, do any damage.

"We've been waiting," the strange voice croaked.

My shoulders dropped slightly. "For me?"

He nodded once, a staccato jab.

"Do you know him?" Andrews whispered.

"Are you with Truevine?" I asked our host.

He gave another low whistle and the dog vanished, moving faster than I would have imagined possible, behind the sarcophagus.

"Come on," the tattered man said, turning away from us.

I looked back at Andrews. His eyes widened.

We followed the man into an area of larger stone crypts, hard to tell how many; they were jumbled and hidden by brush and brambles. The ground was clawed with black moss, the air thick with the smell of decayed leaves. Tumble of stones, knot of vine here and there made all the crypts seem one. Old oak branches overhead looked like exposed veins, bloodless, lifeless but for the artificial animation of the chilled wind. Odd rock angles reflected the gloom, seemed to work at blocking out what little light wandered there. The sun was nearly set, the horizon a red wound.

As we rounded the edge of one wall our guide stopped and a heavy wooden door opened wide, a sick shifting.

"Not really," Andrews pronounced carefully, so there would be no mistake. "I'm not going in there."

I tried to see past the doorway into the tomb—without luck.

"It's warmer," the stranger said, and disappeared inside.

"It is a little cool out here," I admitted to Andrews halfheartedly.

"It is *not* warmer in there." He stood his ground.

I called into the stone building: "Who's in there?"

No answer came.

This structure was solid, gray granite, nearly the size of my cabin, highlighted with hunter green and chartreuse lichens. The wooden door was as big as a drawbridge, riddled with wormholes, crowned with the stern visage of an unforgiving God. I could just make out the quote under it: *Come hither ye blest but depart all ye curst.*

The roof was made of rust-colored clay tiles. Ancient twigs and new pine straw littered its crevasses. After a second of examination I thought I saw fog or steam crouching over it. An instant later the sweet smell of burning hickory made clear the possibility of a fire inside.

"Are they burning something in there?" Andrews said at the same time.

"I think so," I answered, taking a step closer to the door.

"Are they cooking?" His voice lifted. "Smells like barbecue."

Only partially amused that no fear was greater than my friend's appetite, I shook my head.

"There's no telling what's in there."

"That dog's in there," he suggested.

"Probably."

A face appeared in the doorway, someone new.

"Are you coming in or am I closing the door?" said the woman. Not Truevine—older.

"How about if we come in," I suggested, taking a slow step her way, "and *then* you close the door."

"Fair enough," she agreed humorlessly.

"Are you out of your mind?" Andrews didn't move.

"Aren't you the least bit curious?" I said, my eye glued to the woman in the doorway.

"This is what's wrong with you," he said angrily.

But he followed—after a moment.

Before my eyes could adjust to the odd glowing light in the place, I heard the door creak, slam tightly behind us.

By the time white light at the center of the vault receded to amber, I had made out several forms huddled around the fire. A new blaze, it had burned down quickly. It was made only from thick twigs and stems; no large wood fueled it. A column of thin gray smoke shot upward to an open skylight in the ceiling; the draft was perfect.

Silence framed the rest of the air, filled it with unspoken longing. Several of the figures were partly hidden by scarves or hoods, but I was certain Truevine was not with us. These people had helped Able Carter. An intuition.

The desire to pour out story after story was etched deeply on the faces I could see. My chest ached breathing in their desperation. They were frozen, mute, their eyes wild as the ocean and as dark. Waiting.

A younger man, bent and limping, took a step toward me. He was wrapped in a coat that had once been fine, camel hair, double-breasted—now baring and worn at the elbows. I tensed without thinking, and he stopped.

"Dr. Devilin," he rasped, "we need your help."

Shaken by the understatement, and the obvious pain that contorted his face, I couldn't speak for a moment.

The older woman who'd let us in laid another bundle of kindling on the coals, and the room brightened once more.

The scarecrow who had invited us in wiped his nose with the palm of his hand. "We don't like to mix with town folk," he announced, then fell silent, his eyes turned to the fire.

I found my voice. "Who are you? What is this?"

They looked at one another slowly.

The young man in the camel hair coat sucked in a difficult breath and held it for a moment. Then: "We thought you might know us. Know our little community."

"Know you?" A tingling, like a hand that had fallen asleep, touched the pit of my stomach, the back of my neck. I turned to Andrews.

He stood straight, feet apart, balanced, hands shaking a little. He was still in fighting readiness. My old overcoat made him look stockier than he was; he made an imposing figure: face hard, eyes steel.

Reading the questions on my face, the young man motioned for me, then turned toward a darker part of the crypt. "I'll show you."

I hesitated, but the others were watching me with such anticipation— there was no menace in their posture, no threat in their aspect.

I followed.

Every eye was on me. It only took a few steps for me to catch up with the young man. We moved into the shadows.

At the back corner of the place he pointed mutely to an arrangement of debris: broken bits of tombstone, strangely shaped patterns of moss, sticks, other bits of debris all held together by old shoelaces, tied at the back with a knot the size of a tarantula. At the center of this folk sculpture was a geode as big as a human head, cracked open, filled with amethyst colors.

The man stared at me, willing me to understand what the conglomeration meant. I studied it, ideas darting into my consciousness like dark birds, then flying away. It bore some relation to Howard Finster's older sculptural attempts, but without the poetry and Bible verses. As I was about to confess to the man that I had no idea what I was looking at, I caught the glint of something silver in the geode.

He watched my face, nodded slowly.

I moved so that a little more light from the fire could spill into the dark corner, and was finally able to make out what they all wanted me to see.

I took in a gulp of air so suddenly I began to cough violently.

"Dev?" Andrews called out, coming my way.

"I'm all right," I assured him hoarsely. "But my God."

"What?" He bounded to my side.

I had no idea how to tell him what it was. I could only stare at it, suddenly unable to speak.

"Damn it!" he insisted, bouncing.

Where to begin?

Nestled inside the geode was a masterfully wrought antique silver lily.

"This," I finally managed, transfixed, "was made by my great-grandfather. I think."

"What was?" Andrews glared at the pile. "This heap?"

I took a step closer to the pin. "Can you see the little lily?"

He squinted. "In the hollow rock?" He drew closer too, next to me. "Yes. Your great-grandfather? Are you sure?"

"No. And it would be a fairly amazing coincidence. I was just reading his story again."

I reached out my hand without thinking, then pulled it back. "Do you mind?" I asked, turning to the young man.

He hesitated but gave a curt nod.

Instantly I plucked the lily out, took it back to the fire so I could examine it better. By the dim orange glow I could just make out the letters *CB* on the main part of the flower, the only place large enough for the tiny initials. Even though I'd tried to prepare myself for seeing them, I still let out a startled syllable.

"Is it?" Andrews peered over my shoulder.

"See the initials?"

"*CB?* Is that right?"

"His name was Conner Briarwood when he went to Ireland. He changed it to Devilin when he ran to the States."

I heard myself begin to tell Andrews the story, starting with the Irish silversmith Jamison who had taken my great-grandfather as an apprentice. The others drew closer as I went on: the faithless Molly, the gift of the pin, the betrayal, the trial, his narrow escape. I left out the ending, the not-so-happily ever after in America.

To my great surprise, the haggard young man took up the tale.

"Every one of us knows the rest," he began solemnly. "Conner Devilin was buried in this park, clutching the silver lily to his heart. His wife Adele went mad with grief. She left home, came to live here."

I nearly dropped the pin.

"Townsfolk said she was lost in the woods, but this was her home," he said, looking around the crypt. "She dug up the body of her husband, pried the lily away from him, and kept it around her neck for the remainder of her days."

My mind was swimming. "How on earth could you know what she did or didn't do?" I looked around at all of them.

"She started this community. It's named after her."

One of the women pointed to a place over the inside door frame. The name *Adele* had been scratched, very cleanly, in the stone, each letter nearly a foot high.

"I don't believe any of this." My voice cracked with anger. "Why are you saying these things?"

"Used to be called hoboes in her day," the young man intoned. "Travelers. Most don't stay long. Some few take up residence."

"I heard about it in Chicago," said the old woman. How old was she? Twenty? Eighty? Her thick black coat revealed no clue. "*Adele* is a very famous place."

I turned to Andrews. "Am I too exhausted to understand this, or is it all as weird as I think?"

"Weirder," he croaked.

"Who are you?" I demanded to no one in particular.

The young man stepped closer into the light, pulled his hair back, revealing his features clearly.

I studied them, and a slow dawn of recognition grew, contrary to my sense of reality.

"Rud?" My voice betrayed disbelief.

"That's right."

"Who?" Andrews whispered to me.

"Rud Pinhurst," I said, amazed, back to Andrews. "Truevine's first love. He left Blue Mountain over three years ago."

"In town," Rud began his tale around the fire, "I was no good."

He told us his version of Truevine's story, his smithing for the tourists, betrayal of the fragile girl. He added what I had always suspected: his contribution to the girl's legend had been sufficient to make her the witch of our town. He'd continued to spread rumors about her as his health and posture deteriorated. With his aspect failed, demeanor ruined, his bride soon left him, went back to her wealthy family. She sold the home they lived in, with everything in it.

Rud's health prevented his working. His own family had never cared for him, was glad to see him sink. He had nowhere to go.

"I came here to stay. Nearly three years ago," he finished quietly. "I found peace."

Andrews was seated on a stolen lawn chair by the coals. He shook his head. "How do you all live here?" His voice cracked.

"We don't," said the scarecrow who'd whistled at the black dog. No names were offered—or solicited.

We'd all huddled close around the warm glow as Rud told us his history. We numbered seven; most were seated. I stood close to Rud as he spoke, wishing I had my tape recorder.

The woman from Chicago was the only representative of her gender; one of the men was ancient, with no glint of life in his eye; a younger man was very sick, lying in a fetal position close to the fire, covered with several blankets and sniffing, staring at the coals. All were dressed in mismatched layers, filthy pants.

Everyone, however, sported spotless new sneakers, a fashion mystery solved when I remembered the sermon from last Thursday night's prayer meeting at the Blue Mountain Methodist Church: "I cried because I had no shoes until I met a man who had no feet." The collection cage had been set up outside the new meeting hall, contributions of new shoes for the needy had been demanded. Surely that bin had supplied most of our company with its current footwear.

"We only stay awhile, most of us," said the woman from Chicago. "Then move on. It's autumn. Time to move further south."

"Atlanta's nice," the ancient said, affectless, staring into the coals.

"Florida's better," the scarecrow mumbled. "It's warm."

Everyone grumbled. It appeared to be an old argument.

"Sure," the woman said, "if they don't lock you in jail, Alton." She looked up at me. "Florida, in my experience, does not care for the homeless person. You don't see so many bums on the beach, do you? Whereas Atlanta has some degree of tolerance. Underground Atlanta area, Hurt Park or Central City Park, back side of the Omni."

"Omni's gone, May," Rud said gently.

"Always used to be the Omni," she stuttered back, losing her train of thought.

"I'm the only one that lives here currently," Rud told me. "It's my job. When Tess Brannour left me, I tried to kill myself; I wanted to die. But my family would not allow me that. Not even that. Uncle

Jackson got me the job of caretaker here. I had no choice in the matter."

The woman from Chicago, apparently named May, tossed more sticks on the fire. It sputtered up, then blazed. Orange and black shadows danced the walls around us; faces were momentarily more illuminated—I found myself wishing they had not been. Longing and exhaustion painted every one. No deeper thoughts were to be read, however. Everything in the mind was tightly guarded by the mask painted on each face.

"I live in the caretaker's cottage," Rud continued. "Worked here nearly a year before I discovered *Adele*."

"I used to filch things out of his kitchen while he was asleep in his bed," May admitted, grinning. "He never knew."

"I never cared, May," he answered her sweetly. He caught my eye. "I was more dead than alive."

"No one in town knows you're here," I told him.

"That was Uncle Jackson's condition, one of them," Rud said. "I was not to make myself known up here, keep out of sight. Take care of the family plots first, do what I could with the rest." His gaze drifted. "You wouldn't imagine it, but the days go by quickly."

"The rest of us come and go," May picked up. "This is my fifth year."

"You've come here five years," Andrews said, leaning forward. It wasn't a question; it was an expression of astonishment.

"I've been resting here near a month," the scarecrow said. "Trying to nurse Billy." He twitched his head in the direction of the boy under the blankets. "We're travel mates. I can't seem to get him warm enough. He's sick."

He was dying.

"Can't you get someone up here?" Andrews asked Rud, coming to the same conclusion as I had.

"I could speak to Lucinda about someone at the hospital," I added quickly. "Pro bono, no worry."

"We don't do that sort of thing," Rud said. A strange pride edged his words.

Others around the fire nodded.

You don't ask for help from the family that threw you out. Whether the family is called *Pinhurst* or *Chicago,* never look back. This was not a company of beggars; it was a band of outcast travelers. Aid might be stolen from an unguarded kitchen or a church donation bin, but it would never be requested from the people who lived outside the graveyard.

It was Billy's last autumn. Everyone seemed to know it. That was his lot. He was nearly home.

Rud came upon the group in the *Adele* sarcophagus quite by accident—heartbreaking hazard. He'd been pulling weeds around the Angel of Death and caught sight of a woman coming up the hill. When he saw it was Truevine he panicked and ran.

"I came in here." He looked around the room, taking it in, the whisper of a smile at one corner of his mouth. "I'd never been in this one before that. The sudden break with my ordinary routine of moping, weeding, eating, napping, and moping took our little community by surprise."

May smiled.

"The irony was that Truevine already knew they were here." His voice flooded with warmth. "She was bringing them ham biscuits."

"She does a thing with the ham," May began enthusiastically, "which is impossible: makes it smoky, well done, and still tender." She looked at Andrews. "How does she do that?"

"Is there a sauce?" Andrews shot back.

"Nope."

"Too bad," he said, thin-lipped.

"So Truevine found you here?" I asked Rud.

"No," he answered, his voice turning cold again.

If I'd had my tape recorder and we'd been alone, I could have gotten him to reveal what he was hiding, though it seemed obvious. His guilt had crippled him, and he still harbored some feeling for the girl. That was my two-second conclusion.

I took a different tack under the circumstances. "You said you needed my help?"

His face momentarily grimaced a sort of gratitude for the change in subject, then masked again. "Yes."

"It's Ms. Deveroe," the scarecrow said. "She's in trouble."

"I know," I told them all. "That's why we're here: looking for her."

"You know where she is?" Andrews leaned forward.

"She's not right," May chimed in. "A nice girl, but she's not all there in the head."

"Takes one to know one," the scarecrow shot back at May.

"Malmener," she spat back with a perfect accent, her face suddenly alive. "Chatre."

Andrews moved so quickly his chair nearly collapsed. Before I could intervene, his face was nearer to May's.

"Was that *French?*"

The anger left her eyes; she wouldn't look at him. " 'I have not always been as you see me now.' "

Her expression returned to its stony mask once more.

Andrews looked at me, amazed.

"She called him a bully," he couldn't help saying.

"And a neutered animal, I believe," I added.

"We don't ask many questions here," Rud said defensively.

That was all; nothing more would be said on the matter. May's former life—Chicago socialite jetting to Paris, demure teacher of languages in a small girls' school, waitress in an uptown bistro—whatever had taught her French was a closed book. We would never read it. An autumn would come to *Adele* that would find May gone entirely. No one would ask questions then either.

"You're concerned about Truevine," was my deliberate attempt to return us to the task at hand.

"You know what a strange one she is," Rud said quietly.

"I think there's more to her than a lot of people see," I answered.

I hadn't meant it to hurt him, but his eyes winced, and he mistook my observation for something more personal. "Agreed," he said, his voice barely audible above the crackle of the burning twigs. "Most don't know her for what she is."

"She's a kind of savant," I offered, hoping to explain my perception of the girl.

"The point is," he said, stronger, "she's off her kilter just a little at the moment and we need to set her straight."

"Off her kilter?" Andrews finally stood, came next to me. It seemed he, too, could hear the concern in Rud's words.

"Where is she?" I asked plainly.

"She's here," he said. "Close."

"Let me talk to her," I began.

Rud shook his head. "She won't see you."

"Can you be a little more specific about what's wrong with her?" Andrews sneered. "*Off her kilter* isn't exactly a medical term."

Maybe he wasn't trying to sound snide, may just have been his accent.

"I'd take care, Dr. Andrews." The iron in Rud's voice, coupled with the sudden fact of his knowing my friend's name, took Andrews aback.

"I was only asking," he said hastily.

"All right, then," Rud answered, voice still hard, "I'll tell you. Truevine is convinced that she's dead."

Rud told us he'd been awakened by strange noises in the yard sometime Thursday night. The racket was not one of the ordinary sounds of the place and he sensed something wrong.

He dressed, got his shotgun, braved the night. It hadn't taken long to follow the noise to Truevine, sprawled on her parents' grave, shaking.

"I tried to speak with her," he told us, "but she didn't hear me. I knelt down to touch her, get her attention, and she shot up, hid behind the tombstone. She said, 'Can you see me, Rudyard?' She never called me that. I said, 'What do you mean? Of course I can see you.' She said, 'Stay back. Noli me tangere.'" Rud turned to Andrews and snarled, "That's Latin."

"Sort of," Andrews returned, responding more to pronunciation than vocabulary.

"It means 'don't touch me.' It's what Jesus said to Mary after He died." Rud seemed eager to demonstrate his knowledge. "Jesus didn't want her to see He was a ghost."

"You think Truevine said that because she was a ghost?" Andrews could not keep derision out of his voice.

"She believes it," Rud affirmed calmly. He turned to me. "That's the problem."

"She thinks she's dead," I checked.

"Won't let a soul come near her," May whispered. "That's why Rud said she wouldn't see you."

"Well, she's upset," I began, "no doubt because of the events of that night: it's possible she got into a fight with her boyfriend; she may have been witness to a murder. But it's quite a leap to say she thinks she's dead. I mean, that's not the most obvious conclusion."

"I can tell," Rud said stubbornly.

"Latin?" was all Andrews wanted to know.

"It's in the Bible," Rud growled.

"Let me just say this again: *in Latin?*" Andrews was tired; I could hear his stomach gurgle from where I was standing. He was prepared to escalate the argument indefinitely.

"I think the most important thing," I interrupted, "is to find her, calm her down, take her back home. Right?"

I took silence for assent.

"So," I continued, "where is she now? Do we know?"

Glances were exchanged.

"I'll take you," the scarecrow said. "Dog likes me, and the girl gets riled if Rud comes too close."

He started toward the exit.

"Hold it; hold it," Andrews protested. "I'm not going anywhere until we get a few things straight. First: does that dog bite?"

"Sure does." The scarecrow grinned.

"Don't you want to go home?" I coaxed Andrews. "If we get the girl, our mission's accomplished."

Andrews considered the options: spending the night in the crypt against braving the darkness with the hope of dinner and bed.

"Keep that damned animal away from me." He pulled the coat

around himself tightly and jutted his chin in the direction of the exit.

"All right, then," I told Rud.

"If you can get her to go," he said slowly, "what then?"

"I'll see if she needs medical care, get her to her brothers," I told him, "but then I have to notify the police."

"Skidmore."

"Right."

"I figured that," Rud said tentatively, "but I meant more about . . ." He looked around at the small group huddled over the coals and didn't finish his sentence.

"Oh." Every eye was turned my way. "I see. I don't know what to say. I can't lie to Skidmore; I'd have to tell him where I found her. And how it happened."

"You can tell him I found her," Rud said, his voice rising. "He knows I'm up here."

"Skid knows you're the caretaker?" My surprise was short-lived. Of course Skid would know; he patrolled the area regularly. And Rud's secret would be safe with Officer Needle, a trait I greatly admired in my old friend.

"You don't need to mention anything else." Rud's voice calmed a little.

"If Skid knows about you," I said, volume lowered, "what makes you think he doesn't at least suspect the rest?"

"Because I'm a lightning rod," he said. "If I make myself known, they can hide." His face set itself, granite like the walls. "No one knows they're here."

"I don't think that's true," I disagreed. "For one, you remember Hek Cotage? He's seen things. He's talked about them."

Once again the room fell into a silence that brimmed with tension.

"Hezekiah talked to you about us?" May said slowly.

She seemed to know him.

"Not exactly," I answered, turning to her.

"Didn't think so." She settled back. "But you never can tell about a preacher."

If she was only passing through from Chicago, how did she know Hek and his occupation? I began to put together conversations the group might have had about townsfolk when Rud's voice stopped me.

"Reverend Cotage is a special case," he said, a strange glint in his eye.

"We know him," May said before Rud could stop her. "He's one of us."

Rud growled, clearly displeased that she had let it slip. She lowered her eyes instantly to the fire.

"How do you know him, May?" I took a step closer to her. "What do you mean?"

She recoiled slightly, and I stopped.

"May," I insisted.

"The story is," Rud announced from behind me, "that Hezekiah was once, for a very short while, a member of our *Adele* community."

The crackle of the kindling, the smoke that sifted straight upward, took up the silence.

I turned back to him. "Hek? Lived up here?"

"He was wounded in Vietnam," May said softly. "They say."

Junie's ghost story, the way I'd heard it a dozen times, came back to me. Hek had been wounded in the war, wandered, found his way home, married June—a kind of miracle.

"He came here first, before he went home."

"I told you this community has been a part of a hobo network for a long time." Rud's pale smile frightened.

If it was true that the idea had started with my great-grandmother, the gathering of travelers could well have a hundred-year history. Hek had come home from the war less than fifty years ago. It was possible that he'd stayed in the cemetery, gathering strength or courage before going down to find his future. Maybe he'd kept up an association with the group, continued to visit these people. His ministry was certainly strange enough.

Before I could completely put together a picture of Hek's service to the homeless, May struggled to her feet. She opened her coat and pulled the scarf from around her neck. In the dim light I could make out a yard and a half of dirty, torn, peach-colored cloth. Tiny roses dotting the fabric, almost transparently thin in spots. Still, I remembered the pattern.

May was wearing all that was left of Junie's wedding dress.

"I didn't know Hek when he lived here, of course," she said, almost to herself.

"He didn't *live* here," the scarecrow said. "He only stayed a month, they say."

"But he comes back every so often," she went on, as if she hadn't heard her detractor. "Brings food sometimes, and clothes. Brought me a book to read once."

"He leaves everything with me," Rud said. "Never says a word. Usually just sets it on my porch. About every other month or so. I don't think anyone knows."

I was trying to adjust to the knowledge myself.

"This was just a square of cloth in a trash bag Rud set in here," May said dreamily. "But it spoke to me. I got a chance to ask Hezekiah about it one day. I waited on Rud's porch, special."

"She sat there for three days and nights," Rud explained.

"He saw me and almost left, but I showed him I was wearing the cloth and he stopped." May's voice had turned inward on itself; she was clearly no longer in the room with us. "I asked him did he know what it was, I was in love with it so much. He told me it was the remnants of his wife's favorite dress. She cried when she threw it away. Hezekiah told me he couldn't bear to take it to the dump, so he thought someone might get some use out of it, still. And someone did." She closed her eyes. "You can feel their happiness when you touch it." She seemed to drift off.

"Tell him the rest, May," Rud prompted, his eyes piercing Andrews. "Tell Dr. Andrews what it reminds you of."

"In Chartres," she went on, as if she hadn't been encouraged, "they keep the Veil of the Virgin, the head wrap Mary wore when Jesus was born. They show it every once in a while, but they keep it hidden in a cave under the cathedral most days of the year. I saw it once. It was yellow, like this."

I realized then it must have been May who had given Hek a piece of that cloth a few days earlier, to ask for his help with Truevine. But he was frightened, didn't know what to do. All he could think of was dropping strange hints to me in his kitchen. I would have to confront him about it. Did June know about his stay in the community? Had he really stayed at all, or was it a part of the legend of the place? The stuff of future research.

"All right," Andrews said. It was the only apology he would make, but Rud seemed to accept it. Andrews didn't seem to know why he was apologizing.

"I'm more interested in finding out about my great-grandmother," I said to Rud, "but I wonder if there's any way to do that."

"There is," he said curtly, "but don't you think the more immediate question at hand—"

"Of course," I interrupted. "Absolutely right." I turned to the scarecrow. "Shall we?"

"Wait," Andrews protested. "That's it? We're just charging out into the night with a maniac and a mad dog?"

"Who you calling a maniac?" the man bristled.

"I only mean there's a lot to be answered here," Andrews insisted, more to me than to anyone else.

"Agreed," I said, "but Rud is correct. First things first. We have to find Truevine, help her if we can."

"Unless she's right about herself," May slipped in calmly, settling back, eyes mesmerized by the orange glow of the coals at her feet. "If that girl's really dead, there's not much you can do for her."

Ten

The scarecrow, black dog at his side, took us out of the surreal comfort of *Adele* and into the darkness of the night. He pulled his heavy brown coat about him, black scarf flying behind him in the cold wind like a broken wing. Autumn sunset was fast and final; evening had fallen hard, still moonless.

All around, bare tree limbs clattered, high wind slithered through the trees. Leaves dead on the ground were reanimated, danced upward yearning for the air. Bats clicked; dark wings beat the sky.

Past a row of lurking granite boulders, in the opposite direction from the Angel of Death, our guide took us into a low hollow where the wind stilled and the air was damp. Spiders had spun moonbeams of their own, silver shadows of midnight light stretching from tombstone to statue, ruined wall to gate.

"This is far enough," the scarecrow said.

The three of us stood in the center of a group of headstones, in a circle of old oaks, more protected from the night air. The branches overhead, ink patterns, made a dark vault. I scanned the stone, the fallen limbs, the broken wall twenty feet to our right—no one was there.

"Where is she?" Andrews whispered.

"She'll come," our guide answered.

Long minutes passed, shivering. In the silence, every noise was a warning, every sudden movement a threat. An owl, a rat, a leaping toad.

At last: a low whistle, and the black dog lunged forward.

Andrews's breathing increased; my shoulders tensed. I realized I had been grinding my teeth. My jaw hurt.

A second later she was at the wall, barely twenty feet away. The dog planted himself in front of her, his hair bristling. She was wrapped in a shawl or a blanket that covered her head and shoulders, drooped around her. Underneath she wore a man's flannel shirt that nearly covered her dress, the third layer. One hand clasped the shawl at her throat; the other held a heavy, gnarled walking stick, Contorted Hickory, a witch's wand.

She wouldn't look at us. Even though my eyes had adjusted to the night, it was hard to make out her features. If I hadn't been expecting Truevine, I wouldn't have known who was standing there.

"These are the ones been looking for you," the scarecrow said.

She nodded.

"All right, then." He turned and was gone back up the path.

Andrews and I looked at each other, then back at the girl. She stood motionless, almost floating in the cold air.

"Truevine?" I ventured.

"Hello, Dr. Devilin," she said softly, as if she were addressing a memory, not a visitor.

"Can we talk awhile?" It's what I always asked her when I came to her house to record stories or conversations. I was afraid she might bolt if I was too abrupt. There would be no running after her with the dog in our path.

"I'd like that," she answered, her voice still drifting.

"I understand it's the gestalt," Andrews whispered in my ear, "but if I didn't know better, I would believe that was a ghost."

The ether of her voice, the thick shawl, her walking stick: she was the image of a *wraith,* a wandering soul. Anyone would have thought so.

"Can we come closer?" I offered.

She stood mute.

Stars began to blink between high clouds; the moon was making its first tentative appearance. Only two days past full, it would illuminate the whole mountain within a half hour's time. We were in the valley between day and night, blacker than midnight, and the stars did little to lift the gathered gloom.

Without warning Truevine bent, whispered something into the dog's ear. It shot away like a cannonball. She took a step toward us, paused, sat demurely on the stone wall, still clutching her walking stick.

"Stay where you are, if you don't mind." Her voice was a vapor. "But make yourselves comfortable. I have a tale to tell."

Andrews let out his breath, an irritated sound born mostly of hunger and the release of a bit of his tension, trudged over to a fallen branch, sat heavily. The branch complained but held.

I moved a little to my left: a granite rock, cold, mossy, solid.

"We've been looking for you," I began, not looking at her, "for nearly a week now."

"I know."

The air around us sighed sympathetically, trembled the spider-webs.

"We'd like to take you home," I went on, still matter-of-fact. "You know your brothers are worried about you, and the house is a mess."

"I'd like nothing better," she said, her voice flooded with sorrow.

"Well then," Andrews said abruptly, slapped his knees with the palm of his hand, and shot up. "Let's go."

The girl, startled, got to her feet and was behind the wall in a blur almost impossible to believe.

"Damn it," I said under my breath to Andrews. "Sh!"

He froze, realizing he was about to chase her away.

She was poised, ready to fly, glancing backward into the darkness where the dog had vanished.

"You said you had a story to tell us," I soothed. "I always enjoy when you tell me your thoughts. I'd like to hear what you have to say."

"You need to hear it," she agreed hollowly. "But I don't like to say."

"Say what?" I said, glancing to Andrews, willing him to sit.

He sank slowly back to the tree branch, Truevine seemed to relax, though she held her ground behind the wall.

"I have to tell you what I did," she went on softly.

"I wish I had my tape recorder." The Wollenzak was in my truck. She loved to hear the sound of her voice on it. I was thinking she might be tempted.

"I always sound so funny on that thing," she said, and for an instant she was the girl I knew: a smile touched her lips; her tone warmed. There may have even been a blush peeking around the edge of her hood.

"I have it just over that way." I pointed in the direction of the truck.

"No," she said, her voice dark again. "I don't think it would hear me now. And what I got to say, it's not for everyone."

"I'll keep your secret, if you like," I promised. It was not an idle vow. Keeping secrets was a family pride and a town fetish.

"I'll tell you," she announced.

She sat again, a midautumn night's queen.

"Thursday night." She said the words as if they opened a book.

Andrews relaxed, and the branch sagged, creaking. I shifted on the mossy rock, trying to get comfortable.

"Able and me," she sighed, brokenhearted, "we had an argument. Our last words were harsh. He says, 'What'd I care if Harding is your cousin; what he's done is wrong!' I told him church was not the place for such, I called him pigheaded. Then he made fun of my brothers and called them a thief, which they don't do, they don't steal, they catch wild swine, and it's hard work."

She looked to me for agreement. I nodded, encouraging her to continue.

"He was accusing Harding of something awful." She looked around. "But I can't see how it mattered. The dead are dead. What do they care where they leave the remains? What does corn care for a husk?"

"You knew what Harding had done," I guessed.

"You can't walk around them woods much without you come across it," she admitted. "Me and the dog, we seen many a earthy vessel."

"You weren't frightened?"

"I always felt someone watching over me," she said, looking around at the trees, "in these woods."

"But you still told Able about it. You disagreed with him."

"I say, 'Let the dead bury the dead.'"

"You wanted him to let it go. Stop his investigation."

"I did," she said firmly. "But he got so angry about it. He cussed me; then he took my arms and grabbed this big old flannel shirt I was wearing, like to tore it." She seemed about to burst. "It's his, you know, this shirt. Anyway, he grabs it and I says to him, 'Take your hands off me.' He did right away and I lit out like lightning."

"You ran into the woods."

"Up the mountain," she said. "I didn't know where I was going."

"He followed you."

"He did." Her voice cracked. She sipped a breath. "Wish to God he had not."

"What happened?"

"He followed me. I heard him coming." She tilted her head to one side, as if watching the events unfold in her mind. "I couldn't see how he caught up to me so quick. I run fast, and he didn't take out after me right away. I know that. But there he was, close behind me."

"You saw him."

"I didn't look around," she said very softly, "but I could hear him running, trying to catch up. He was breathing like a bellows. He never walked around the woods as much as I did, so I reckon I was in better shape. I believe it was his job which kept him indoors a lot, you know, and did not allow for exercise."

"But he caught up with you," I said, trying to get her to return to the story.

"Grabbed me from behind," she said, "couldn't get his breath to speak, and I punched my elbow into his guts as hard as I could." She focused on me a moment. "If you grow up the only girl in a band of brothers like I got, you figure how to wrestle rough."

"You hit him in the stomach," I said. "You didn't turn around."

"Uh-huh." She swallowed, her eyes glassing over once more. "He took a tumble, hard. Thud on his head. Made me sick to hear it. By the time I turned around, he was at the bottom of the ravine. I got my bearings." She tried to focus her eyes on me. "I was close to your house."

Andrews and I exchanged a quick glance.

"I took a tumble in my mind when I seen him lying down there. It was still dark; I could barely make him out. But he weren't breathing that I could tell." Her voice nearly gave way. "I couldn't move. My gut got sucked up through my head, and I swear to this world I wasn't there anymore."

"You weren't there?" Andrews interrupted.

"I flushed right out of my body." Her breathing was thick and broken. Her hands trembled.

"There was more." I waited.

"Uh-huh." She gulped. "That's how I knew I killed him."

"How?"

"I seen him again, at the top of the ridge, coming my way. His ghost was playing the death scene over again, the way some revenants do." She looked up. "They do."

"You saw Able running toward you?"

"Full in the face, arms out, red as a beet, wild." Her pitch had raised, and her head was palsied. "I was so scared. I got me a tree branch to fend it off. Swung out so hard I took a tumble backward myself. I stopped his ghost, though, and I didn't look back. I got up and ran and ran and ran until I couldn't move no more and I fell to the earth all done in."

That was all. She was incapable of any more speech, sipping little breaths, nearly doubled over.

I stood and took a step her way.

The dog appeared out of nowhere, bounded in front of her, a guttural menace in his throat.

"I only want to help," I said to the dog calmly.

It stopped growling.

"I only want to help," I repeated in slow, reassuring tones.

It sat, its eyes still locked on mine.

"For God's sake stay where you are," Andrews muttered between clenched teeth.

His panic was a little contagious, and for a second all I could think about was the dog's teeth.

In that moment, Truevine stood.

"I've only come back to tell you these things so I can rest," she said, her voice more air than sound.

"Come back?" Andrews said.

"From the grave," she answered.

She was gone, the dog behind her, before I could catch my breath.

Andrews and I found ourselves after a moment.

"Come on," I said, and lit out after her.

"Wait!" he called, planted to his spot. "Damn it."

I didn't stop; she was already gone into the shadows.

I raced up the incline, bounded the short wall. There were more trees past the pile of stone and everything was black. Ahead I heard the tarnish of leaves, the sick snap of wet wood. I followed by sound more than sight.

I knew the dog was waiting for me, teeth gleaming. I knew Truevine lived in this yard and I was a stranger. I still thought I could overtake her.

Behind me I heard Andrews running, lungs stoking his heart.

The path through grave markers and dead grass turned abruptly at a small sarcophagus, unusual because it was made of marble, not granite stones. The noise of her escape had evaporated ahead of me.

The name chiseled over the entrance to the crypt was Carter. I stopped.

Andrews caught up with me, stood panting.

Wordlessly I jutted my chin in the direction of that name.

He nodded. I motioned for him to go around to the back of the structure. I'd learned my lesson from Able.

Andrews agreed and moved as quietly as he could around to the right.

I steeled myself.

"Truevine?" I called out.

Whistle of the wind through the tombstones answered.

"I don't think she's in there!" Andrews called in a stage whisper anyone within a hundred yards could have heard.

I shook my head, called again. "Tru?"

A small scraping sound came from within the crypt.

"Everything's all right," I offered, my most soothing tone.

A catch of breath assured me she was inside.

Her voice confirmed it a second later. "Nothing's all right."

"I don't know what's in your head, Tru," I said, inching my way toward the entrance, "but Able's fine." I glanced up at the name carved in marble. "He's not buried in there, in his family crypt. He's with Skidmore Needle in town, very much alive. He's more worried about you than your brothers are."

"That's a lie."

"Please come out," I encouraged her gently.

"Because we're not coming in," Andrews stated flatly, his voice muffled by distance and stone.

"Is the dog with you?" I asked as casually as I could.

"He does what he likes," she answered softly.

"Can I come in?" I took another step toward the doorway.

The crypt seemed made of a single creamy block of marble, no seam anywhere to be found. Moss had not taken its wall as had happened with many of the other structures. The roof was marble too, as far as I could tell, and aside from a few fallen branches, it was clean. The doorway was not guarded by a gate or a door, it was an open rounded arch, and several six-inch angels, wings wide, danced around the Carter name. Smaller by a fourth than the *Adele* building, it seemed patrician, understated, wise in the gathering moonlight.

The moon had come up over the mountains, past full but bright in the polished sky. Night seemed to mirror its glow, and a wide halo circled it. I only had a moment to consider that it was exactly the color of the Carter crypt when another noise popped loud from inside.

"Truevine?" I called out, forgetting caution and lumbering through the door.

The interior was small; the walls were thick; the last remains of generations of Carters lay hidden behind marble squares. It was little more than a long hallway with a small urn at the back wall—no windows, no back door. The ceiling was high, no opening there, no way out but the way I'd come in.

Which made it impossible for me to understand why I was alone.

"Dev?" Andrews called after a moment.

"Come on in," I sighed.

His face appeared in the doorway, backlit by moonlight.

"Where is she?" he whispered. "Where's the dog?"

"Not here," my voice cracked.

"What do you mean, 'not here'?" He took a step in. "Did they get past you?"

"No."

"Then . . ." his voice trailed off.

A few moments' examination of the place yielded no explanation of the girl's disappearance, no hole in the wall, no skylight. The only way in or out was the arched entrance.

"All right then," Andrews said, brushing off his hands, "I think *now* would be time for dinner. Etta's lunch is a dim memory. Was that today? Seems like a week ago."

He turned and exited the tomb.

"We have to . . . at least we should go back and tell Rud what's happened," I said, following him. "What she said."

"I'm not sure what she said."

"I can't quite get it right in my mind either," I had to admit. "We're tired and hungry and it's been a really long day."

He trudged ahead of me silently.

The trail back was quiet enough to make us both uncomfortable. We'd grown used to the wind and the night noise. Everything was still, waiting. I was glad to see the *Adele* building appear in the slant of moonbeams.

"It's just occurred to me," I said to Andrews as we neared the door, "that we don't know what families are buried in this building."

"What families?" Andrews repeated. "I assumed since it was so close to your grandfather's grave—"

The door creaked open, silencing him.

"Sh." Rud held his index finger to his lips.

He stepped outside with us, pulled the door closed behind him. His face seemed made of smoked glass in the silver light. It was deeply creased around the eyes, the jaw unshaven, the lips dry and cracked.

His camel hair coat had once been fit for opera, fine dining, the Ritz. He wore it now as a wound, wincing as he walked. His hair was cut short by a pair of scissors, an obviously homemade bit of grooming. He did not sport new sneakers; his feet were sheathed in duck hunting boots, expensive, relatively new—watertight and warm even in subzero temperatures. He had not cut himself off from the world entirely; the boots seemed the sort that might have been purchased through a catalog.

He stood silent, waiting for us to speak.

"We saw her," I began.

"But she didn't come back with you."

"She talked. She does seem to think she's dead."

"Her mind," Rud said, struggling for a way to say what he was thinking, "has always been a delicate place."

"Yes," I said, "but not one given to complete delusions, nothing of this variety."

"Something happened to her," he snapped. "She needs help."

"And you can't get close enough to do anything yourself," Andrews interjected.

Rud's head spun around so fast his neck popped. "You can go home now."

Home clearly meant Atlanta, not my house.

"Gladly," Andrews told him pleasantly. "Although I'd have to say that your permission wasn't the thing holding me back."

Rud took a step.

"We were just going to go for dinner," I intervened. "Check in with Skidmore. We've been out all day, a long cold day. We'll be in better shape tomorrow." *And I've really already done what I set out to do*, I thought. *I've found Able; that's all Girlinda wanted.*

I tried to tell myself that the rest was inconsequential, but I knew I wouldn't ignore an overwhelming desire to see these events to their conclusion. Even Andrews, I was betting, would not be willing to let things go.

Rud seemed to sense something of my thoughts.

"Rest is good," he sighed, clearly a man who could not find repose of his own.

"We'll come to the caretaker's cabin tomorrow," I said reassuringly.

"Early," he grunted.

"As soon as I'm up," Andrews told us both pointedly.

Andrews was a late riser, left to his own devices, and it was clearly his intention to stay in bed through the next morning. I let the issue be for the moment.

"Everyone's asleep in there?" I asked Rud.

"Some are," he said, his voice sinking back into his throat. "Sleep comes hard to May, for one. She knows she's safe, but she won't close her eyes until she's certain everyone else is out."

"Do you know about the murder?" I thought to catch him off guard with the sudden change of subject.

"I do." His voice didn't change one iota; his eyes were still; his breathing never altered. Years of practice masking anything internal had allowed him to shift gears without skipping a beat.

"I'd like to know how," Andrews said. "And *what* you know, exactly."

"It was in all the papers," Rud sneered slowly, not even looking back at Andrews.

Our town didn't have a paper. Most news was disseminated through church bulletins and gossip, the latter being the faster, more reliable method. I was certain the press in surrounding towns had gotten wind of what was happening over at the mortuary. It might have even made Atlanta television. But that had nothing to do with Rud.

"We need to let Skidmore know everything," I insisted.

"I don't have any information that would help in that regard," Rud said like a man being interrogated.

Impossible to read, his eyes were absolutely vacant.

"All right, then," I said, "we'll be off. We have a little hike back to my truck." I looked around. "Glad there's a moon out. See you in the morning."

"Or sometime tomorrow." Andrews, true to his evening's pattern, was slow to follow. I could almost hear his brain trying to figure out why I wasn't asking more questions. But he was either willing to trust me or too tired to care.

He waited until the truck was in sight, close to the Angel of Death, before he spoke up.

"You keep doing that," Andrews said. "First you let the Deveroe boys get away with hanging your friend, you don't tell Skidmore, then . . . I don't know, you leave off questioning everyone just when the answers would be juicy. What the *hell?*"

He was exhausted, famished, disturbed by the sight of so many bodies, baffled by the encounter with living ghosts. Everything about the day, the *Adele* community more than most, had long since lost all reality.

"Things don't boil here," I said slowly. "They simmer."

"Like the food at Etta's." Hard to tell if his smile was motivated more by hunger or derision.

"The fact is," I went on, unlocking the truck, "you can't just jump at anything in this town. It'll run away. You have to approach things on the diagonal, saunter up to them, talk about the weather before you ask about the murder. Things here take time."

"Things are buried deep," he countered. "That's what you always say."

"People keep themselves locked," I agreed.

"So it takes a while to dig them up," he went on, his voice stammering. "Except of course for Truevine Deveroe, who doesn't seem to have been buried deeply enough."

His laughter exploded and was contagious. The day had taken its toll, and we were hysterical for a span of five minutes before I started the truck and pulled away from the cemetery.

Etta's place was closed by the time we got into town, much to the vocal dismay of Dr. Andrews. Most of the town was dark. We went to Skidmore's office, one of the few bright windows on Main Street. He was waiting for us.

Able was in lockup, dead asleep. He'd told Skid he wanted to stay in a cell. He was exhausted, and jail was the only place he felt safe enough to close his eyes.

We filled the deputy in on most of what had happened—omitting certain wayward members of our cast, commenting on the cemetery's caretaker.

"Maybe I should have mentioned you might run into Rudyard Pinhurst," Skid said when we stopped talking. "How's he holding up?"

"He knows about the murder," I said, "Maybe I'll speak with him again, but he seems much more concerned about Truevine than anything else. I don't think he'll talk about what more he might know until we settle that."

"So you don't believe that she's dead?" Skid's voice was flat, but his eyes sparkled.

"I'm keeping an open mind." I returned his gaze.

"You saw her up there earlier today?" Andrews asked Skidmore. "That's what Dev thought you were saying when we left."

"I saw her."

"Well, why didn't you get her?" Andrews appeared to be growing increasingly amazed at everyone's lack of sense.

"I saw her," Skid said calmly. "Then she disappeared. I was looking where she'd gone when Dev called with Able cornered in the crypt. She was gone. Like a ghost."

"Christ!" Andrews exploded.

"Let's go home," Skid said. "Linda's got supper in the oven."

Andrews leapt to his feet.

The Needle living room offered us its usual clutter: tumbling children's toys, floors so clean they mirrored. The fireplace popped, flanked by indoor ferns and potted red mums. The house was warm as summer. I shed my jacket instantly, hung it by the door.

The kitchen sang a familiar clatter of dishes and silverware. Girlinda was humming; the children were helping. The thick sweetness of cherry pie filled the air.

"Remind me," Andrews said, taking off his coat. "How many kids have you got?"

"Becky's eight now; the boys are ten, eleven, and twelve."

"Uh-huh." Andrews managed to make his syllables insinuate.

"You'uns come on in the kitchen." Girlinda's voice always lilted, but she sounded happier than usual—certainly lighter than she had a few nights ago when she'd asked us to look for her brother.

She appeared in the doorway in a man's dress shirt, untucked from pale jeans, red house shoes. Her figure filled the frame, and every centimeter of body shone. A genuine Christian compassion, a capacity for love that a thousand churchgoers claim to every one who actually owns it, was at the foundation of Girlinda's DNA. That much was clear from looking at her, and it made her one of the most beautiful human beings on the planet. No one who knew her, no one who met her, thought of her as a large person. The departed Sheriff Maddox had occasionally attempted to bait Skidmore by referring to her as *fat*—it only made Skid laugh. "God gave her a little extra room," he said once. "What she's got inside wouldn't fit to anything smaller."

Amen.

She hugged my neck, did the same to Andrews before he knew what was happening.

"You found him," she said. Her hand flew to her mouth; her eyes glistened. "Thank you, boys."

Andrews blushed.

"There's a lot more to this, you know," I told her softly.

"Able didn't kill a soul," she said. "I love him, but he's a mousy boy, scared of his shadow." She sighed, "I reckon him and Truevine's a match made in heaven."

"Heaven doesn't mind setting up dates for witches?" Andrews grinned.

"That girl," Girlinda said, shaking her head. "Bless her." That was all.

"What?" I asked her. "You don't think she's got a gift?"

"You have to be really smart to know all about that," Girlinda said, slipping back into the kitchen.

Andrews exchanged an amused glance with me before we followed.

"You don't think Miss Deveroe has the brains to be a sorceress?" Andrews teased.

The kitchen was even warmer than the rest of the place. The white worn table was groaning under a weight of culinary treasure. Light seemed to come from everywhere, the white oven, the whiter sink.

We took our seats instantly.

"I don't think I realized how starving I was," I sang out, "until I smelled all this!"

"What's for supper, hon?" Skidmore said, scrubbing his hands at the kitchen faucet.

"Fried chicken, chicken livers, chicken and dumplings . . ." she trailed off, examining the stovetop.

"That's just the meats," Skid assured us. "We've also got seventeen vegetables, most of which had been cooked for all day in a half a gallon of fat."

"Greens," Girlinda said, as if it were a given.

"Collard," Skid whispered to Andrews.

"Black-eyed peas," she went on, "carrots, potatoes, field peas, cut-off corn panfried in an equal amount of sugar; coleslaw, fried okra, and celery dressing." Her head bobbed up, she smiled our way. "That's all."

"Good," Andrews said, barely controlling his glee. "And what are the rest of you having?"

The children clambered into the room, hugging us, shouting at one another, arguing among themselves. The meal began.

Half an hour later, the younger members were gone again. Television murmured from the den. Andrews and I were still working on our plates; Skid was sipping coffee; Linda was pulling cherry pie out of the oven.

"When your husband is elected sheriff," Andrews addressed her very seriously, his mouth full, "he'll have less time for you. He'll stay late at the office. Your relationship will falter. Eventually the marriage will end. When that day comes, I stand ready. Consider yourself automatically proposed to." He looked at Skid and me. "I say this in front of these witnesses, it's a pledge I will honor with my life."

"Nice try, city boy." Skid grinned. "You couldn't keep up with this woman. She'd wear you out in a month."

She blushed, swatted her husband's shoulder.

"I'm just saying," he assured her.

"It's just coming clear to me," Andrews mumbled past the napkin wiping his mouth, "that your brother-in-law is the county coroner, Skid. That's got to be some kind of crime-busting cartel here in Blue Mountain."

"He didn't take his job that seriously," Skid said lazily, "until here recently."

"Courting Truevine takes up a lot of time, I assume," Andrews said, eyebrow lifted.

"Have you ever seen that girl's front garden?" Girlinda asked me. "It's a wonder."

"I was just thinking that the last time I was up there."

"No, I mean it; she's something unusual." Girlinda pursed her lips. "Garden's just an example. I love my brother, but he's a sort of boring boy. Truvy's a very interesting person. It ain't she's a witch or that nonsense. It's more how much there is to her spirit that makes me worry about their courtship—I'm not sure Able can keep up with her."

"You admire her," Andrews said plainly.

"That I do." Linda smiled to herself.

Skid's eyes were on me. "You're quiet."

"Harding Pinhurst was a worm." I leaned back in my chair.

"The important thing," Andrews said, "is that you don't hold a grudge."

"He worked overtime when I was in high school," I sighed, "talking to everyone about my mother's adventures. I was his special project, always. If I didn't have a fair alibi, I think Deputy Needle ought to be considering me for his murderer."

"In the first place," Andrews said, "I was asleep. You could easily have slipped out, done the job, and then gotten me involved. Except for the fact that you feel guilty about nearly everything in life and you'd never have gotten past Saturday morning without confessing. Which is why you're bringing it up now, by the way: guilt. You're glad he's dead."

"I could host a party."

"Is there something you're not telling us?" Andrews grinned. "Seems a petty bit of the past to hold on to."

"When my father died I was sixteen," I began slowly. "My mother didn't come to the funeral, but Harding and some of the other boys did, outside. They set off firecrackers and scared us all, accidentally caught part of the mortuary on fire. Volunteer fire department had to be called; the funeral was a fiasco. When Harding took over that same funeral parlor a few years back, I was still at the university. He sent me a card telling me that he was changing the place over to a crematorium; he'd gotten the idea from my father's ceremony. He's the one who was holding on to something."

Andrews took a quick gulp of coffee. Skid and Girlinda avoided eye contact.

"All right, enough of that." I pushed my plate away, sat back in the chair. "I've been thinking."

Skid looked up.

"Finally," he said.

Andrews looked between Skid and me, momentarily lost.

"He's about to declare," Skid confided in him, happy to change the subject. "Haven't you wondered, just a little, why he's not been telling you and me what to do, how to handle this mess, considering all that's happened?"

"Now you mention it," Andrews said, setting down his cup, "that does seem odd."

"Get ready." Skid folded his arms, slumped a little in his seat.

"I want to take Able with me," I began, ignoring their attempt to belittle my plans, "and go to the cemetery tomorrow. I want to arrange a meeting between him and Truevine. I think it's the only way to proceed."

Girlinda burst out laughing.

We all turned her way.

"I mean, you see why that's funny," she explained, sliding a wedge of cherry pie my way. "You know what day it is."

Of all people, Andrews realized first: "You want to get a witch and a murderer together in a graveyard *tomorrow*." He took my pie.

"Tomorrow." I still had no idea.

Andrews sank his fork into the golden crust. "It's Halloween."

Eleven

When I was young I began studying folklore as a way to escape the sordid peculiarities of my family but came to realize that my studies only resulted in assuring me that there was no escape from the past. The discipline of folk study, an intellectual archaeology, yielded treasure after treasure, and all of it was mined from the bizarre affinities of the larger human family.

In 800 B.C.E., for example, the Celts moved into England, bringing with them a notion that the evening before November 1 marked the end of an old year, the beginning of winter, when the festival of Samhain (pronounced *"sow-en"*), Lord of the Dead, was celebrated. All departed souls were permitted to return, visit the living. Anyone who wished not to be bothered wore a mask so that the ghosts could not recognize family members. The other world was notoriously cold. Huge bonfires were lit to keep the worst spirits at bay, invite the rest to a feast.

When the Romans took Britain in 54 B.C.E., they did what Rome had always done: they assimilated local beliefs and called them Roman. They added touches of their own to Samhain festivals: creating centerpieces out of apples for Pomona, Roman goddess of the orchards. Bobbing for apples was a popular custom of the ancient empire.

When Emperor Constantine the Great was baptized on his deathbed in 377 he began Rome's association with the new Christian church. By the year 835, Pope Gregory IV did what that church had always done best: he assimilated local beliefs and called them

Catholic. He moved the celebration for martyrs, called All Saints' Day or All Hallows' Day, from May 13 to November 1, aligning Celtic and Catholic celebrations. The days of reverence for departed family members became the church's time to honor murdered saints. The evening before this feast day was called All Hallows' Even, shortened by slack-tongued revelers to Halloween.

The tradition of begging door-to-door is an Irish addition, only several hundred years old. Farmers collected food and drink for town feasting and bonfires. Anyone who helped was blessed, and the stingy were threatened with bad luck. When Irish Catholics came to America in the massive immigration of the 1800s, the custom of trick-or-treating came with them. We may similarly credit the Irish with a custom of carving a pumpkin, though the original idea was to hollow out a turnip, put a burning candle inside to light the way as the evening grew dark.

The old celebration lasted three days and nights when time ceased and anything was possible. Gates and locks were left open; cattle and horses were scattered; lunacy reigned. We may mention it was no mere coincidence the fact that Samhain was the time of year when herds were culled. Old, sick, weak animals were slaughtered; leaves spilled from the trees; corn husk towers stood silhouetted in the moonlight—death was everywhere in nature. Witness the old County Waterford Halloween trick-or-treater's chant:

> Straw in the windows and close the doors. Rise up housewife, go inside womanly, return hospitably, bring with you a slice of bread and butter the colour of your own cheek, as high as a hare's jump with a cock's step of butter on it, coming in hills and going in mountains; you may think it would choke me, but, alas! I am in no danger.

All cultures, all customs, twine together at the origin of our species. The pull of those very first beliefs still tugs at us, still spins us around, shows us what we are.

"Listen to this!" I called to Andrews, book in one hand, espresso cup in the other. " 'Halloween seems to have been of old the time of year when the souls of the departed were supposed to revisit their old homes in order to warm themselves by the fire and to comfort themselves with the good cheer provided for them in the kitchen or the parlor by their affectionate kinsfolk. It was, perhaps, a natural thought that the approach of winter should drive the poor shivering hungry ghosts from the bare fields and the leafless woodlands to the shelter of the cottage with its familiar fireside.' "

Light rolled in, a golden message from the sun. Darkness would never triumph over such brilliance. It was, however, a message that could be easily forgotten after midnight, in the blackest hours—I knew from experience and my own frequent battles with memory.

"Very nice," he mumbled, still not awake. "What is that?"

"Sir James Frazer's *The Golden Bough*," I answered. "Nineteen twenty-two. You see how this idea applies to the lost souls in the place they're calling *Adele*."

The image of the group huddled around the orange fire among the dead bodies and cold stones was a coal in me.

"I suppose."

"Although maybe we're all wandering spirits," I said softly.

Andrews looked up, coffee poised exactly halfway between table and lip. He was in a sweatshirt, baggy jeans, and thick socks, a costume made more comical by the erupted disarray of his hair.

"How very winsome," he muttered, accent exaggerated as his diction.

The morning had come on slowly. We'd both slept in; I couldn't remember falling asleep and I didn't move for nearly ten hours, a record for me. I'd wandered downstairs in my robe and slippers to find Andrews, heavy-lidded and incoherent, trying to start the espresso machine. A few minor adjustments and the addition of water coaxed it into working. One cup apiece and a few minutes later we were slumped at the kitchen table, reading, musing. It was nearly eleven.

"I mean what's the difference between you and May?" I asked him.

His cup drifted back to the table.

"Manchester, male, doctor, blond, good-looking, and—by the way—*not* homeless," he numbered off six fingers, "just for starters."

"Given." I rubbed my eyes, yawned. "But I meant, of course, the larger sense. And what's her story, do you think? How is it that she speaks French?"

"A few words does not a language make," he pronounced carefully.

"You know what I'm talking about," I shot back, irritated.

" 'There but for fortune,' I'm assuming."

"Exactly. Was that so hard?"

"I'm not going back up there, you know." He picked up his cup again, sipped loudly. "I'm not about to be a part of your little play among the bones."

"Are you serious?" I glared. "You'd miss the opportunity of a perfect Halloween? Not to mention seeing the conclusion of our little adventure."

"How will it be any conclusion? We don't know who killed Harding Pinhurst, which is the crux of the biscuit."

"You really are a complete loss, you know?" I heaved a leaden sigh. "Truevine killed Harding. Accidentally."

He stopped in midgulp, eyes far off.

"That's your conclusion?" he asked, the realization of what the girl had told us the day before dawning slowly.

"Harding had come to the church to confront Able," I began. "Do you remember my saying I thought I saw something outside after the meeting on Thursday night?"

"I told you it was shadows, the way the moon moved or something," he said.

"It was Harding; he heard the couple argue. He stayed out of sight, ran after Truevine to convince her to plead his case with Able. She thought he was Able, wrestled him. He fell, hit his head. Just as she would have gone down to see after him, and incidentally discovered he was *not* her fiancé, along comes the real Able. She panics."

"Because she's a strange girl," he interjected.

"Thinking he's a ghost," I agreed, "she fends him off, stumbles. When Able recovers, she's run off. He thinks the body in the ravine is hers. Before he can go and check on her, he's scared off by her brothers."

"Only it turns out not to be her brothers but the three drunks we saw Saturday morning."

"Well, no." I bit my lower lip. "You see the problem with that."

Andrews was beginning to wake up. "There's a lot of coincidence keeping everyone from checking on the body in the culvert."

"Concentrate." I had to stand. "The chief concern is timing: Able and Truevine were there at the edge of the culvert late Thursday night."

"Yes?" He still didn't understand.

"And the drunken teenagers found the body early Saturday morning."

"Oh my God, you're right. They couldn't have frightened Able away." He set down his coffee cup. "Is he lying?"

"I don't know." I walked to the kitchen window. "Clearly that's why they didn't mention seeing Able or Truevine. I'd wondered about that."

"Well, that puts a different light on everything." He pulled on his earlobe. "The body lay in the ravine a whole day. A missing day."

"I think I might have taken a walk there Friday morning before you were up. I usually do." I rubbed my eyes. "It's so hard to concentrate given the magnitude of what Harding's done. After the invasion of those images it's hard to remember other things, do you find?"

"Not to mention that Truevine's a lot more disturbed than I'd thought," he agreed, "thinking she was batting a ghost in the head with a tree branch. Able's equally off saying he killed her when he never even touched her. Take a step back from it, none of it holds up."

"Right." I turned to him. "And we haven't even mentioned the question of why Harding was naked."

"I never wanted to think about that, but there's a larger problem for me." He leaned. "Everyone in your town has a bizarre fascination with death. They talk about it at church; they laugh when they see it; they have covered dish dinners and raffle drawings at funerals. Those drunken boys, ones that found the body? They're prime citizens of your little Creepy Junction. What's the matter with you-all? Why can't you just put the dead in the ground and forget about them like decent people?"

"Are you finished?"

"Necrophilia is like the town *hobby*." He set his cup down, nodded once.

"Death is comforting." I stood.

"No. There's nothing remotely reassuring about it." He watched me move to the counter.

"Everything dies. When you do, your tribulations will be at an end. That's a comfort."

"Do we have to talk about this?" He held out his cup.

"A belief in the solace of death is essential to an agrarian culture," I told him, taking the cup out of his hand.

"This is hardly an agrarian culture," he stammered. "Shops and gas stations and the tourism industry hold this berg together. And businessmen would rather talk about anything than death."

"All right, don't come with me, then," I said flatly.

The espresso machine sent white vapor upward. It curled around the sun slanting into the kitchen, as if it were avoiding the light.

Skidmore was understandably concerned about letting a murder suspect out of jail to meet with a witch in a cemetery on Halloween. He trusted me, but if word got out that I was tromping around the graveyard with his prisoner, the election campaign would surely suffer. It was the sort of thing that would give his adviser, Tommy Tineeta, an aneurysm. The plan was to avoid mentioning anything about the tryst I had in mind. To anyone.

Which is why I wanted Andrews with us. Without meaning to, he was quite capable of leaking information, or *flooding* same if alcohol were involved. I didn't want him wandering down to Gil's, for example, sipping lightning, musing about our adventures to total strangers. Not only would it make things more difficult for Skidmore, but it could jeopardize the invisible community I had promised to protect.

I called down from my bedroom, pulling on a fresh pair of black jeans. My appeal was to his sense of literature.

"Think what a perfect Poe moment you could have."

"No," he countered from downstairs, "it would have to be after dark to be ideal, and you're getting dressed now. It's barely after noon."

"It'll take a while to get Able out of lockup and up to the grave-yard."

"Two in the afternoon is not midnight. It ought to be around midnight."

"How about a chance to challenge May?" I appeared to him at the top of the stairs. "Test her language skills."

"What possible thrill could I find in that?" He had planted him-self on the sofa, reclining, tousled head on pillow, eyes closed.

"Are you going to sleep?" I couldn't believe it. I bounded down the stairs, a deliberate clatter. "You've just slept twelve hours."

"Ten."

"What kind of host would I be," I said shifting approaches, "to leave you alone and palely loitering while I have all the fun?"

" 'Palely loitering'?"

"Isn't that Shakespeare?"

"Not by a long shot. It might be Keats or Shelley, some *belle dame sans merci* sounding crap, I think," he told me drolly, "but it's hardly Shakespeare."

"Are you sure?" I knew it wasn't. I sat on the arm of the sofa.

"Look," he said, sitting up. "You stick to your five-thousand-year-old boring stories, how would that be? Leave genius of the ages to me."

" 'There are more things in heaven and earth, Horatio, than are dreamt of in your philosophy.' ' 'Tis now the very witching time of night.' "

"Yeah," he shot back, standing, "*Hamlet*'s a big one for the supernatural, but you should have gone with the Scottish play for witches."

"Aha!" I leapt to my feet.

"What?"

"No other group on earth is as superstitious as theatre people." I grinned. "You couldn't bring yourself to utter the name of the play even in my house. The closest theatre you could curse by saying it out loud is seventy miles away at Young Harris College."

"Force of habit." He avoided my eyes.

"Uh-huh. Do you whistle in the dressing room? Do you ever say the words *good luck?*"

"I avoid what makes actors nervous. They're skittish enough as it is."

"Continuing the infantilization of an entire profession." I turned and headed for the door.

"You know, you could bite me right about now." He followed.

" 'The time when screech-owls cry and ban-dogs howl, and spirits walk, and ghosts break up their graves.' "

"All right, that's a fairly obscure one for the likes of you," he admitted, right behind me.

"It's *Henry IV,*" I said proudly.

"*Henry VI, part 2,* actually," he corrected, pleased.

"Better put on some shoes and get your coat."

"What?" He stopped.

We were on the porch steps. He seemed surprised; the conversation had carried him outside without his realizing it.

"It'll get cold later," I said, not looking back. "We may be out awhile."

"Oh, right," he said absently, ducking back into the house. "How on earth do you know that *Henry* quote?"

His shoes were by the door, coat on the hook above them.

" 'Graves have yawned,' " I went on, opening the truck, " 'and yielded up their dead, and ghosts did shriek and squeal about the streets.' "

"Stop it!" He appeared again in the doorway, pulling on my old overcoat.

"*Julius Caesar.* There's more."

"No," he ordered. "Should I lock the door?"

"Pull it to; it's all right."

I started the engine; he hurried to the passenger side.

" 'Vex not a ghost.' " I added Vincent Price to my voice. " 'He hates him that would upon the rack of this tough world stretch him out longer.' "

"*Lear,*" he said, but his voice was softer.

"What?" I heard something in his tone.

"How much does that last quote apply to Rudyard Pinhurst? There's a man stretched out on the rack of the world if ever there was one."

"He's not the ghost," I reminded Andrews.

"Really?" He settled in his seat, slammed the door. " 'Were I the ghost that walked, I'd bid you mark her eye, and the words that followed should be "Remember mine." ' *Winter's Tale.* He's the most haunted man I've ever met, obviously still in love with Truevine. Guilt's a ghost that torments everyone, but him more than most."

"Is that Shakespeare too, that last part?"

"No," he said, smiling. "that's me."

"It's good." I pulled the car onto the dirt road. "True."

We drove awhile in silence. All the leaves were gone from the trees; the sky above us was shredded by naked limbs, threatened rain.

"You think Rud is more haunted than I am?" I said when we were down from the mountain and turning onto the paved road.

"God, no," he said instantly. "I meant more haunted than any *normal* man. You're way off the scale. Category of your own."

"Good." I rolled my head a little to pop my neck. "Wanted to keep my title intact."

"You know you didn't trick me into coming with you," he said, watching long rows of stacked corn sheaves out his window.

"I know," I agreed. "You just wanted to appear reticent. Keep the Cool Crown."

"You have your reputation to maintain," he said, settling into his seat. "I have mine."

Getting Able out of jail was a breeze.

"I reckon I'll take the prisoner home with me for lunch," Skidmore told the other deputies, yawning, "so you'uns can get yourself a bite, not have to worry over him. Plus, let him see his sister."

His coworkers agreed it was generous of Deputy Needle. They all liked him, backed his election bid for sheriff. No one had cared for Sheriff Maddox, whose funeral had been a lonely affair. Skid was the man for the job.

The others checked out. Andrews and I sat mute. Skid watched his fellows leave, remained seated quietly for two or three minutes after they were gone.

"Strictly speaking," he said slowly, "what we're about to do is *not* legal."

"Couldn't you say the prisoner has vital information about the crime scene," Andrews began, "and you have to take him there to confront the . . . something?"

"Yeah." Skid nodded. "You see a lot of that on the television. But the caretaker's cabin at the cemetery is hardly the crime scene. The idea behind incarceration, as I understand it, is to keep the criminal from getting out. By and by if I keep letting criminals loose, I could get a slack reputation."

"Whereas telling your colleagues that you want to take the prisoner home for a visit with his sister and a home-cooked meal . . ." Andrews trailed off.

"Is something folks around here could understand," Skid returned pointedly. "*Whereas* if I tell anyone that I'm taking said prisoner to the boneyard for a visit with a girl who thinks she's dead, there ain't that many who would understand. You see the difference."

"I do," said Andrews contritely. "One's Mayberry; one's Addams Family."

Skid turned a jaundiced eye my way. "How does he know all this old American TV?"

"There's some cable station that shows the things over and over again," I sighed. "He's addicted."

"Okay." Skidmore stood. "Let's go."

He headed to the cells.

Skidmore's squad car lead the way, Able in back. Andrews and I followed in my truck. We'd explained the idea to Able three times, but he still wasn't sure what we were doing. In the end the notion that he could see Truevine for himself, confirm she wasn't dead, was the thing that most convinced him to go.

"Able certainly did have trouble following our conversation," Andrews mused, watching the squad car ahead of us.

"Maybe being locked up and accused of murder is distracting him." I tried not to ride Skid's bumper, but he was driving more slowly than I wanted to.

"Little thing like that," Andrews said. "I guess it would bother some. So your grand scheme here is to get the lovers to confront one another, thus jolting Truevine back to reality, easing Able's mind . . ."

". . . and getting to the bottom of the murder," I finished. "Wouldn't it be nice to solve that, make sure I'm right?"

"Oh, *that*. So things can return to normal here in Pleasantdale." Andrews cracked his window a little. "This smell—old leaves, cut hay, whatever else it is—it's incredibly . . . evocative." His voice softened. "I don't often think of home, you know. But when I was a kid, nearly every autumn Dad would take us all to a fall carnival in the town where he was raised."

"What was it like?"

"Don't reach for your tape recorder; it wasn't anything special. Cheap rides, crass booths, candy apples—but there was a haunted house that was something. Old school. Witches and ghosts; someone would tell you grapes in a bowl were eyeballs, make you stick your fingers in it, that sort of thing. Terrific." He rolled down the window a little bit more. "Smelled just like this."

"How is your father?"

"Same." He sniffed the air. "I don't think he'll leave the hospital."

"When are you going home?"

He pulled on his earlobe, a perennial unconscious gesture when he was distracted. "Probably not until his funeral."

I wanted to ask him why he wouldn't go home sooner, speak with his father before it was too late. The thought set me thinking about my own father, our tangled relationship. Clouds were rolling in. The day grew darker quickly as we turned off the highway and up the mountain.

My parents were itinerant entertainers, carnival performers. Father was a prestidigitator of some merit. My mother was his lovely assistant, whose moral fiber wove a unique cloth, a cloak she wore to disguise her true self. Theirs was a match made in another reality, one where fidelity, concern, parental responsibility all were unknown, unused qualities. My father's death was a curiosity to most. My mother's funeral was lonelier than Sheriff Maddox's bleak ceremony.

Since my parents' touring enterprise, *The Ten Show,* had been the concoction of Tristan, the self-named Newcomb Dwarf, I'd met him several times when I was young. He had died and left the show to my parents by the time I was in grade school.

Tristan Newcomb had once tried out for the St. Louis Browns. His father, Tubby, had refused to allow him onto a church little league team in Chattanooga when he was ten, embarrassed by his size. Tristan practiced every day in private and became the best ballplayer in Tennessee by the time he was in high school. When he graduated he took a bus to St. Louis, hoping to replace Eddie Gaedel, the renowned three-foot, seven-inch specialty hitter. Gaedel had made all the papers when he was walked in a game against the Detroit Tigers in 1951. Gaedel died in 1961. Tristan, who claimed to have Eddie "beat by an inch," thought to replace him. But management explained that Eddie's contract had been a joke, a freakish entertainment. They weren't really looking for short players.

Tristan left St. Louis that night, came back to Blue Mountain, the town that had exiled his father. He started the strangest traveling show in American history, as far as I know, something so far removed from Andrews's gentle English country fair that it was difficult to believe they had both existed on the same planet.

Without meaning to, a father influences a son. A son does things to prove himself to the father, even a distant one, a demented one— even one who's dead.

So I did not ask Andrews about his decision to stay in America while his father died in Manchester. Instead I slowed my truck and kept a safe ten feet behind the police car all the way up the mountain.

"I haven't told you about my visit to the Deveroe place," I said to Andrews as we pulled up to the cemetery entrance.

"Something happen?"

I told him about Truevine's "house seal" and my opinion of it, as well as the strange feeling I got from Donny.

"She's really shaping up to be my kind of girl," Andrews sighed. "Weird beyond all recognition *and* a secret genius."

"Keep an eye out, would you," I said to him as we turned onto the rough roadway into the place. "You never know what you might glimpse."

"Skidmore can be closemouthed," Andrews said, his eyes scanning the yard, "but weren't you a little surprised that he knew Pinhurst was the caretaker up here?"

"A little."

"And don't you think Skid knows about the vagrants?" he went on, lowering his voice.

"Seems he would, doesn't it." I shifted down to first; the police car crept along in front of us.

The caretaker's cabin came into view as we topped a small ridge. It was beginning to rain; translucent blue lines blurred everything.

Rud was sitting on the porch, shotgun in his hands.

The squad car came to a stop. Nothing moved for a moment.

Rud stood up slowly, barrel of the gun pointed at the floor of the porch. He held up his right hand for an instant, gave one short wave.

Skid said something to Able; then the deputy got out of his car; Andrews and I followed suit.

"You've got a gun," Skid said plainly.

"Had trouble last night," Rud answered, "after Dr. Devilin left. I believe it was the Deveroe brothers."

Out of the corner of my eye I could see Able twist around, searching the perimeter for any sign of his tormentors.

"We're here on official business," Skid continued. "There was a murder last Thursday night up by Dr. Devilin's house. It appears to have involved Able Carter, who is in the back of my vehicle."

Rud nodded without looking at the car.

"He's a suspect. We believe the other person involved is Truevine Deveroe." Skid's plodding diction seemed more out of bad television than his own mind. "I have reason to believe she's here on this property. I'd like to find her and take her in for questioning." Skid looked at the ground for a moment. "I don't have a warrant. It's just questioning."

Rud shifted his weight onto one leg. "Did you write that down and rehearse it?"

"No," Skid grinned, his face relieved, "but I've been studying on it all the way up here. How'd I do?"

"Very official." Rud's stone face showed no hint of humor. "I'll try to get it just like that if Uncle Jackson asks me about it."

"*When* is the word," Skid assured him. "Not *if*."

"Okay," Rud said impatiently. "Can we go now?"

"Sure." Skid looked back at the car. "Able, you ready?"

"Ask him did he chase off the Deveroes."

"I've never seen them here in the daylight," Rud answered. "Never once." He held up his firearm. "I've got a gun."

"Gun?" Able squirmed in the seat, his voice barely audible through the unopened car window. "You seen them boys recently? You better take a cannon."

"Able," Skid said, opening the door, "I understand being nervous about them after what happened—"

"You don't understand *dick*," he interrupted. "I was hanging by my neck from a tree!"

I kept my eye on Rud. He didn't show the least surprise at Able's statement. Despite Rud's ability to mask his inner self, I got the impression that the incident was not news to him. As it happened so close to his kingdom, I wouldn't have been surprised if he'd seen it.

"I didn't mean that," Skid said, holding the door. "I meant that I see why you'd be nervous under the circumstances. I'm telling you I won't let anything happen."

I heard the promise in Skidmore's voice. I believed it.

Able heaved a sigh, pulled himself out into the misty rain.

"If I get killed up here," he said to Skid, "my sister's going to be very upset with you."

"She'd get over it," Skid said softly, hand on Able's shoulder. "She don't care for you that much."

Able smiled for the first time, I was guessing, since Thursday night.

"We'll start at her parents' grave," Rud said, launching himself off the porch.

Without a further word, he set off down the path in the direction of Davy and Eloise.

Somehow the rain encouraged the landscape in the graveyard to be more serene, almost comfortable. Little blue drops caressed the stones; the high cloud cover was nearly white. Sunlight found its way, however nimbus-filtered and feeble, onto everything.

The Deveroe parents' grave was not attended.

"She could be anywhere," Rud said.

"I know you-all saw her," Able said to me. "But are you sure of what you saw?" He was shivering a little.

"We talked to her," Andrews said impatiently.

"You know what I mean." Able continued to lock eyes with me.

" 'It is not only the souls of the departed,' " I quoted as best I could remember, " 'who hover unseen on the day when autumn to winter resigns the pale year. Witches then speed on their errands of mischief.' "

"*Not* Shakespeare," Andrews said wearily.

"No," I assured him. "Frazer's *Golden Bough* again. It's been on my mind lately."

"You don't know what you're dealing with," Able said, rasping.

" 'Those departed, gone before,' " Rud began very softly, " 'sleep in peace, return no more. Some poor souls that peace ignore. The witch's grave is an open door.' "

"Jesus." Even Andrews heard the bizarre menace in the caretaker's words.

"A witch is not permitted to die like the rest of us," I explained to

Andrews. "Death is not, to her, a closed portal. Entrance between this world and the next is left open. In some cases dying only makes the witch more powerful. She works unhindered by a material body."

"That's what Tru believes," Able said to Andrews, imploring him to understand. "That's why she'll be hard to talk to. She really thinks she's wandering between life and death."

"The hell she does," Andrews answered flatly. "Who would believe that crap? A girl who understands geothermal pockets and manages those three brothers is not the sort who loses herself in rubbish." He cast his eye over the landscape. "She's hiding because she's scared. She was witness to a murder. Or worse. And that's why we've got to find her—show her she didn't kill you." He tossed a glance Able's way. "Keep her from harming herself. It's why we're here, your spooky fun aside." He pulled the coat more tightly around himself. "Now. I'm getting wet; I'd like to round her up before it's dark. So let's get on with it."

"I reckon that says it," Skid agreed, a slight glint in his eye.

"After you," I told Rud.

He assented with a single lift of his chin and trudged past me into the trees.

Two hours later we still hadn't found the girl. Our eastern side of the mountain would begin to lose light by four-thirty or five. The rain had not increased, but steady mist had soaked us all to the bone. Everyone was shivering.

"I've *got* to dry out and have something warm," Andrews announced, glancing at his watch. "I suppose it's too much to hope that you'd have tea in your cabin."

Rud refused to look at Andrews. "Darjeeling, green tea, Earl Grey, valerian, and something called *Calm* that I think has tarragon in it."

"I could murder a pot of Earl Grey." Andrews didn't bother to keep his enthusiasm low.

"And some scones," Rud went on, his tone grown arch. "Maybe a cucumber sandwich."

"Oh." Andrews looked away, realizing Rud's derision. His shoulders sagged; a short blast of air escaped his nostrils.

"Let's put on a pot of coffee," Skid said, starting back toward the caretaker's cabin.

We slogged silently through the mud and weeds. I dared look once at Andrews; anger ground his jaw tight.

Everyone's mood shifted, however, when we entered Rud's cabin. It was immaculate. I don't know what I'd been expecting, but I found the place freakishly clean. It was comprised of one large room with an exposed sleep loft upstairs. The downstairs was divided into four perfectly distinct areas. To our right was the kitchen, very modern, all chrome. To the left of the entrance was the dining area. An ancient French farm table, oak, sturdy as a boulder, nearly filled that quarter of the room. Close to the far wall sat a leather chair and matching ottoman, both luxuriously well worn, the color of coffee with a little cream. They faced a window the way chairs in more modern homes might have aligned with a television set. The back corner comprised an office, furnished only with a rolltop desk, standing Tiffany floor lamp, 1920s desk chair. On the tidy desktop I noticed an open ledger, one small book, a single well-sharpened pencil, and an expensive thin laptop computer.

Rud's face showed no change, but his voice was noticeably lighter. "Let's see," he began, and moved instantly to the cupboard above the sink. "Earl Grey, you said."

"You mean you *do* have it?" Andrews stammered.

"And scones." Rud turned. His face was strangely lit from within, and he was smiling, an expression that appeared to use muscles generally dormant.

"I thought," Andrews started but seemed to lose his concentration.

Rud pulled a sheet of homemade scones from beneath a towel on the counter by the oven.

"I make them with rolled oats and fresh cream." He turned on the oven and slid the sheet in to warm them. "They achieve a significant texture that way. Now: butter." He moved to the tall chrome refrigerator.

"If you pull a cucumber sandwich out of there, I'm moving from Dr. Devilin's house in here with you."

"Alas," Rud said, still smiling, "*that* was mocking."

"Still." Andrews held his eyes on the oven, waiting for the scones. Their scent began to perfume the warm air of the cabin. "My grandmother made them this way, with rolled oats. She was from Aberdeen."

Rud produced gleaming tea globes from a drawer. "Earl Grey all around?"

I nodded, mute. Able stared blankly.

Skid, at a loss, managed, "I'd take a cup of coffee, if it's not too much trouble."

"Of course." Rud took out the Earl Grey, turned on the kettle. "I'm afraid the only place for us to sit is around the dining table, if that isn't too much of an imposition."

The more I stared at Rudyard Pinhurst in his element, the more my heart broke, realizing what he had given up in life. All that was left of enormous family wealth and position, a sumptuous elegance, was to be found on his face, entertaining in the afternoon, offering scones he'd baked on the lonely off-chance we'd come back to his home and taste them.

Once we were settled at the table, our refreshment arrived in due time. We sat in silence awhile, warming, gathering thoughts.

"Where the hell is she hiding?" Skid said at last, taking his cup of coffee with both hands, warming his fingers.

"I don't mean this to be a sore spot," Andrews mused, failing in his attempt to sound casual, "but it was mentioned that she shied away from you, Rud. Could that be the reason we're having difficulty?"

The scones were gone; they'd been perfect, not too dense; buttery; filling. Light was beginning to fail in the east as the opposite horizon grew red. Night birds took up their song. Evening was settling in.

"Could be," Rud sighed heavily. "I suppose."

He stood, switched on the light above the table, which only made it seem darker outside.

"You'uns think I'm crazy," Able said, "but I'm half-scared to find her."

"Don't start this again," Andrews objected, setting down his teacup.

"No," Able answered, "I've been studying on this. She thinks she killed me; that's what put her in her current mind."

"But Dev's idea—" Skid began.

"I know," Able interrupted. "He thinks to shock her back to us, but that ain't what I'm studying on." He looked around the table. "She didn't kill me; she killed Harding."

"I was wondering if you'd realize that," I said.

Able turned to Skidmore. "That's why you want to find her. You want to bring her in."

Skid avoided his eyes.

"She won't do in jail." Able's eyes implored me. "She couldn't take it."

"It was an accident," I offered. "Everyone will see that."

"Maybe." He nodded. "But she's a person who can't sit in that lockup, bars and concrete. She'll die." He turned to Skid. "You got to keep her at home with you, or something at least, Skid."

"The law don't make that kind of exception," Skidmore answered uncomfortably.

"You'd do it if you weren't running for office," Able spat back bitterly.

"Gentlemen," Rud intervened, his voice the soul of calm, "I'd prefer not to disturb the peace of my table. We haven't found her yet, and we may never at this rate." His lips thinned. "Reluctant as I am to agree with Dr. Andrews, *I* may be the problem. Allow me to suggest that you get back out there, unaccompanied, before it gets completely dark." He gazed out the window, his voice turning from frost to glacier. "I recommend the far corner, where the Newcomb graves are. We haven't been to that section yet."

Skid stood. "Right."

I finished my tea; Andrews skated his finger over the plate in front of him, gathering up the last crumbs of scone.

Able didn't move.

"I don't want to go back out there," he said slowly.

There was more than mere concern for his fiancée in the voice.

"The whole point of our being here," Andrews said wearily, "is for you to go back out there."

"Come on, brother," Skid coaxed.

Able looked to Rud for help, but Rud was still staring out the window.

"Okay," Able said hoarsely. "Let's do it."

We were out the door without another word. Rud stood in the archway watching us for a moment. We heard the door close as we turned onto the path that would lead us to the Newcomb corner of the cemetery.

Contrary to what might have been expected, twilight shadows added nothing to the ambience of the landscape. There may be a degree of strangeness that no environment is allowed to exceed, and our graveyard had reached its limit.

We walked in silence. I suspected that none of us had any hope left of finding the girl. We were loud men trudging through an overgrown landscape—hardly a difficult group from which to hide.

The path to the far corner of the yard went upward through an unused half-acre or so: brown grass, gangly wild privet, a gnarled rhododendron or two, a kingdom of *nigella* pods each the size of a baby's fist—eerie, alien, bending in the night wind. Someone had sown the area with a flower called love-in-a-mist, and these brown, devil-horned seed pods were all the autumn had left of them.

We topped a small ridge; the Newcomb area was revealed.

Tidy, well-arranged, uniform to a fault, the graves and vaults were significantly out of step with the rest of the cemetery. It was impossible to miss the fact that the entire section had been spotlessly groomed recently. No weeds, no stray growth—only sterile order.

"Rud does his job," Skidmore said softly. "Let's start with the big one."

We started down the slope, headed for the largest of the structures in the center of the area.

"Hang on," Andrews said after a step or two. "I thought his job was to care first for the Pinhurst family holdings here."

Skid stopped. I took in a breath.

"What?" Andrews said to me, noticing our new tension.

"It never occurred to me—but of course you wouldn't know," I answered slowly. "Pinhurst is the maiden name of the woman who married Jeribald Newcomb."

"Tubby," Andrews said. "The one who started the family curse. The one who got the name of the town changed from Newcomb to Blue Mountain."

"Right."

It took him a second. His eyes widened, and he scoured the graves all around him. "Pinhurst *is* Newcomb."

"Most of the Newcomb family left for Chattanooga when all that happened," I told him, "and the ones that stayed took the maiden name, Pinhurst."

"We don't talk about it," Skid said.

"But I've just realized you wouldn't know that," I apologized to Andrews. "Sorry."

"It's a kind of salient fact," he objected loudly. "Wait." He rubbed his face. "This means Rud is a Newcomb."

"Rudyard Pinhurst," Able chimed in, "is the illegitimate son of Tristan, The Newcomb Dwarf."

"I've got to sit down," Andrews managed, looking around for a spot. "This is huge!"

"We kind of take it for granted," Skid said, not looking anywhere. "Plus, we don't talk about it much, like I say."

"It's Peyton Place from hell." Andrews found a convenient stone bench a few steps from where he stood. "Little people can have normal-sized children?"

"Of course," I answered.

"You said *illegitimate*," Andrews went on. "Who was the mother?"

Skid looked at me.

"It was always rumored that my mother was the culprit," I said lightly. "No surprise, she was prodigiously promiscuous, as I have explained to you many times. But in the end a girl from Tifton, Georgia, claimed the child was hers, looking for a bit of the family money. Tristan had dallied with her when the *Ten Show* toured near her home. Tests were performed; her maternity was confirmed; she was paid and never seen again."

"Christ." Andrews shook his head. "No wonder Rud is such a mess."

"Good-looking boy, though," Able offered. "You know he and Truvy . . ."

"She loves *you*, Able," Skidmore said comfortingly.

"I know," he answered, but his voice shook a little.

"Well, this is more news than I can absorb in a day," Andrews said, keeping his seat. "Rud makes scones the way my grandmother used to, and by the way, his father was a famous dwarf." He peered at me through the dim light. "Any chance you're making this up?" He surveyed the place again. "You'd have a right. It's the perfect stage."

"What sounds unbelievable on first hearing," Skid began philosophically, "becomes commonplace in a generation."

"It don't seem that odd to us," Able explained.

"Did you ever meet Tristan?" Andrews asked me.

"Toward the end of his life, I've been told. I think I was four or so, don't remember it."

"And he left the traveling show to your parents when he died."

"Perpetuating the rumor of his relationship with my mother."

"I've seen pictures," Able said. "He wasn't strange-looking. Aside from the height. I mean he was . . . proportional."

"His limbs and features were not stunted," I explained, "and I recall Mother's telling me his laughter was very musical and engaging."

"This is why you kept telling me all those Newcomb stories." He was beginning to piece things together. "This is why Rud had all that money, not just from his rich ex-wife. And it explains a lot about Harding Pinhurst, too." He slumped. "Wait. And Truevine is their cousin. God!"

"Hold on," Skid told him. "It's not as bad as you think. You can't hardly find anybody up here that's not related to someone else in some kind of way."

"Weren't but five or six original families settled on Blue Mountain," Able added.

"Everybody's somebody's cousin," Skid concluded. "I know it's a bad joke from a Yankee comedian, but if you count fourth or fifth cousins, hell, even Dev and I might be related."

"Stop." Andrews held up his right hand. "I've heard enough. The conceptual bliss of ignorance has never been clearer to me." He stood. "I can't think about this right now. Let's just get on with the show." He looked about. "Where to?"

"Seems appropriate, under the circumstances," Skid answered, grinning, "to head for Tristan's grave."

"Lead on, Macduff," Andrews said gamely.

He started down the slope, into the Newcomb yard, headed for the largest vault.

A lone figure, swathed in black, sat hunched over the reclining marble image of Tristan Newcomb. Skid was first in the entrance, frozen, transfixed by the tableau. The crypt was sparkling, looked polished. Two torches, depended from iron wall sconces, blazed bright as day. The figure was so still, I thought for a moment it might be a part of the carving, but the head moved when Andrews gasped.

A bone white hand, rough and gnarled, beckoned.

No one moved.

"This carving is very lifelike, I believe," the voice whispered reverently.

I took a step inside, past the others. "May?"

She looked up. "There is a plethora of fine statuary here in this place, you know, not just the Angel of Death." She looked back down at the recumbent Tristan as if he were her child: pietà by Dalí.

"What are you doing here, May?" I asked gently.

"He's just sleeping," she said serenely.

"May, damn it." Skidmore powered into the vault. "You like to scared me to death."

Andrews and I exchanged a lightning glance. He failed to resist the question on both our minds.

"You know this woman?" he said to Skid.

"Yes, God," he answered, exasperated.

"I thought you were Truvy," Able said, shaken.

"She's not here," May said, having difficulty focusing. It was clear she'd had a drink or two.

"You shouldn't be out, sugar," Skidmore chided, moving closer to her. "It's rainy and cold."

"Rud said wait for you here after I found Miss Deveroe," she said grudgingly. "Always do what Rud says do. Funny watching you all traipse around the yard."

Skid looked back my way, addressed her. "Rud told you to wait for us here? You saw us walking around the graveyard for two hours and you knew where Truevine was?"

"Always do what Rud says," she repeated, softer. "Supposed to take you to Miss Deveroe."

"Was he leading us around to *keep* us from finding her?" Andrews asked, instantly suspicious despite scones.

"And he took us to his house to give May time to complete some task," I mused.

"Where is she?" Skid demanded. "Where are you supposed to take us?"

"So come on." She stood.

May did not speak further but wafted past us out the door, into the night. We watched mutely for a moment.

"Are you coming or am I going?" she called, her voice receding.

Skid snorted, twitched his head in the direction of her question, and followed. The rest of us seemed to have no choice but to follow.

"You know about May?" Andrews drew up beside Skid and whispered.

"I know it won't do no good to ask her anything when she's drunk," he muttered. "We just have to follow after and see what happens."

"In spite of the fact that Rud's been planning something," I insisted.

"I mean," Andrews said pointedly, "you know about where she stays."

"I do. It's a little game we've come to play." His voice was tired. "I pretend not to notice them; they convince themselves they're eluding the law. Rud takes good care of them. Aside from how weird it is, I can't see the harm."

In other cities, states more northern, the law might have been less willing to be eluded. But Skidmore's brand of Christian charity gave enforcement a kindness in our county that was unique. I breathed a silent hope, not quite a prayer, that he would win the coming election if for no other reason than May's well-being.

We followed her along the edge of the yard, close to the fence. The rain had let up, but the clouds refused to break. Now and again they would part, curtains, allowing the spotlight of a rising moon to wash everything white. At the back corner of the yard, the well-worn footpath on the other side came into view.

"May." I drew up beside her. "This is where you saw Hek Cotage the other day."

"He's a handsome man," she said dreamily. "For a minister."

"He didn't recognize you," I went on, "until you gave him a bit of the cloth you wear around your neck."

"It's a pretty fabric," she answered.

"You didn't mean to," I said, my voice lowered, "but you frightened him."

"He does not care to remember much about the time he spent here," she reasoned. "And therefore he is occasionally discomforted by the thought."

She found a sag in the fence, stepped over it with a grace more becoming a young girl than a lost soul.

"We're leaving the cemetery?" Skid called.

"If you want to see Miss Truevine we are," she said, not looking back.

"I'm not sure," Able said, coming to a halt. "I don't think I want to do this."

May was already several yards ahead of the rest of us.

"Hold on," I said to her, but she barely slowed.

"May!" Skid barked.

She stopped, still not looking back. She wobbled a little.

"Deveroes won't come into the cemetery," Able said, shivering a little. "But they're out there somewhere, and they want me good. You'uns go on. I'll wait here."

Skid took him by the elbow and encouraged him to step over the fence.

He did, but his breath was filled with little fear catches.

Without warning, May started up again.

"Where are we going?" I called to her.

She remained mutely intent, headlong into the woods.

I caught up with her as the trail sloped upward into tall cedars, wild purple-leafed rhododendrons.

"May, what did Rud tell you to do?" I insisted. "Where are you taking us?"

"The Newcomb mansion," she whispered deliciously. "It's haunted."

On a dare when we were fourteen, Skidmore and I spent a night in the old Newcomb place. Long abandoned, it clung desperately to the hillside, too tired to support itself, too terrified to fall. Lower rooms had been sacked beyond redemption, but anyone brave enough to venture up the wide broken oak staircase to the upper floors could be treated to a glimpse of former grandeur.

Skid and I took flashlights, sleeping bags, matches, sandwiches, NuGrape. I had a book; he brought a transistor radio. My parents were gone, as usual, touring; his were asleep by eight, no trouble for him to sneak out.

The place was gray, all semblance of paint long gone. The roof was fairly intact, but a tree had fallen during some storm and caved the porch. Its dignity shattered, the house endured a constant humiliation of toads and bugs and field mice crawling over its moldering innards.

Nothing much really happened that night long ago. We were scared teenage boys, challenging each other farther and farther into the house. The second floor still had rugs in some rooms, high chandeliers, even some furniture. We found a bedroom on the third floor, cozy, our size, two beds—servants' quarters, I guessed—with an amazing granite mantle adorning its fireplace. I'm ashamed to admit we broke up chairs to burn, set a blaze in the hearth. After a casual dusting, a check of the darker corners under both beds, I piled my sleeping bag onto the bed closest to the fire and settled in.

Neither of us slept a wink. Wind, mice, owls, branches scratching at the roof—the night was alive with a thousand sounds; each could have been approaching death. We were forced to converse through the night. A gentle rain began around two in the morning and made our little room cozier, masked the other noises.

That conversation was the first adult talk either of us had ever had. I suppose everyone comes to that experience at a certain age. For the first time in our lives we discussed all of life's true meanings: Kathy Holliman's improved profile, the world according to me, God and His Plan, scurrilous local politicians, my family's foibles, something called "Cathy's Clown," a song by the Everly Brothers that was Skid's favorite—an old forty-five of his father's that was made significant by Skid's unrequited affection for Kathy Holliman.

The night passed more swiftly than either of us would have thought possible. By the time I was trying to explain the analogy of Plato's Cave for the third time, Skid sat up, pointed to the windowsill. There was sunlight washing it. We'd survived.

" 'There's more of gravy than of grave' to that place," I said to May.

"You quote Charles Dickens," she confirmed.

"You constantly amaze me," I told her.

"But you know," she went on, "memories can haunt a place just like a spirit can."

"I know."

"Hold on." She dropped to her knees; her voice changed dramatically. "Damned new shoes. Always come untied. Look at these new laces, though, pretty, ain't they? The old ones always got like a spider caught up in its own web, all tangled up." I assumed this was her attempt at adding to the Poe-like ambience of our endeavor.

The woods were a dance of moonlight and shadow. Wind swirled the dead leaves from the ground into fairy circles, made dull castanets of the smaller oak branches. We emerged from a thicket of laurel and the house came into view.

I hadn't seen it in years, but it didn't look remotely like the place Skid and I had invaded. The porch was gone, tumbled to the ground. The tree that had caused the damage so long ago was well decayed. Not a single pane of glass remained anywhere. The front door was missing, giving the facade a gap-toothed appearance. Boards had fallen from the exterior; ivy had taken one wall entirely. Even the bricks in the chimney tops had cascaded: a ruined crown.

Skid whistled unconsciously behind me. "Time has *not* been kind to this place."

"Is that so?" May stood, turned around slowly. "Well, you show me the place where time *is* kind. I want to go there."

"Truevine's in that place?" Able gazed at the mansion in the pale light.

"Well," May answered, head to one side, "let's go see."

I had a moment of expanded perspective, sucked momentarily out of myself looking down on our little group as we trekked the last hundred yards to the house: shivering coroner, Shakespeare scholar, county deputy, lonely wanderer, failed academic. I watched us walk, kicking up leaves and shambling in the dark, judged us the perfect group to trespass in a haunted mansion, and returned to my body.

The interior of the house was no less ruined than the sad facade. Nothing of the soul of the place remained downstairs. Floorboards were gone; walls were covered with mold and mildew; moss had taken hold of the stairs. The staircase, once a grand avenue, was an impossible dilapidation and seemed incapable of supporting any of us.

Everything creaked: floors, walls, the trees outside. Skidmore's flashlight barely made its way through the gloom.

"Miss Truevine?" May's voice startled us all.

There was no answer.

"Hope she's not left and gone," May muttered to herself.

A sudden scratching to our right turned all heads. The flashlight's beam stabbed wildly about the room, settled on the black dog in the doorway to the parlor.

"There you are," May said, as if addressing a small child.

The dog sniffed.

"Ms. Deveroe!" Skidmore called out. "It's Skidmore Needle, I need to see you now." His voice was firm but somehow not remotely threatening.

The dog turned its head, hearing something we hadn't. It gave a small, short whine.

"All right," said a voice within the parlor. "Go."

The dog shot away, past us and out the door.

"Can we come in?" May asked.

"I've been waiting," the voice said. Impossible to tell who was speaking, I only assumed it was Truevine.

Skid went first; I fell in behind. Able and Andrews didn't move at all. The flashlight beam scoured the parlor, found the cloaked figure standing by the mantel. The marble fireplace was huge, a carved standing lion flanking each side. A mirror hung over it, so caked with dust and cobwebs it had no hope of reflecting anything. Otherwise the room was bare.

She turned.

"They say you have Able with you." Her voice was wracked with doubt, shaking. "But that can't be." Her eyes quickened. "Unless my spell worked."

"Tru?" Able parted Skid and me, stepped into the room.

A sudden intensity of light burst from Truevine's face, and the armor of tension melted from Able's shoulders. They moved without moving and were in a locked embrace without another word. The hood fell from her head, and her hair tumbled, soft, slow. Her black cloak seemed to enfold them both.

I held my breath, afraid to break the image.

They pulled back, staring at each other. It seemed they were conversing, but still no sound was made.

"This is romantic," May said after a moment.

The mood shifted instantly. The play was over. We were six exhausted people in an old abandoned house in the middle of the woods. The fact that the calendar read "October 31" held no significance whatsoever. It was just another night.

"Ms. Deveroe," Skid started up again, maintaining his official tone, "I've got to speak with you."

"Look," she said, her voice barely a vapor on the air. "I did it. Able's alive."

"And so are you, ma'am," Skid said, a little softer.

"I," she stammered. "I reckon I must be."

Able petted her hair, kissed her cheek. "It's all right now. We'll be all right."

All her ghostly behavior seemed to collapse; she was a young girl again.

"I'm so sorry, Abe," she said, close to tears. "I hate we had a fight."

"It was all my fault," he said, pulling her closer. "I'm an idiot; you know that."

"No such thing," she nuzzled her head in the hollow of his shoulder. As I watched her with Able, my opinion began to shift. The winsome spirit act seemed a complete contrivance. The romance of her image as a savant, powerful in a knowledge of ancient lore, evaporated. It was replaced by something that was much more likely: a simple, lonely girl in school whose only refuge from tormenting classmates was to veer strangely, take up the mantle of derision as a garment, wear it, own it. It was an image with which I was passingly familiar myself. Truevine Deveroe was a dropout with few prospects, impossible siblingry, and an irredeemable reputation. Her hopes were all pinned to the man at her side, someone who would take care of her, work to ease the sting of life. Theirs would be a small life in a smaller town, and I was entirely envious.

"Can we go now?" The show was over for Andrews, who must have sensed something of what I was feeling.

No ghost, no witch, no spooky mansion. Why weren't we home by the fire?

"That seems right," Skidmore said. "Let's all go on back into town."

"Except me," May piped up.

"Good night, May," Skid said pointedly.

"Okay, then." Without eye contact or further rumination, May was out the door, swallowed by the night.

"Come on, kids," Skid said, his deputy's voice giving way to something gentler. "Show's over."

"Christ, am I suddenly tired." Andrews rubbed his face. "What a day this has been."

"Dev?" Skid took in the place for the first time. "You remember when we spent the night here, back in the younger days?"

"Never forget it," I said, unable to keep the smile from my lips.

"That night," he said, struggling a little with his thoughts, "was the first time I thought about a lot of things. A lot of big things."

"It's the house," Truevine said.

We stared at her.

"The house wants you to think about the big things." She looked up at the mirror. "So it can feel better. About itself. It's old, wants to be a teacher—"

"That's enough," Andrews interrupted.

"Let's *go*," Skid insisted.

I was about to make my own comment when the black dog shot into the room, panting. It rounded Truevine's legs and cowered behind her. I turned toward the front door. Anything that could frighten that animal had my full attention.

"Skid?" I said uncertainly.

He put his hand on his pistol. As far as I could determine, he never had time to do anything further.

Someone set off fireworks outside.

I felt a white burning in my chest, a draining numbness in my arms. My knees hinged, gave way. The floor hit my shoulder, then the side of my face. All feeling was muffled; a blanket surrounded me, no sound, no sensation. My stomach was seized by a fierce icy hand and everything began to glow phosphorescent, brighter and brighter all around me, until there was nothing at all.

Twelve

"Fever?" My great-grandmother Adele stood over me.

My eyes were closed, but I knew her voice.

" 'O, what can ail thee, knight-at-arms,' " she said, " 'Alone and palely loitering? The sedge has withered from the lake, And no birds sing.' "

"I said that to Andrews. It's not Shakespeare."

"It's Keats."

"That's what he said."

" '*La Belle Dame sans Merci*.' " Her voice was everywhere.

"Why are you here?" My voice was only in my head.

"I was going to ask you the same question," she said, "but I guess you came looking for me."

"No."

I could hear her let out a breath. "No one came looking for me."

"I'm sorry."

"It's all right," she went on after a moment. "I can tell you a story. I did that once or twice when you were little."

"Story?"

White silence filled my head.

"Nancy was a pretty girl," she began. "Her great-grandmother educated her. Not with books, but sedge and hazel, weed and water, rock and salamander trails. Some called her a witch.

"Nancy worked as a cook in a rich man's house and fell in love with Randal, the son. He was in love with her too, but his parents would not allow the union. In those days a cook and a lord were not permitted to marry, especially if there was a whisper of witch-craft.

"The boy was sent to sea. He sailed Baffin's Bay, where the whale fishes blow great spikes of water.

"Nancy could not bear to be without him, so on the eve of Samhain she put on her cloak and took out her mortar to grind up some hemp seed for a charm and to sow some in a beckoning circle:

> " 'Hemp-seed I sow thee,
> Hemp-seed grow thee;
> And he who will my true love be
> Come after me
> And show thee.'

"She said it three times, turning in a circle, looked back over her left shoulder, and standing there was her love, Randal, pale as snow. She ran to kiss him, but in her haste she spilled the seed, the spell was broken, and he vanished.

"She wept bitterly from that night on, unable to concentrate on work, eating little, sleeping less.

"Not three weeks later she got a letter that told her worse news.

" 'Nancy,

" 'Our ship foundered in Baffin's Bay; your Randal was on deck. Without warning he dropped to his knees; the blood left his face; he lay dead, as if his spirit had been ripped from this body. A moment later he revived, shrieking. "I saw my Nancy," he said. In his madness to get home to you, he jumped overboard to swim home, and froze. His last remains are here on board and will arrive at length.'

"The news was signed in the captain's hand.

"It took near six months for the ship to come home with its sad cargo. But the story does not end there. The girl did not know the power of her spell.

"When Randal's body was returned, it did not go quietly to the grave. The spirit, still confused by the witch's magic, tried to go to her once more. At midnight it broke the bonds of its coffin, found a horse, and rode to Nancy's door.

"The girl saw only a rider coming, furious and fleet. In her guilt, she took it for a murderer, sent out from Randal's father to punish her. She fled, terrified, never recognizing her love in ghostly form.

"She ran through sedge and hazel, weed and water, rock and salamander trails, past a circle of hemp. He gave chase, calling her name, until they came to the blacksmith shop in our town.

" 'Help!' she cried when she saw the glow from his bellows.

"The smith appeared, a red-hot iron in his hand. He saw the girl's distress and reached out his hand. But the undead spirit leaned down and grabbed the unfortunate girl's dress, a pale yellow gown twined all about with rust roses. The smith raised his iron and burned off the dress from the rider's hand, saving our Nancy. She fell, more dead than alive. The rider howled, believing Nancy no longer loved him. The horse, frightened to madness, leapt over the cemetery wall, gone.

"The smith took Nancy into his shop, where she lay weeping, asking only that she be taken to Randal's grave, that she might see her love one last time. A priest was called, the doctor came nigh, and Nancy's mother made three in attending to her, but none could prevail. Before the first light of day, the poor girl died.

"They took her body to the graveyard, where they found, on Randal's grave, the corpse of a colt, drenched in foam, his eyes bulging, his tongue swollen round. The grave was fresh dug, no grass, no moss.

"And beside it: a piece of Nancy's dress, burnt from the smith's iron.

"She was buried beside him, in a simpler grave. And all around their graves, all tell the tale, on October thirty-first there grows a circle of hemp and the lovers are permitted one embrace before they must return to their cold coffin prisons.

"If the moon is near full, you can see them to this day, twined in a true-lovers' knot, between the midnight and the dawn, on the eve of All Saints' Day."

I felt the icy touch of my great-grandmother's hand on my cheek.

"That's a ghost story," she whispered, "from long ago. I used to tell it to you when you were a baby, do you remember?"

She fell silent once more. A slow-growing warmth surrounded me, taking the chill from my skin, seeking to penetrate my bones.

"Oh." Her voice shimmered. "You're not staying."

Thirteen

Samhain is New Year's Day on the Isle of Man, the last Celtic hold-out against Saxon invasions. A new fire is struck, the old one dies, and from the sacred flame torches are taken. All the hearths of the island are rekindled, fortunes are told, and the future is reasonably assured. The fire of the new year restores all spirits; its orange glow is the liveliest soldier against the gloom of the night. Bonfires blaze.

> On the last day of autumn children gathered ferns, tar-barrels, the long thin stalks called *gàinisg,* and everything suitable for a bonfire. These were placed in a heap on some eminence near the house, and in the evening set fire to. The fires were called *Samhnagan.* There was one for each house, and it was an object of ambition who should have the biggest. Whole districts were brilliant with bonfires, formed an exceedingly picturesque scene.

The most effective is a circle of fire, burning iron-hot. It is made on the highest spot, and a stone is put in the circle for every member of every family in the town. When the fire is out, the stones are examined. Any found moved or damaged were taken as a sign: within twelve months the person whose stone had been so disturbed would be cast out of the circle of the living.

Fourteen

"I think I saw his eyes move!" Andrews's high-pitched tone betrayed great distress.

"I don't think so," Able answered.

"No, honestly," Andrews shot back. "Come here."

"Mind the stones," Truevine's voice entreated urgently.

"You're going to burn the place down," Andrews argued.

Where's Skidmore? I thought.

Truevine was whispering something low and I was desperate to hear it, but the lovely warmth that was flooding my arms and legs was distracting me. I could feel the touch of a hand on my heart, hear the crackle of the fire in the hearth. I wanted to open my eyes, but they wouldn't part, the way some dreams won't allow the sleeper to awaken.

Flashing red light stabbed my eyelids. Car engines raked my ears. Heavy footfalls disturbed my slumber. Vague voices barked commands; rude hands roughed me.

"Time of death?" someone said.

"Stop!" Truevine's imperious voice pierced the din. "Do *not* pick him up!"

More voices mumbled, but the jarring ceased; I relaxed.

"Oh my God, Needle, come look at this." I didn't recognize the voice. "I thought you said he was shot."

"He was." Skid's voice was clawed and ragged.

"There's a dab of blood. But see here."

"Mind the *stones!*" Truevine's voice triumphed again.

"What the hell?" Skid whispered. "There's no bullet hole."

"Right," the voice said.

"So what killed him?" Skid asked softly

When I was finally able to open my eyes, I could make no sense of what they saw, as if a brief chapter had unfolded without me.

I was lying in the middle of the parlor, tumbling bits of the abandoned Newcomb mansion all around me. Strangers surrounded Andrews and Able Truevine sat in the corner closest to me, rocking back and forth praying or whispering to herself, eyes closed.

I was in the center of a small circle of stones, black, each with a slight hollow indentation where a candle sat. I tried counting, for some reason, but was unable to focus on numbers; I suppose there were twenty or more.

Skidmore was by himself, staring out the window.

I sat up.

For a moment, no one took notice.

I rubbed my eyes, absently put a hand to my shoulder where it ached.

One of the uniformed strangers close to Andrews happened to turn at that moment and catch me out of the corner of his eye.

His gasp took him backward, into another officer, and he began choking violently. All eyes turned first to him, then my way.

I looked down at myself, trying to determine what they were staring at. The room had fallen crystal-still, poised.

"What happened?" I said.

Everyone remained frozen.

"Fever?" Skidmore said strangely, his hand steadied on the windowsill.

Truevine opened her eyes, sighed, and collapsed on the floor.

Everyone rushed to my side.

"Fever?" Skid repeated, trying to stare through my eyes into my head.

"My chest hurts."

One of the deputies laughed. He was wearing a uniform different from Skid's.

"You got shot, brother," Skidmore said, his voice shaking. "You were dead."

"What do you mean, *dead?*" The sound in my throat was barely mine.

"As in 'pronounced dead on the scene' dead," he returned, trying hard to pull himself together.

"Deveroes." Able was white as milk. "They were outside."

"They didn't mean to shoot you," Skid said, gathering strength. "They were shooting at the dog. Didn't even know we were in here."

"You don't know that," Able shot back belligerently.

"I'm really thirsty," I managed, still unable to recognize the sounds I was making.

Everyone's attention was on me; my eyes were distracted by movement in the corner of the room. Truevine had recovered herself, stood, and was moving past us out of the room.

"I'll be damned if I can explain this," a man in gray said to Skid.

I focused on him; he was an emergency medical technician, beefy, shave-headed, young.

Skidmore leaned in to me. "You got shot, Fever, did you know that?" He was speaking as if I were five.

"I don't think I was shot," I said, gaining energy by the second. "I'm not bleeding, it doesn't hurt that bad, and I'm conscious."

"You were dead three minutes ago," the ambulance man chimed in.

"Stop saying that," I sniffed. "Who told you I was dead?"

"This." He held up his stethoscope. "No heartbeat, no pulse, no eye movement, no breathing—just exactly like a dead guy. I've seen my share."

"Didn't I hear you say there was no wound?" I looked down at myself. It was a little bloody and my coat was ripped open, but otherwise I seemed fine.

"That's just one of the questions I have," the ambulance man said, straightening up.

"Truevine did this," Able said softly. He was staring at the stones and candles.

"Give me the two-second tour," I said, looking up at Skid, "could you do that?"

"Dev, you don't know what you just put me through."

"No," I said, "I don't; that's why I'm asking you to tell me what happened."

"You know he won't let up until you do." Andrews had stood mute, unable to speak. When he did, his voice was shaky, but his face beamed down at me.

"The dog ran in here," Skidmore sighed, resigned. "Shots were fired from outside; you went down; I went out. Deveroe boys were running away. Andrews was yelling his head off. I saw you'd been shot, ran to the squad car to call the ambulance, called the state troopers who were here to investigate the mortuary; we all came back. When the medical personnel got here, they did their best, but you were already gone."

"In the meantime," Andrews took up, "Truevine set up these stones all around you; she had them in a little sack. She told Able to get candles; they were in the pantry in the kitchen. She set up this circle, despite my protestations, and started some voodoo ceremony."

"It included dabbing this on your chest." The ambulance man held up a bloody square of moss the size of a kitchen sponge.

"What is it?" I asked him.

"I'd like to know," he said, "but the girl won't talk to any of us, just keeps rocking and praying."

"We'll figure all that out," Skid said licking his lips. "Right now it don't . . . I'm just . . . damn, Fever, you were really gone."

"I may want to discuss that later, in private," I said, scrambling to get to my feet, "but I wouldn't mind getting out of here at the moment. I feel strange."

"Yeah." Skid blew out a breath. "Let's get everyone together."

"I'm taking him in to the hospital, Deputy," the ambulance man chimed in. "He needs medical care, don't you believe?"

"I need a good rest in my own bed," I insisted, standing, pushing past everyone.

"Where are you going?" Andrews protested.

"I'm trying to stop Truevine," I answered, still dazed, headed in the direction of the front door, "since the rest of you won't."

They all turned toward the front entrance.

The girl had disappeared.

The next part of the evening was a blur. Weaker than I'd thought, I sat down in front of the house outside, doggedly resisting evacuation to the hospital. A shroud of shock had settled over me; I could feel nothing.

Loud argument from everyone about my medical condition seemed vague to me, far away. In the end Andrews saved the day, waving his university identification, claiming to be a medical doctor, promising everyone he'd take care of me. There was some heated discussion, someone wanting to know why Andrews hadn't done anything earlier. Skidmore finally lent his support to Dr. Andrews, and it was settled.

The ambulance departed; Andrews fetched my truck and drove me home; Skidmore took Able back to lockup; state patrol went into the woods after the Deveroe family unit.

I must have fallen asleep in the truck, groggy getting into my house. But Andrews had a roaring blaze going after a while and brought me a cognac the size of a country iced tea.

A few sips warmed me inside almost as much as the fire bathed my skin. I settled back onto the sofa, covered with a thick quilt, doing my best to concentrate on the events of my demise.

"Go over everything again, do you mind?" I said to Andrews. "What happened to me?

He'd poured himself a glass equal to mine. It was already nearly half-gone. He sat slumped in the chair beside me, shoes off, feet up on the table.

"All right, let me clear my thoughts." He took another gulp, a deep breath, and closed his eyes. "We were about to leave the haunted house with Truevine safely found when her dog came barreling into the place, yelping, scared to death. That, of course, got our attention. I was thinking there was some sort of huge animal or something that scared it. Skidmore got out his pistol and headed for the front door, when a bunch of shots were fired, I don't know how many. Glass broke; a couple of bullets must have hit the walls; there were little plaster explosions. It all happened so fast, I didn't even react. The next thing I knew, you were on the floor."

"Was I bleeding?"

"I'm sure you were; I didn't see it right then." He sipped again. "Skid barked something over his shoulder and ran off into the woods. I don't think he saw you go down. I could hear yelling outside, but no more shots. Truevine took charge inside, a remarkable command. She pointed; we did what she said. I thought maybe she'd had some sort of folk doctor training the way she was ordering us about, the mouse that roared. I found some blankets upstairs, which was an adventure in itself. You ever try climbing that staircase?"

"A long time ago. It was more intact then. Go on."

"Anyway, upstairs at the house of Usher there are still a few sticks of furniture. I found a bed with linens still on. The top layers were useless, mostly mold, but underneath was a blanket and some sheets that I thought might do under the circumstances."

"Could we skip the fascinating adventure of the bedclothes and get on with what was happening with my dead body?"

"It's always about you, isn't it?" He finished his cognac, hoisted himself out of the chair, lumbered into the kitchen. "The point is, what with the navigation of the wacky staircase and the time it took to find decent linens, I was gone out of the room you were in for, I don't know, as long as ten minutes maybe. When I came back, it was a scene from *The Exorcist*. She'd laid out that circle of stones all around you, set candles; they were all burning. The girl was huddled over you, dabbing at your chest with some hunk of sod, and I use the term advisedly."

"I *was* bleeding."

"You were then," he affirmed, pouring out another healthy drink. "A lot. Able was hunkered in a corner, I stood for a moment in the doorway, uncertain what to do. It was just so weird."

"What was she saying?"

"No idea." He waved his glass grandly.

I pulled the quilt aside, unbuttoned my shirt. There was a welt the size of a nickel on my left pectoral muscle barely two inches from my sternum—and my heart. It was purple like a bruise, black on the edges, ragged, very nasty. I sat up.

"Come over here, do you mind?" I wrestled my shirt over my shoulder, exposing my back. "Is there anything there?"

He clicked on the lamp beside my head, peered down. "Yeah." He leaned in. "Like a black mark, a jagged hive or something."

"About the size of a quarter."

"Roughly." He straightened. "What is it?"

I lay back down, pointed to the similar mark on my chest.

"Hey." He reached out and poked it.

I winced.

"Still a little tender?" He pulled back his finger.

"Hurts like hell," I answered, pulling my shirt back on. "My whole shoulder does, like it's been broken, run over by a truck, and stapled together with rusty pins."

"Descriptive. What are those welts?"

"Just hear me out," I began.

"I hate when you start that way," he said wearily, retreating to his chair once more.

"These are the entrance and exit wounds of the bullet that went through me. The Deveroes told me once that they use bullets that are very smooth and thin, coated with some sort of oil. Their bullets go through clean."

"Why would they do that?"

"I remember they were very proud of the idea." I tried to concentrate. "Something about not having to bother finding and removing shot from the innards of their kill. They thought it was a brilliant time-saver . . ." I floundered.

". . . effort-saver . . ." he offered.

"Something," I soldiered on. "Also claimed it was kinder to the animal."

"They really are morons," he mumbled.

"No matter. I think that's what they shot me with."

"They were shooting at the dog," he reminded me.

"I believe that. I was just unlucky."

"Are you serious?" He sat up, the cognac beginning to flush his face. "You're the luckiest bastard I ever knew. You were dead, and now you're fine, all in the space of a couple of hours."

"All right, I'll give you that," I told him, settling back on the sofa, covering up again.

"How do you think *that* happened?"

"I think Truevine is privy to a certain moss or lichen in those woods that has the ability to stop bleeding and heal scars, bind wounds."

"That wouldn't begin to describe it," he said, clearly not agreeing. "What kind of a remarkable medical breakthrough would that be?"

"It would be something," I admitted.

"Voodoo nature crap."

"Twenty years ago everybody in the medical community laughed at echinacea and Saint-John's-wort, that sort of thing. Look how they've come into common usage."

"You can't seriously compare the new age herbal marketing boom," he began, sneering, "to the kind of thing you're talking about. The medical establishment doesn't take Saint-John's-wort any more seriously now than they did then."

"I suppose you're right," I said. "I still think Truevine gave me a stone circle healing."

"Yeah, tell me about that." He shifted in his seat. "What was with the stones and candles?"

"Oddly," I said more softly, "I was thinking about that while I was unconscious."

I told him about the stones in the fire circles on the Isle of Man. I wavered on the edge of also revealing that my great-grandmother had come to me, but I was still unsettled by her voice, the story she'd told.

"While you were out," he said, smiling down at his glass, "you recited part of the introduction to your doctoral thesis to yourself?"

"Sort of." I had to agree it was a little amusing. "I think I was in shock from the bullet. Maybe my heart did stop, or maybe I went into a kind of coma."

"The ambulance guy tried to revive you," Andrews said, avoiding my eyes. "Pumped your lungs, massaged your chest, gave you two jolts from the whatever-you-call it."

"Defibrillator."

"If you say so. He pronounced you dead." He took a healthy swig. "I'll tell you what: saying it now is worse than when it was happening. At the time I think I was probably in shock too; it didn't exactly register. Couldn't believe it. I was staring down at your dead body and I was thinking, *That can't be right*, like it was a misadded column of numbers or something. You know?"

"No."

"I mean now I'm starting to get really freaked out about it," he went on, "but at the time, I was calm. Cool as a cucumber." He looked down. "Christ."

"I think the body has a way of helping you out in those situations," I offered soothingly. "You get some kind of natural anesthetic; you cope biochemically. It's supposed to be like that."

"All I know is that Able and I were helpless," he said, words trembling in the air, "and that girl knew exactly what to do."

"She's a concern," I said, staring into the fire.

"How do you mean? The murder?"

"No. A few days ago I had her pegged as a genius, the Einstein of natural phenomena. When I saw her in the cemetery, later in the house, it was clear she was a simple girl with an IQ lower than most, making the best of her limited abilities, coping with a difficult social situation. Now I have to come up with a third portrait."

"She's a shy girl," Andrews said simply. "You always do this, you know: make too much of the mystery of the eternal feminine. She's a person with no more or less strangeness and charm than anyone else. Sit down with her when this is all over, if you can, and try to get past your furtive little fantasies and academic attempts to *solve* her. Just talk. Maybe you'll meet the real Truevine Deveroe."

I raised myself on one elbow, eyes wide, forehead tingling.

"I don't know if it's that I'm tired—or that I've been shot and pronounced dead—but I think you've forced a bit of old-fashioned satori into my mind."

"Sorry?" He squinted my way.

"I'm saying I think you're right. I've tried to see Truevine as an icon, the embodiment of a certain ethos, a human reliquary, repository of ancient lore. That's a lot to pile onto one young person with a fifth-grade education from Blue Mountain, Georgia."

"I'd say," he agreed, settling in.

"You really pegged a foible of mine."

He raised his glass. "To pegged foibles."

"Nice going, Andrews," I said warmly, lying back under the quilt.

"Actually, this is what I'm always on about," he said evenly, swirling the cognac in his glass. "Takes a bullet through your heart before you'll admit I'm right about anything."

"Well, be fair: you weren't *right* so much as you were pointing to something right," I corrected.

"Uh-huh," he grunted. "Aren't we lucky that bullet missed its mark?"

"Or it wasn't a *silver* bullet."

"Well, there you are," he said, drinking. "I'd be quietly planning my very touching eulogy now instead of enduring your increasingly faint praise."

"I shudder to think what you'd say at my funeral."

"If you like . . ." he offered.

"Not for a thousand dollars," I told him.

The fire settled to gold, the room was warm. Outside the night may have been wet and cold, filled with black dogs and wandering spirits, but there beside the hearth everything was bathed in light and the world seemed finer to me than it had in recent memory.

Fifteen

The next morning I was up and making espresso before I remembered I'd been dead. I'd apparently fallen asleep on the sofa by the fire; Andrews had gone upstairs to bed. The sun was out, seven in the morning, world washed with rain, sky as brilliant as a polished stone. The espresso machine roared; my head was as clear as the air.

Cup in hand, I moved deliberately to the trunk in the back corner, the story my great-grandfather had written. The light wasn't as good there; the western window had not yet been touched by the new sun. Some corners remain dark even on the brightest morning.

I clicked on the nearest lamp, the cold thrill of its touch engendering more memories of Adele. The lamp had been made from a crystal candleholder of hers, a hole up the middle for the power cord, a cheap socket. What had once depended on wax and match now gave illumination with a touch. The age of miracles was safely at hand. But the lead crystal was cold and seemed not to care as much for electric brilliance as candle flame. Its light was characterless and empty.

The trunk complained when I opened the lid. I had reached for the story of the lily so often that it felt odd just to stare down at the contents. Comparison to coffin too obvious, I tried to filter everything I saw and everything I was feeling through my discipline as a field collector. Start from the beginning: What did I see in the trunk? Look at it with new eyes.

I tried conjuring up a memory of the day the trunk arrived, but that was no use. The thing had not been remotely important to me until I had grown a little older and could understand the melancholy poetry of is contents.

I returned my attention to the immediate, taking note, with only a modest embarrassment, of all the burnt sage stems littering the interior. Reading the story always brought ghosts, and the smell of smoldering sage was the only thing that banished them.

Yellow paper, scent of cedar, torn lining where I had looked for the silver pin Conner had made—it was all as familiar as my own face. I wanted what I had always wanted from this casket: answers, some explanation of a certain kind of human nature. What made a man capable of emotion that could not be extinguished—no matter what a woman did? Such inquiry only brought me to more personal questions. Why was my mother incapable of fidelity? What in my father's nature had allowed her to wander? Did I have those same propensities? Was there anything in the trunk or the story that would admit me to the chamber of my own heart, explain some of the dark corners there?

Alas, overwrought self-examination aside, such answers are simply not to be found in furniture. I closed the lid.

Maybe I'd wanted to conjure my great-grandmother's ghost, ask her about the strange community she had founded. I still didn't believe she'd done it, though evidence seemed to support the notion.

But the day was too bright; All Saints' Day, lonely spirits were cast out. Let the dead bury the dead. Once planted, a corpse is best left in the ground. Gloom could not linger. It turned to mist in sunlight and was gone. Even the dark corner where I sat seemed brighter as the sun rose.

"Should you be up?" Andrews stood at the top of the stairs, wrapped in a patchwork quilt, rust and gold against a buttery background.

"I'm fine," I answered, getting to my feet.

"Doubt that." He began his descent, mock regal in his robes.

"I feel better than I have in a year," I insisted, going for more espresso.

"God," he whispered, "look at that sky."

"Coffee?"

"I could *murder* a cup of espresso."

I started the machine, caught my sleeve on its edge, only then realizing what I was wearing.

"Maybe I should change," I said. "I'm still dressed in the clothes I died in."

"And shower," he added. "God knows what voodoo gunk Ms. Deveroe used to swathe your wound. It smelled like a bog."

"I won't be a moment."

I took the stairs three at a time, bounded into the bathroom. Peeling the clothes away, I felt refreshed just standing naked. The water began to steam the room; sun from the window infused it with white luminescence.

The shower was heaven; its warm pounding urged my shoulder muscles to relax, neck knots to untie. For Andrews, I'd put out some guest soaps, an unused Christmas present from some student. They smelled of lavender and honey. In the heat and light, those smells were spring. I was transported. The mountain was covered in new wild primrose, blackberry blossoms, air thick with white song: chickadee, whippoorwill, cardinal.

"Are you staying in there all day?" Andrews's voice from the other side of the door roused me from my reverie.

"Sorry." I turned off the water. "Didn't I just come up here?"

"You've been showering for forty-five minutes!" he called through the wood. "You're clean!"

"Are you sure it's been that long?"

"All right, half an hour," he sighed, "but I'm hungry."

"There's a surprise," I said, grabbing a thick white towel.

"What are the odds," he went on, "that we could lay about today? Do nothing?"

"Not that good," I told him, briskly thrumming my head, drying my hair. "I have to find Truevine; my job's not done yet. And aren't you the least bit curious about who killed Harding Pinhurst?"

"I thought we said Truevine did it," he said. "Accidentally."

"Do you really believe that's what happened?" I wrapped the huge towel around my upper chest; it still dragged on the floor.

I opened the door; the steam spilled out into the hall. Andrews was leaning, back against the wall, staring into his cup.

"Who killed Harding Pinhurst?" He wasn't talking to me. "And who scared Able off that same night, if anyone did?"

"Is it just coincidence that the drunken teenagers stumbled on the body," I continued, moving toward my room, "when the Deveroe boys, who were avidly looking, couldn't?"

"What if it was that black dog?" Andrews's voice grew excited.

"You're an idiot, you know."

"All right," he conceded, "but get dressed, would you. We have to go find Truevine Deveroe."

I stopped in my doorway. "Now all of a sudden you want to find her."

"Dev," he said slowly. "Do you know what I'm thinking?"

"Hardly."

"She may be in some danger." He pulled his left earlobe; his gaze was vacant. "The scarecrow and his dog, that's my theory now. The scarecrow killed Harding; the dog was protecting the girl. But she knows who did it, and she's hiding out from the murderer. And he's looking for her. He wouldn't do anything with all the other home-less people around him, but once he's got her in the woods alone, I'm afraid he might kill her too, keep her from telling Skidmore."

"Completely far-fetched," I pronounced.

But I moved quicker. Out of the towel, into new clothes, a sense of urgency swelled in my chest like the chill of a gunshot wound.

" 'In that sleep of death, what dreams may come,' is that how it goes?" My truck was barreling around the mountain, nearly fifty miles per hour even on the treacherous turns, veering to the edges of high overlooks, a panoramic view of the deep valleys into which the truck would surely plummet. We were careening toward the Deveroe place. We'd already argued about leaving the house. He'd threatened to call the hospital if I set foot out the door. A second shouting match erupted over whether to go to the cemetery or the Deveroe cabin, a third about calling Skidmore. In the end Andrews had been forced to give up in favor of the vibrancy of my enthusiasm and superiority of my weight. We were careening toward the Deveroe cabin, unbeknownst to Deputy Needle.

"Yes, *Hamlet*." Andrews clutched his door handle, grinding his teeth. "Why?"

"When I was out, shot, I had a strange dream." Wanting to dissociate myself from any taint of the previous day, I had found my old black leather jacket. It was good against the wind but left something to be desired in the arena of warmth, so I was also sporting the dark green turtleneck Lucinda had given me for my birthday, and black corduroy pants.

"We should have called Skidmore." He was barely paying attention to my conversation. He'd been less concerned with fashion and appeared to be wearing exactly what he had worn the day before. "Look, I want to get there too, but is it necessary to go this fast?"

"I can usually distract you with a good game of 'Shakespeare Quotes,'" I said, slowing the truck a little.

"I'm in fear for my life."

"Don't you want to hear the dream I had when I was dead?"

"Look," he said, relinquishing the handle and turning my way, struggling with his seat belt. "You've gotten about as much mileage out of the 'when I was dead' game as I can take. Could we leave it be?"

"Sure." I could see out of the corner of my eye he was upset.

"Okay, tell me your damned dream, if you think it's so important."

"That's just it," I told him. "It *is*, somehow."

"Stop the presses." He turned again, squirming in his seat. "Alert the Jung Patrol. Dr. Devilin's had a dream."

"A dream," I went on, ignoring his tantrum, "is a message from the subconscious to the conscious mind, a telegram. I know something that I don't know I know."

"Diction Check."

"My subconscious has taken in some facts that my waking mind has ignored," I explained. "When I was unconscious these facts surfaced, but they came in a code."

"All right," he conceded, "I'll sort of buy that."

"In the form of a ghost story," I went on.

"Appropriate." He was beginning to calm. "So tell."

In shorthand I told him the tale my great-grandmother had given me, the nature witch, the lover called out of his body, the rescue by the blacksmith, the ghostly couple united on All Hallows' Eve.

"Is it a story you already knew?" he asked when I was done.

"Not that I'm aware," I answered.

We were nearing the cabin. I slowed the truck.

"What does it mean?" he said, eyes glued to the door of the Deveroe place.

"What do you think?"

"Too distracted now," he whispered, as if the boys could hear. "Do you really think Truevine came home? Is she in there?"

"We have to eliminate the obvious before we go chasing through the woods again," I said, voice equally still. "I'm not certain how capable I am of a third day romping through the corpse-infested forests of my childhood."

"Which should be the title of your biography."

The cabin was still, even as the truck rolled its last few feet toward the front walk. No shifting of curtain, no crack in the door—not a sign of life.

"Are they hiding?" Andrews wanted to know.

"Not likely. What do you think those boys are afraid of?"

"Nothing in this world."

"Exactly," I agreed. "They're not home."

"Are we getting out?" His voice was barely audible, and he was clutching the door handle again.

"I am." I shoved the door open and was headed for the cabin before Andrews knew what to do.

"Truevine!" I called into the house. "It's Dr. Devilin!"

Helloing the house used to be a common custom in Blue Mountain, in most places in the hills. Always a good idea to let the occupants know you're coming, identify yourself. Sneaking up on a family like the Deveroes could get a body shot, and I'd had enough of that for one week.

The house remained still.

I heard Andrews getting out of the car behind me, but I kept my eye on the front door. I didn't want any unpleasant surprises heading onto the porch.

The first step creaked loudly. I froze, but that didn't take the sound back. I half-expected to see a face in the doorway, but there was still no evidence of occupation.

"Boys?" I called again. "It's just me. And Andrews. No Deputy Needle."

Silence reigned.

"There's no one here," Andrews said, frozen on the walkway somewhere behind me. "Can we go now?"

I turned. "What are you so nervous about?"

"Are you out of your mind?" His voice rose. "These are the people who shot you last night!"

"They didn't mean to," I explained reasonably.

"Oh my *God*."

"They didn't even know we were in the Newcomb place." I stepped up onto the porch, went to the window. "Do you really think they would have shot into the house if they'd known their sister was inside?"

He paused. "Good point."

I put my hand over my eyebrows and pressed my nose to the window, hoping to see through the opaque curtains into the cabin. I could only see shapes and shadows. Nothing was moving.

"Should I check the door?" I said, still gazing in the window.

"No, Christ!"

"Hey." I turned to him. "Come up here. You've got to feel this thing at the doorway. The geothermal shot."

"Not for a thousand dollars," he said, not budging, "to coin your phrase."

"Come on," I urged. "It's really—" My words stopped short when my eye fell on what was arranged neatly in the sunniest part of the porch corner.

"What is it?" Andrews asked urgently. "Do you see them?" He readied himself to run.

"No."

Standing in the corner were two clay pots planted with sedge and contorted hazel, ringed in dried weeds, as well as a wooden bowl of water, a smooth black river rock, and a dead salamander.

"You've got to see this." I moved toward the arrangement.

"I'm not putting my hand in some blast of hot air," he insisted, "just for your amusement."

"Not that," I said, inching closer to the sunny corner, eyes locked on it. "There's something on the porch."

"What is it?"

"It's a collection of things," I said, bending down, "from the dream I was telling you about."

That was enough. He started toward me. "What do you mean?"

"The exact phrase my great-grandmother used," I said to Andrews, "was 'sedge and hazel, weed and water, rock and salamander.'"

"You remember it that precisely?" He took the steps, staring down at the circle of weeds. "You know, I think this is weed."

"Unusual in Truevine's garden," I admitted. "There's not a weed anywhere. It must have come from the hillside up there."

"No, Grandpa," he chided. "*Weed*, pot, grass, marijuana."

"What?" I peered down at it.

"If memory serves," he assured me, "that's what it looks like."

"Hemp!"

"I guess some people call it that." He eyed me sidelong.

"I didn't tell you about the hemp circle the girl made in the story," I said, my words quickening. "That's what brought her lover's spirit from Baffin Bay to her side."

"So you're saying all this stuff was in your dream just like this?"

I stared down. "Something like it."

"Well, you don't need to sound so spooky about it," Andrews said calmly. "It was here when you came to visit the boys the other day.

You said yourself that you may have seen something your conscious mind took in but didn't register." He dismissed the assemblage in the corner with a flourish of his hand. "Exhibit A."

"Oh." I let out the breath I'd been holding for a while. "You know, I might have." I saw the things with new eyes. "In fact, this stone? Could be one I picked up when Dover dragged me. So why did this gunk come up in the dream?"

"You understand this conglomeration," he said slowly, "is a not unlike the assemblage of stones and trash in the corner of the *Adele* crypt."

"It is."

"And anyway, why would these particular things manifest in your subconscious? Why hemp, for instance?"

"Wild hemp," I answered him, "not the smoking kind, the rope-making variety, grows as a weed here. The symbology is clear: the plant that makes rope works in a spell of binding."

"Makes sense," he admitted, "in context." He bit his lower lip. "Hang on." His voice picked up. "You mean this is the spell from your dream. Truevine was trying to call back her lover's departed spirit—something she said in the Newcomb mansion."

"She thought Able was dead," I agreed. "She believed this would bring him back to her." I nudged the stone with my toe. "And it did."

"You've got an idea," he said, watching the side of my face. "You know something."

The brothers being nowhere to be found, I told Andrews we were going to speak with Hezekiah Cotage. His church was not far away. We'd clear up a few things about his past, and I'd order them in my mind. Andrews didn't understand, but he'd chosen to give up thinking too hard.

The church, a white box in the middle of the woods, gleamed in the slant of autumn sunlight. All the saints of the day had apparently decided to look in on Hek: the grace of illumination, the air, a carpet of surrounding burgundy leaves, made the plain little building seem a cathedral. We pulled up close to the door. There were no other cars.

Inside voices were lifted in song, page 65 from the new 1991 edition of the Sacred Harp book, *Sweet Prospect*. "Oh, the transporting rapt'rous scene that rises to my eye, Sweet fields arrayed in living green And rivers of delight."

Andrews and I sat in the truck, unwilling to disturb the sound as it wrapped around us like a clean autumn wind, bracing, washing away darker thought.

The singing ended. A moment later an older couple appeared in the doorway; affectless and slow. They moved without speaking onto the path that wandered down the mountain. One by one the rest of the parishioners exited the church. I got out of the truck.

Hek came to the door.

"I thought I heard your truck," he said. "Is that Dr. Andrews?"

Andrews got out the passenger side, waved.

"You missed the service," Hek said.

"We heard the last song, though," Andrews said, shaking his head. "I still can't get used to that harmonic structure; it's very strange."

"Simple," Hek said proudly. "Ancient harmony."

"Have you ever recorded that stuff?" Andrews asked me.

"There certainly are recordings of the music," I said, "lots of good ones, but when I hear them I'm always a little disappointed. It's impossible to capture the feeling of that sound."

"You have to be in church," Hek agreed, "to hear those hymns right. You want to come in, talk?"

"I do," I answered.

"Thought so." He disappeared back into the church.

We followed.

"You mow the lawn since I was here last?" Andrews asked, teasing. It had been over a year since his most recent visit. "The place looks cleaner."

"Got a new paint job," Hek said, not looking back over his shoulder. "New roof."

"Collection plate must be full," Andrews said, looking around the inside of the place.

"All donated," Hek said absently.

Walls were whitewashed; benches were sturdy; the floor was worn but swept clean. Windows were clear; light poured in like honey. At the far end of the tabernacle was a stone bowl that served as baptismal font and the starting place for Hek's wild, rambling sermons.

That bowl had once been at the center of controversy: was it an imitation artifact or the holy grail? To the faithful it was a sacred relic; to a doubting academic community it was simply an aberration. Time had rolled over those troubles like a river and all had been washed clean. The congregation still came to church, Hek still handled snakes and promised a fiery hell without God. A rage of contention had scoured the church. In the end Hek cared for his flock and they believed the word. That was enough.

"Hek," I began, unable to take my eyes off the golden floor, "I have something I want to ask you. It may be uncomfortable."

"If you want me to wait outside . . ." Andrews offered.

"Nothing is hidden from God," Hek said quietly.

He took the aisle seat on the first bench. I sat opposite him, Andrews lingered farther back.

"I've put two and two together," I began.

"Hope you got four," Hek said evenly, eyes locked on mine.

"And I've spoken with May."

I stopped, let that sink in for a moment. Silence was kind, softening every thought.

"May," he said at last, a sigh.

"She gave you that piece of cloth in the graveyard the other day."

"She did."

"Why didn't you tell me that?" I leaned in, closer to him.

"June don't know about that part of my life," he answered, dulcet tones. "She had enough suffering when I was gone; I always thought it best to leave out that part of my story. Seemed right: let the dead bury the dead."

"A thought which has occurred to me a lot lately," I assured him.

He let out a long sigh. "Good. I was afraid you had some notion to tell June, tell the deputy about them people up there." He lowered his voice. "I still take a basket of food or such up yonder every now and again."

"I know."

"Always glad to see May's still around. See her every year about this time."

"She's migrating." I saw her face in firelight. "Moving south from Chicago."

"But not to Florida," he added, a gleam in his eye.

"I believe she has a little crush on you."

He blushed. "Shoot."

"Hek," I said, my voice stronger, "you deliberately told me about seeing some mysterious apparition in the graveyard and taking that cloth from her. You wanted to make me curious, investigate, maybe find May and the others."

"I did."

"You didn't want to tell me about them, but you wanted me to find them."

"Correct."

"Why?" I folded my hands, waited for an answer.

"Truevine." That was all.

He stood.

"Wait," Andrews jumped in. "That's not nearly enough."

"It's all I care to say," Hek said solidly. "Got to get on home. June'll be waiting."

"You wanted me to find Truevine," I said, following him as he strode toward the door.

"And?"

I stopped. He was testing me. Sometimes he, along with a handful of older men in town, wanted to prove they were just as smart as someone with a university education. Hek had done it to me many times before.

"There's something more you wanted me to find up there." I started after him again.

"Besides the hobo camp?" Andrews asked me.

"Something to do with the murder," I said louder.

Hek was through the door without looking back.

"Why doesn't he just tell you?" Andrews fumed. "Why does everyone up here think that telling you anything is like a mortal sin?"

"Frustrating, isn't it," I commiserated, smiling.

"But it doesn't matter to you," he said, calming, "because he confirmed something in your mind. I know that look." He shifted, sighing through clenched teeth. "You're as bad as he is. You not going to tell me what you're thinking, are you?"

"I'm just thinking. It could be nothing. But I've decided we shouldn't proceed any further without at least trying to speak to Skidmore. I suspect he might already be gone into the woods looking for Truevine again. Maybe that's the reason no one was home at the Deveroe household."

I headed the truck for Skidmore's office.

Andrews glanced at his watch. "It's after ten. You don't think he'll be in his office."

"No, but somebody may tell us where he went. We could catch up with him." I looked up at the polished mirror of the sky. "Nice day for it."

My old green truck took the last corner of downhill road comfortably, slowed coming onto the blacktop. Everything seemed clearer than it had the day before, crisp air focused, a window wiped clean. The fields, tan sheaves of corn, golden rolls of hay, bore no resemblance to the dreary gray rags we'd seen in the rain.

In town, the police station appeared empty. We pulled into a spot right in front of the door. There was a note. I climbed out; Andrews stayed put.

" 'Dr. Devilin,' " I read aloud from the note written in Skidmore's hand, " 'you might join me at the mortuary if you read this note before noon.' "

He hadn't signed it. I peeled the Scotch tape, crumpled the note, stuck it in the soft leather coat pocket.

"Let's go to the mortuary."

"Great." Andrews slumped. "I suppose it's too late for breakfast at Etta's."

"She stops serving at eight."

"And luncheon is not served . . ." he began.

". . . until eleven," I finished.

"Fine." He gazed longingly at the dark diner's window.

The open sky seemed reflected everywhere, in the glass behind the word *Etta's,* on the hood of the Ford; even the road glistened glass beads of sunlight.

"The world looks different this morning." I couldn't keep the notion from lifting the corners of my mouth. "Town looks nice."

"What's different," Andrews mumbled, "is that we haven't seen a living soul. Diner's closed; police station's closed; no one's on the street. Body snatchers, that's my guess."

I eased off the accelerator. He was right; there was no one around. Gil's was vacant; the few cars parked around were empty and still. No one was walking. It would have been just as odd, of course, to see a flurry of activity in our quiet hamlet, but everything suddenly seemed as abandoned as the Newcomb mansion.

"No one at Gil's," I told Andrews, nodding in its direction.

He stared silently, eyes widening. He knew what it meant for that place to be empty: it was possible the world had come to an end and Andrews and I were the last to know.

The mortuary was surrounded. A hundred cars, police sedans, state trooper vehicles, news vans, old Chevy station wagons, new Mercedes coups. We had to park off the road.

"Mystery solved," Andrews told me climbing out of the cab. "Everyone in the county is *here.*"

"Looks like it." I followed close behind him. "Must be some news story about the bodies, finally."

"But would everyone in town be here for that?" He tried to see around the house. Still no sight of anyone.

"Absolutely," I confirmed. "If there's a big wreck on the highway, we all come out to look."

Without warning, the front door of the mortuary burst open and a crowd of reporters erupted onto the porch. The first people out were running to their cars and vans, some shouting into cell phones. The next wave included familiar faces, merchants and town people, moving slower, wagging heads.

Behind them all Skid stood in the doorway.

He watched the chaos, caught sight of us, beckoned.

We moved through the throng, denying eye contact to anyone, onto the steps.

"I guess your story broke," I said, gazing out over the frenzy.

"Just finished my news conference," Skid affirmed. "Look at 'em go."

"This won't do your election any harm," Andrews said sagely.

"Any publicity is good publicity," Skid sighed, "is what Mr. Tineeta says. Come on in."

He turned and stepped over the threshold, into the relative darkness of the front room of the mortuary.

Door closed, silence was cotton to the ear.

"Body count," Skid began with no ceremony, leading us toward the back rooms, "is up in the three hundreds now."

"Jesus," Andrews said softly.

"How could it be that no one knew about this?" I said as we came to the door I'd found locked from within.

"That was one of the questions at my news conference," Skid said, enjoying the phrase a little too much for my taste. "The fact is, people did know about it. Just not the right people."

"Deveroes," Andrews stated flatly.

"The people who live up at the cemetery," I whispered, afraid someone might overhear.

"They don't live there," Skid corrected at a normal volume.

"They're only passing through. That's why we call them transients."

"Is that what we call them?" I gave him a sidelong glance, returned my attention to the locked door before us. "I probably should have told you this before. I didn't just discover the trapdoor to that room; I broke into it. The one that's . . ."

". . . locked from the inside?" Skid finished calmly.

"It wasn't hard to get in," I told him. "Got a knife from the kitchen, lifted the hook."

"So you know it don't look a thing like the other lab." He pointed to the cleanest room any of us had ever seen.

"Right. So you've gotten in."

"Through the trapdoor in the cellar you told me about." Skid leaned against the wall.

"Would someone *please* tell me . . ." Andrews fumed.

"Near as I can piece together," Skid told us, his voice veering dangerously close to the official, "Harding Pinhurst was never a mortician."

Andrews and I exchanged a questioning look.

"Didn't have a license, never filed a death certificate, a single burial record, nothing."

"How is that possible?" Andrews folded his arms.

"Harding's Uncle Jackson made him take this job," I guessed. "Set it all up."

Skid grinned. "Damn, you're pretty good."

"Why do I know that name?" Andrews said to himself.

"Rud said it," I answered.

"The man who made Rud take the caretaker's job." Andrews's eyes lit. "He's the godfather of Blue Mountain."

"Harding had him a few boys he'd hire to take the bodies out to the state woods," Skidmore went on. "Guess who?"

"Deveroes," Andrews shot back.

"They don't do *everything*," Skid chastised.

"They shot our boy, here," Andrews said, tilting his head my way. "That's enough for me."

"Didn't mean to," Skid said.

"The boys who found Harding's body Saturday morning," I interrupted, "are the ones he hired to dispose of his customers."

"Batting a thousand today," Skid said, impressed.

"Those drunken teenagers?" Andrews asked, trying to understand it.

"So they could have known about the enmity between Harding and Able," I went on.

"Which is why they were so eager to accuse Able that day," Andrews concluded. "Or did they even have something to do with the murder?"

"Don't know," Skid said slowly. "But I do believe they were looking for a place to dump more bodies when they found Harding."

"Christ!" Andrews said. "That close to Dev's *house?*"

"How long has this been going on?" I asked Skid. "How many years has it been since Harding took over the mortuary?"

"What's that, five years?"

"For that long he's been throwing corpses into the woods," Andrews said, "and no one's known?"

"I was saying that the transients up at the cemetery knew," Skid allowed. "And, of course, the Deveroes, all of them."

"Truevine knew." I stared at the wall beside me.

"The bodies were all covered up with red clay," Skid went on, "and pine straw, impossible to see—or smell. Until recently."

"Red clay has the additional benefit," I declared, "of being acidic, increasing the decay rate of the bodies."

"This doesn't make any sense," Andrews said.

I assumed from the falter in his voice he was trying to get his mind around the facts as much as I was.

"It seems like as much trouble to do . . . what he did," Andrews continued, "as it would have been just to bury the bodies the right way."

"It's hard to figure," Skid admitted.

"You said 'until recently.'" My eyes narrowed. "What changed?"

"It appears," Skid told me, "that Harding was planning to do something new with the bodies. He uncovered a bunch of them, rented some earthmoving equipment, and had it brought here."

"To the mortuary?" Andrews shook his head.

"No, to the state land," Skid said, casting his eyes in that direction. "Turns out Jackson Pinhurst has been working on a deal with the state of Georgia for a good many years. It finally went through. That government property over yonder? It ain't set to be a park like everybody thought. It's going to be Georgia's biggest landfill operation, all three hundred acres."

"No." I looked up.

"Disgusting, I call it." Skid seemed very calm under the circumstances. "Trash from all over the state shipped up here to my town."

"You're not so upset about it," Andrews said accusingly. "You've got something up your sleeve."

"I do—"

"One thing at a time," I interrupted. "For God's sake tell me what's been going on here at the mortuary."

"Far as we can tell," Skid responded, "Harding spent all his time drinking, messing around in Atlanta, that sort of thing. He's definitely not a mortician. He had no education of any sort after his prep school days. Apparently the family wanted him to go to college, but he didn't get in—on the recommendation of the headmaster of his prep school."

"The headmaster recommended that he *not* be admitted?" Andrews asked.

"The mortuary, please, is our topic," I said impatiently.

"Shoot," Skid laughed, looking around the place. "This ain't a mortuary. It's a big old house—where over three hundred counts of fraud were perpetrated on the public."

"But *why?*" I said. "That's what I want to know. Why did Harding do it?"

"He was insane," Andrews offered. "All that family inbreeding and bad blood."

"Harding Pinhurst didn't give a damn about anything in this world," Skid said, cold as the grave. "Dev, you probably don't even remember an incident when we were in grammar school about some little bird eggs . . ."

". . . where Harding broke one open in front of a bunch of other boys," Andrews finished, a little amazed that he was remembering the story.

"I always thought, after that incident," Skid went on, "Harding would come to no good. Which is apparently what happened."

"Do you remember the nickname our friend acquired after that?" Andrews asked Skidmore.

"Nickname?" Skid's brow furled. "*Fever* isn't bad enough all by itself?"

"There you have it." Andrews turned to me. "You're the only one who remembers the nickname. But everyone remembers Harding's bad behavior."

"They'll remember it a lot better after today," Skidmore said, taking another look around the empty mortuary.

"Amen," Andrews said. "So who killed him?"

"Dev?" Skid looked at me.

"Andrews thinks it was one of the nameless homeless," I began, "the one who calls the dog sometimes."

"Scarecrow," Andrews chimed in, "we call him."

"I know who you mean," Skid sighed. "He does look like that. What makes you think he did it?"

"He's creepy," Andrews said without thinking.

"He's harmless enough," Skidmore said, but his voice was very dry, his eyes boring a hole in my head.

"I'm more interested in finding Ms. Deveroe," I said, avoiding Skidmore's burning glare. "Andrews also has the idea that she's in danger. I agree."

"She saw the murder," Skid agreed, "and whoever did it is still out there."

"Good," I sighed. "So you don't think Able's guilty."

"Not really."

"And now we don't think Truevine did it either?" Andrews asked, checking.

"I keep asking myself how the body got naked," Skid mused.

"I have an idea about that," I said, nearly to myself.

"I don't like to think about it," Skid went on. "It's clear that Able was about to have Harding brought up on charges for all this mess here. Although Able didn't know the extent of the problem."

"Harding knew how close he was to getting arrested," Andrews said, his hand raking the part in his hair. "Able and Truevine argued; Harding overheard, knew it was all coming down . . ." Andrews stopped.

"What?" I asked him, wondering why he hadn't finished his thought.

"Now," he answered slowly, "I'm back to thinking Able did it. Or Truevine, accidentally—what we were thinking earlier."

"Something happened that night," Skid said, "that was sufficiently traumatic as to scare Able and Truevine fairly bad. Make them act stranger than they normally do."

"Which is going some for her," Andrews said. "Although she does seem the sort to be frightened of a shadow if she attaches some supernatural import to it. But Able's more levelheaded, isn't he?"

Skid pushed off the wall. "Okay." He headed toward the back door, through the kitchen.

"Where are you going?" Andrews asked, surprised.

"I think I've given the reporters and townsfolk enough time to clear out," Skid said, pulling his coat around him. "State troopers have a sufficient number of things to do." He held the door for us, beckoned. "Time to let Dr. Devilin have his way. He's got ideas. I'd like to see what they are."

"If you can goad them out of him," Andrews complained, "you're a better man than I am. He's got the town disease: genetically incapable of discussing anything important, don't you think?"

"I'd rather not say," Skid deadpanned, pushed the door a little farther.

"You're a riot." Andrews looked to me.

"But I'm right about Dev," Skid said softly. "Look at his face."

I buttoned my coat.

"All right," I said, mind spinning like a carnival pinwheel, "let's go."

Sixteen

Sun was beginning to warm the air; a cloudless sky allowed light to flood the tops of hills. Still, down in the hollows where the dead bodies were it was cold and dark as dusk. We alternated between these two worlds, walking up into the light, down toward darkness, over little rises. If walking was good for clarity of mind, it was also a quicker way to the cemetery than driving from the mortuary.

"Where are we going?" Andrews asked suspiciously. He was game, but he enjoyed his whining.

"I'd like another visit with our friends in the *Adele* community," I said. "I want to check in on Billy."

"Who?" Andrews asked, stumbling behind us.

"The sick boy by the fire, remember?"

"Oh," he remembered. "Right. Why?"

"I want to see what he's wearing."

I took the silence behind me to be a form of derision.

"I have about a hundred ideas shooting around up here," I told them without looking back, rubbing my temple, "and it would be better if I didn't struggle to verbalize them until I have something concrete to show you both; would that be all right?"

More silence trailed me.

I marched perhaps ten feet in front of the other two along a path I thought would avoid stray state troopers and further grisly discovery. The shushing of leaves urged the quiet, emphasized it, imitated the sound of rushing water.

The last ridge taken, our most populated graveyard came into view. Touched by sunlight, scrubbed by the first day of November, it seemed a village, a picturesque Disney impersonation of a cemetery.

Down the barely discernible path, toward the center of the larger crypts, I stopped short, taking it all in, waiting for my companions to catch up.

"See something?" Skid said softly, straining his eyes over the gray and brown.

"I'm looking," I said hesitantly, "but I can't tell where the so-called *Adele* crypt is. It all looks different in sunlight."

"Like a park," Andrews agreed, pulling up beside me. "I think it's that way." His hand waved indefinitely.

I turned to Skid. "You know, don't you?"

"I usually just go to Rud's cabin," he answered uncertainly. "This place is always confusing to me."

"Let's go on until we're attacked by a big black dog," Andrews said dryly. "Then we'll know we're on the right track."

"Excellent," I agreed. "Lead the way."

"Shut up."

"It's got to be one of those." I pointed to the group of eight or nine large stone crypts not a hundred yards away.

"Seems right." Andrews held his ground.

"Come on." I started in that direction.

Down the slope the scene was no more familiar. It seemed I hadn't been in the place for years. Bronze sun poured over everything, softening gray wreckage to blue statuary, black moss to green decoration. Even waterless brown hulls of weed waved sweetly in the clear cold water breeze.

Luck, then, was our only ally. A voice to our right turned our heads.

"Finally," May said exasperatedly.

She was beckoning us around a low wall, her neck wrapped in June's cloth, a shawl we had not seen before over her shoulders. She turned; we followed.

Between tumbled gravestones and small marble vaults, the familiar doorway appeared. In the clear noon I found it quite attractive, ornate deco ironwork in the upper corners, relief carvings of peaceful angels adorning the front wall.

May was already through the door.

"Hold it," Skid said.

He took the lead, hand on his holster.

"What are you doing?" I said, laughter edging the words.

"You think the Deveroe boys might be around?" he said, peering into the darkness.

Biology chose that moment to release me from the protective cocoon of shock that had supported me for twelve hours. My knees gave way like hinges; my head narrowly avoided a jagged tombstone. I plunged into darkness.

I woke up with fire in my face.

Low coals glowing red and white three feet from my face startled me, I jerked backward, felt cradling arms.

"Sh," she said. "It's all right. You're safe."

Truevine held my head with such tenderness I felt a pinch in the corners of my eyes.

Andrews was sitting next to us; Skid stood close at hand. Other faces, sweet, soot-covered, sad, held me in their gaze.

"He shouldn't be out," Truevine said softly, petting my forehead. "After what happened to him."

"I told him," Andrews said tightly. "Try making that man do something he doesn't want to do."

"Can't be done," Skid confirmed.

"What are you doing here?" I gazed up at Truevine's version of the Madonna.

"Hiding from you'uns," she said matter-of-factly.

"She come to look after Billy."

I couldn't see who had spoken, but it was the scarecrow's voice.

"Billy." I sat up. "How is he?"

The room was exactly as it had been before, orange and red, dark and warm, huddled, lonely, strange. Among the living faces I could clearly see the ghost of my great-grandmother, driven into the forest by wild heartbreak, losing the man she loved, knowing he didn't love her. How had her mind turned, digging up her husband's grave to snatch the memento of his true love from lifeless fingers? What had been her plan? Or is madness primarily defined by its lack of maps? Founding an invisible homeless shelter had certainly not been her design; that was clear from the vacant look on her face. She was staring toward the arrangement of items in the corner, the geode where the little silver lily lay. I could barely see her through the smoke, but I was certain she was there, gazing into the darker shadows.

"Billy's gone," the scarecrow choked.

Only then did I notice the bundle across the coals from me. A breathless heap, his face still exposed, Billy stared into the warmth without expression.

"I was too late," Truevine said, without a hint of sadness. "Billy's done now. Gone home."

I reached toward him absently, then looked up, found the scarecrow's face.

"I'm sorry for your loss."

"He's past caring," the man said, hollow, eyes vacant. "Excuse me. I got to step outside a moment."

I watched him go, then scanned the room for the dog.

"Where's your pet?" I asked Truevine.

"Dog?" She smoothed her dress where I'd been lying. "He's not my pet; he belongs to himself."

"It's not around," I tried to confirm.

"Can't say," she answered, sighing. She seemed sleepy or drugged.

"I passed out?" I checked with Andrews.

"Only a second ago." He stared down. "We barely got you inside, she took your head; you woke up. It happened in nothing flat."

Gaining focus, I gave further search for other players. Rud was not in evidence.

"Once again," I addressed May, "you were waiting for me?"

"She thought you'd probably find her," May answered, indicating Truevine. "Knew you were headed this way, came anyway to help Billy. She's a good girl."

"Where did you find Ms. Deveroe," Skid asked, his voice seeming harsh compared to everyone else's, "to get her here?"

"In the woods," May told him serenely. "I know a thing or two."

"Truevine," I said, trying to get her to look at me, "you saved my life last night."

"That I did," she answered. "I'll expect something back."

"I know."

Hard laws of retribution and fairness were etched into us both by the mountain, the air, our parents, our different churches—hers was a green cathedral, mine came with a card catalog, but they were our religious homes nonetheless. It was clear to both of us that I owed her a debt, one I would pay without question. No matter that her service to me had been mostly in her mind, partly in a certain esoteric knowledge of plants.

"I've been studying on Harding Pinhurst," she went on, "and I believe I know what happened now. Last Thursday night."

"Ma'am," Skid said, still hard, "I'd like to hear about that."

"All right." She shifted in her seat. The color of the coals flushed her face rich with warmth; her eyes were far away, at peace.

She was not wearing the black cloak we'd seen the night before. A plain dark dress, heavy gray sweater, a man's black construction boots, and thick gray socks were her costume. She'd changed clothes.

"You've been home," I said simply.

"Followed the boys," she assented. "Give them a piece of my mind about shooting into the old mansion. They're a cussed bunch sometimes, and that kitchen's a mess."

"They were happy to see you."

"Not when I told them they'd shot you dead."

"Are they home now?" Skid interrupted.

"No," Andrews, Truevine, and I answered as one.

"You went by there this morning before you came to my office," Skid accused me.

"They weren't there," I dismissed him, and turned back to the girl. "But I saw your charm on the porch."

"It was a good'un." Her face tensed a little. "That was the problem.

I thought I would bring Able back from the dead, but he wasn't dead after all. So it just messed things up."

I didn't know if her brothers had confessed to hanging her boyfriend or not. Best leave that a family matter, but I thought perhaps her charm had worked better than she realized. I turned my full attention to the subject.

"It brought Able to you in some other way," I coaxed her.

"In the Newcomb mansion." She nodded. "Last night. That's when I knew what happened. Able's not dead, and thank God for it. But I don't know if this is worse."

"What's worse?" Skid stepped in closer.

"Able was trying to protect me," she said, her voice losing its gentle lilt. "He didn't mean it. I believe he pushed Harding down that hill." She looked Skidmore in the eye at last. "That's not murder. You see that. He was saving my life."

"You think Harding was trying to kill you?" Skid's voice finally softened.

"He wanted to, yes."

"Why?" Skid knelt down next to her.

"Well, because I'm the one told Able what Harding was doing with them bodies."

Truevine Deveroe, in her daily exploration of her mountain, learned new things every day. She had barely gone to school, but the university of geography had tutored her mightily. She knew every inch of the terrain within ten miles of her house, in any direction. She knew plants that had no names, lizards that were unique to our county, mosses that grew under granite. Her mother had fostered this education, passing on information from women whose knowledge could trace roots to the beginning of European culture. For millennia these women and thousands like them had guarded nature, protecting its secrets from men, keeping facts about their earth from being forgotten. It was a kind of knowledge I had thought vanished from the earth. Listening to Truevine talk about what her mother had taught her, I thought there might be a drop of true folklore left to be squeezed from Appalachia yet. A great vindication of my academic study washed over me. Such was not Truevine's point, of course. She simply wanted to assure us all that finding dead bodies—animal, plant, human—was as natural to her as coming across a fallen tree. But she'd been greatly disturbed by sheer numbers in the section of her domain close to the mortuary. For several years she simply avoided the area. A casual word slipped here and there in conversation meant only for his ears had alerted Able's suspicions. He'd finally investigated. They'd fought about the subject more than once, the last time on the night in question.

"Able was going to file charges." She squinted. "Harding was a no-account, but he's kin. I asked Able not to do it. Lordy, we fought. He's a strong-willed man."

"The point is," Skidmore said impatiently, "that you think Harding somehow knew you were the one who told Able."

"He knew." She gave s single nod.

"How did he find you over there by Dr. Devilin's house last Thursday?"

"I told him to meet me and Able at the new church hall that night," she said, unable to fathom that we hadn't known that fact. "That's why we was waiting outside."

"For Harding." I moved closer to her, sensing something in her voice.

"But he never came before I got mad and run off. Or at least that's what I thought." She stared off again. "But he must have been standing by, and heard. I lit out; Harding came after me. Able not much later."

"We heard him say he wasn't going to chase after you." Andrews folded his arms, glaring down.

"What accounts for your amazing powers of memory?" I asked him.

"A background in theatre," he shot back, "and single malt scotch."

"But he did," Truevine managed to get in. "Able did come for me. Wish to God he hadn't."

"Because you believe, now, that Able attacked Harding to keep him from killing you." Skid was no more receptive to the idea than Andrews had been.

"That's what's in my head."

"But you told us before that you had popped out of your body." Andrews assumed the tone he'd used on May.

"I did," Truevine said, shifting uncomfortably.

"And then yesterday you thought you'd killed Able." Skid leaned closer to her. "Why are you coming up with this new mess now?"

"Leave her alone!" May barked, sensing a growing tension in the room.

Still a little thickheaded, I used the distraction of her voice to shoot my hand to Billy's blanket, toss it back.

Billy had on layers of clothes given him to keep him warm. The top layer consisted of a very fine tweed jacket; Marks and Spencers was my guess. The pants were gray wool, pleated, too large for Billy's frame. It was the kind of outfit a young man in our town would wear to a church meeting.

"What the hell are you doing?" Andrews stammered, stepping back from the body.

It seemed to me he was just coming to grips with the notion that it was a corpse. After what we'd seen in the woods, Billy's last remains were nothing.

"I believe if you check you'll find that coat and pants belonged to Harding," I said to Skid. "That's the only reason Harding was found naked. Someone wanted to keep Billy warm."

The boy was pencil thin, chalky white dry skin red in patches. It was possible he'd died from a simple combination of pneumonia and dehydration.

Truevine had done her best, comforting him, giving him a salve for his itchy rash. He'd died without speaking. She told us she was happy for him; his suffering was done. That night he would walk in sweet fields arrayed in living green by rivers of delight.

Skidmore'd been the one to put a hand inside the nice tweed coat and read the words *handcrafted by Winton Pfife for Harding Pinhurst III.*

"Who gave Billy these clothes?" He looked around the room carefully, then addressed me.

"Of course," Andrews realized, "there's no reason you would know that the scarecrow was Billy's chum."

"Is that true?" Skid asked May. "He and this boy travel together?" She avoided his eyes.

I rubbed my eyes, still a little weak. The light was dim, shadows amber and rust-colored. May sat by Billy's feet, avoiding my stare.

"Someone's missing," I began, "besides Rud—an old man, barely said anything, vacant stare."

"Left early this morning," May muttered. "He didn't talk much."

"Someone left?" Skid said, eyes on May. "How long ago?"

"Sun came out today and it looked like good walking weather. He'll make it to . . . what's that town where they pan for gold still?"

"Dahlonega."

"It is my belief," May pronounced, "that's where he'll be."

"How was he dressed?" Skid sighed, taking out a small spiral pad and a pencil.

"He had new sneakers." May grinned.

"I've noticed," Skid said to her, "that everyone does." He knew where they'd come from.

"He had whiskers," Andrews chimed in. "And if you tell your cohorts to look for a bearded zombie in new shoes I guarantee he's the one they'll pick up."

"He did bear a lifeless eye," I agreed, getting to my feet.

"Description," Skid insisted, glaring at May.

It occurred to me then that Skid was in his policeman's mode and may have seen all the residents of *Adele* as potential problems, whereas I saw them more as members of a community. Theirs were cold relationships, borne of necessity, fear, privation, but something about the bond they forged—as much to the place as to one another—was meaningful.

"Sorry I brought it up," I said slowly, "about the old man. I think the scarecrow is a greater concern, don't you? He just lit out of here."

"Damn it." Skid moved quickly toward the entrance. He poked his head out, looked around, confirmed his suspicion.

"There you are," Andrews said plainly, "as I've said all along: the scarecrow did it."

"I'm not eliminating the old man!" Skid shot back.

"That guy?" Andrews shook his head. "He couldn't snap a twig; he'd never muscle an angry man fifty years his junior."

"Maybe," Skid said, slowing, "but I got to have him picked up."

"It was the scarecrow," Andrews said emphatically, "and he's escaped!"

"Stop calling him that," May said softly.

"We don't know his name," Andrews shot back. "You don't give out names here."

"You don't listen," she mumbled, staring into the coals. "People don't listen to us."

"Do you know his name, May?" Skid demanded.

"Maybe I do and maybe I don't," she said stubbornly, not looking up.

"I don't have time to argue with you now," Skid said, shoving his pad and pencil back into a pocket. "He can't have got far." He took off for the door.

"Do you have a motive in mind," I began, "for his killing Harding?"

"You don't think Harding had a wallet in those nice wool pants Billy's wearing?" Skid said from the entrance gate. "It's gone. I checked every pocket."

"You did?" Andrews said, impressed. "What are you, like a magician? I never saw a thing."

"I have to go out there and find that man," Skid said again, slower. "Maybe he didn't mean to kill Harding. But the wallet, the money, that could be a motive."

"But you're not running after him," Andrews said.

"I need more help," he said, staring out over the graveyard. "Plus I have to take Truevine in, call an ambulance for Billy."

"Not sure about this robbery motive," I ventured. "Does it sound all that plausible that the scarecrow was lurking in the woods at night on the off-chance someone might happen along with a wallet?"

"I can't make up my mind," Skid said, embarrassed to admit it. "But I'm not going off half-cocked, chasing through the cemetery again. Not without I think it out a minute."

"'Some sudden qualm hath struck you at the heart,'" Andrews quoted, "'and dimmed your eyes, that you can read no further.'"

"*Hamlet,*" I guessed. "It's a play about a man who can't make up his mind."

"*Henry VI, Part II,*" Andrews corrected. "You quoted it earlier."

"I did?"

"Deputy Needle, here, is struck with a qualm," Andrews repeated. "Now he doesn't think the scarecrow did it."

Blue Mountain is a small town, not sophisticated. For example, its deputies are not issued personal body radios the way some servants of a larger municipality might be. We had to walk back to the mortuary where Skid's car was parked. We had to call the hospital for Billy's body, the state troopers for help in finding our suspect, and of course we needed the car to take Truevine to jail.

She was in custody, though that word was too strong for her circumstance: no handcuffs, no harsh words. Skid simply asked her if she'd mind coming into town to visit Able. She came silently, Mona Lisa smile and all.

Andrews wondered why we didn't just go to Rud's cabin, break in if he wasn't there, and make calls. Skid told him that Rud had no phone, which Andrews found impossible to believe, twice asking me what century I thought it was. It made for an amusing walk back.

I tried to engage Truevine in a more useful conversation.

"Thank you for helping me the other night," I opened. "And just now."

"It's all right."

"You know the moss you used to help stanch my wound is something in which the medical community would be quite interested."

"No, they wouldn't," she said softly. "What'd make them listen to a dumb old country girl? Best just keep all that nonsense to myself. That's what Able says."

"I see."

"He's smart."

"Able's concerned for your reputation," I told her as gently as I could. "Isn't that one of the things you were fighting about the other night?"

"Shoot, Dr. Devilin," she laughed, "you're not so old you don't know young'uns argue when they're in love. Didn't you ever fight with Lucinda? She's real sweet. You know you ought to marry that'un."

"That's the consensus," I agreed, "but I'm more interested in you. Able doesn't want you to make too many spells anymore. Wants to save your position in the community."

"Able wants a normal wife and family," she said, swallowing, remembering a speech she'd heard, it seemed to me. "The things people say about my life'll be forgot in time if I let go of the ways."

"The ways your mother taught you about plants and stones and animals in the woods, you mean."

"Yes, sir."

"Truevine." I slowed a little. "It's my opinion that if you forget those things, then something important will go out of the world. It would be a poorer place. I like you just fine the way you are."

"Well, thank you, Dr. Devilin," she answered sweetly. "That's a plenty coming from such as you. But I know why you say it."

"Why's that?" I asked.

"You're just like me. You have *ways* too."

"Well, you're right, in a way," I said indulgently, an amused parent. "Although I take a somewhat more psychological approach. These things are more metaphorical than actual to me."

"Maybe." She kicked up a trio of brown leaves; they whirled, settled back on the ground. "But I seen her too, you know."

"I'm sorry?"

"Adele," Truevine said. "Your great-grandmother. I seen her in there too, in the crypt amongst the others. You want me to keep my ways so you won't be the only one of our kind left on Blue Mountain."

We walked the rest of the way in silence.

The ride back into town was, to my relief, primarily consumed by a discussion of food. Skidmore insisted we all ride to town together, mostly, I thought, so he could keep track of us. Andrews sat in front with the deputy, I tried to relax sitting in back with Truevine. Andrews put in an enthusiastic bid for Etta's. Skidmore didn't have time to eat.

"There's a fugitive loose, Dr. Andrews." Skid's voice was clipped, his ears a little red.

"Deputy Needle," Andrews explained archly, leaning over the seat and speaking to Truevine, "is running for office. He's more concerned with how things look than hospitality to a guest."

Nine times out of ten that sort of kidding would have provoked a smile from Skidmore. This, alas, proved the tenth time.

Brakes squealed, pulling the squad car to the side of the road; Skid slammed the transmission into park.

"You're on vacation," Skid said to Andrews, tightly coiled. "I understand that. But a man's been murdered, Dev's been shot, my wife's brother got hung up by his neck, and there's three hundred bodies in my backyard. If I'm short on manners, pick any one of those as my excuse. But if you bring up my election one more time, I'll put you in the jailhouse and come up with a reason to keep you there. Are we clear?"

"Absolutely," Andrews sputtered, face drained of all color.

The rest of the drive was dead quiet.

In that stillness I took a moment to reflect. On many occasions I'd seen old Sheriff Maddox exhibit such angry behavior, but this eruption was something of a rarity for Skidmore. For the first time I worried that being sheriff would not be the best thing for my oldest friend.

The deputy allowed Truevine to talk with Able while he tried to figure if he wanted to arrest her. Andrews and I slipped out for a bite at Etta's. We were both as curious as we were hungry but reasoned that asking questions in front of Skidmore would only exacerbate the dark mood. Skid allowed us to leave only after we promised to return within half an hour's time.

Etta's place was unusually slow. We walked past her into the kitchen. Her white eyebrows fluttered. I found fresh yellow wax beans, bright cold beets, country fried steak, just enough to tide me over. Andrews on the other hand heaped his plate: fried chicken, chicken and dumplings, stewed apples, black-eyed peas, buttered grits, chopped greens, a dab of sweet potato casserole on top. He was barely able to manage his iced tea glass.

We took a table by the window. He somehow managed to eat a million miles an hour and still talk.

"I've had it," he fumed. "There we are, the murderer in our grasp, and we trek back to town so Deputy Dawg can validate his own gestalt. Meanwhile, the scarecrow is halfway to Donegal or whatever the gold town is called."

"Dahlonega."

"Either we chuck it," he went on, "or we get back up there as soon as I'm done eating and catch the bastard ourselves so I can have some peace in my vacation!"

"I guess it is a little disconcerting to think about all those people roaming the hills around my house," I said calmly, forkful of wax beans in hand, "while we're watching old movies on television and drinking illegal liquor."

"Damn right," he affirmed, biting into his chicken leg. "Creeps me out. Like maggots crawling on those dead bodies."

"All right, first," I stopped him, putting down my fork, "I'm eating. And second, those people who live in the cemetery are hardly maggots."

"They don't *live* there," he shot back, in a clearly derisive imitation of the scarecrow. "They only stay a month or so."

"My point is—"

"Why isn't your point," he interrupted, "to finish your meal and go get the scarecrow?"

"Because he didn't do it," I said simply.

"Of course he did it." Andrews shook his head. "You're the one who came up with the genius idea that Billy was wearing Harding's clothes, and Billy certainly didn't get up and take them off Harding himself. Scarecrow is the big brother figure; he's the one who did it."

"He's the one who took the clothes," I agreed, "but he's not the one who killed Harding."

"You're not back to Able or Truevine?" He looked wildly out the window. "I'm really tired of this. And, incidentally, how are you going to have a happy ending if the young lovers did it?"

"It's not a play, Winton."

Startled by the uncharacteristic use of his first name, he stopped eating. "Well, of course it's a play. It's a perfect Shakespearean construct: the old lovers, Hek and June; mythic lovers, Davy and Eloise; broken lovers, your great-grandparents; false love, Rud; righteous young love: Truevine and Able."

"Nicely worked out," I sighed, "and I'm impressed you remember all the names and relationships, but you're making a perfect phenomenological mistake."

"Oh, here we go," he groused, shoving his nearly empty plate away from him.

"Seriously," I went on, "you're ordering events and relationships according to your own perspective. You're making them fit your preconceived notions rather than letting them be what they are."

"And what are they?"

"They are what they are," I assured him. "I'm not making the same mistake as you."

"And how does this Let-It-Be attitude get us any answers or any action?"

"If you're finished eating," I said, taking a final swig of iced tea and standing, "I'll show you."

"Christ." He shoveled in the last large forkful of chicken and dumplings, chased it with a loud gulp of iced tea, and shot out of his chair. "You know who killed Harding once and for all. You're positive."

"I'm pretty sure." I dropped a twenty onto the table. "Luncheon is on me."

"You're damned right it is, Sherlock."

The afternoon wasn't exactly warm, but the sun had done its best to heat the asphalt; the air didn't bite. The sky was pale, dotted here and there with black birds, dark pinches of night, reminders of the sky's true color.

"Damn it." Andrews stopped short. "Your truck is still at the mortuary."

"It is."

"So where are we going?"

"We have to get Skid," I said, heading for the storefront station. "We promised."

"Do we have to?" Andrews fell in beside me. "He was mean to me."

Skidmore was still at his desk, head in hands, exactly as we'd left him, staring at blank paperwork.

He lifted his face at the sound of the door.

"Eat?" he said.

"Did," I answered.

"Good?"

"Mm."

"Andrews?" He looked back down at the papers. "Sorry I snapped. Don't usually do it."

"I know you don't," Andrews responded, as kind a voice as I'd ever heard in his mouth. "Nothing for which to apologize at all, you know. Entirely my fault."

"No," Skid began.

"Do you mind if I interrupt the Benevolent Society," I interjected, "with a spot of relevance? I think I'll go back to the cemetery one last time, round up Harding's killer. Would you like to come along?"

Skid sighed, leaned back, bore into me with a gaze that threatened a return of behavior for which he had just apologized. "Say what?"

"Leave the girl back there with Able," I continued, "get into your squad car, and let's go."

"Who are we going for?" he wanted to know.

"I'd rather not say until I have to." How often had that sentence been uttered in my family, my town?

"Dev!" Skid's exasperation spat out the syllable. "I'm afraid this is one of those times—"

"Do you ever remember a time," I interrupted, "when you didn't want to tell people, Andrews for instance, some fact or other because you were afraid they might mess it all up?"

"Hey," Andrews objected.

"Uh," Skid growled.

For a second I felt certain Deputy Needle hovered on the brink of tossing me into the cell next to Able. But after that second passed, he blew out an exhausted breath, stood, spoke to the deputy nearest the cells, hoisted up his pants, and shoved past me out the door.

"He'll make a great sheriff," Andrews whispered, watching him go.

"That's just what I'm afraid of," I agreed, following Skid out the door.

Seventeen

Rud's cabin was locked, no one home. Skid had parked the squad car close to the door; he and I stood on the porch.

"We really need Rud for this?" Skid said finally.

Rud's porch was swept spotless. The porch roof rafters didn't have a single spiderweb; even the doorknob seemed polished hard, as if November wind had scrubbed it clean.

"Yes," I said slowly, "we do."

Andrews sat in the car, glaring. He was clearly ready to go home, the adventure done, cognac set before him in front of a cozy fire. Following through to the bitter end was never his forte; I'd told him so many times. Directing a play, he'd lose interest a day or two before technical rehearsals; writing a paper, he'd often have his secretary pull the last pages together, like a doctor at the end of a strenuous operation: "Nurse, close for me, would you?" Didn't keep him from being brilliant, just kept him from being entertained by endings.

"We'll be done in a little while," I assured him impatiently.

"Didn't you say the same thing yesterday just before you got shot?"

"Sh." Bad luck to bring the subject up in a graveyard, I thought.

"Where to?" Skidmore's tether was short as well. It was clear he was frustrated by the way I was handling the situation.

"Close to the Angel of Death," I pronounced, "we'll find the grave of Truevine's parents. And not to be dramatic, but would you mind taking the safety off your pistol?"

"Do I have to go?" Andrews slumped in the backseat of the car.

"We might need a little rugby-style help," I encouraged him.

"With that tired old bag of bones?"

"Come on," I urged. "You don't want to sit in the cold car when you can have a nice warm jaunt."

"*Jaunt.* That's your choice, that word?"

"Would you just—"

"Fine," he interrupted, throwing the door open and heaving himself out of the car with massive effort. "Let's go."

Some of the sheen on the first day of November was wearing thin. Many of the saints, their work done, had gone home. The sky was losing the edge of its former luster; the sun was on a downward turn. Though it was still a lovely afternoon, the air now held certain promise of night and a November not far from snow, gray days that lasted a few hours attached to cold nights that went on forever.

The yard was quiet, no wind. Weeds stood their ground, seemed less yielding than the headstones, each one a bookmark in the archives of our town: a child, a mayor, a man no one knew.

The Angel of Death came into view.

"I think it would be best," I said softly, "if we went separate paths to Davy and Eloise."

"Surround him?" Andrews asked wearily.

"I'll go straight in," I continued.

"This is very irritating." Skidmore was grinding his teeth. But he'd also taken out his gun, safety off. "I'll go right."

"Christ on a cross," Andrews muttered, and headed left.

The grave site was fifty feet away, longer for the other two as they made their way around other headstones and the few smaller crypts that lay between us and our goal.

I went straight for the Angel.

From behind its wings, a darkness of crows suddenly ascended, tattering the air with their loud complaint. One crow was an omen, ten a warning—something that, to my peril, I did not heed.

Instead I stepped up my pace, fearing what had attracted the crows. Rounding the statue, I stumbled, fell forward, grabbed the stone hem of the Angel's garment to steady myself, and came face-to-face with the scarecrow.

He lay on his back, head haloed in syrupy blood. Crows had already pecked out one eye. The back of his head was caved in, a rotten pumpkin, black and oozing. His lone eye stared toward heaven, a thousand questions still lurking just behind the pupil.

Before I could straighten and call out, the black dog was on me. It was snarling softly; no intention of warning or scaring me, it wanted a kill. Teeth were bared at my neck, eyes wide and wild.

The force of its lunge knocked me backward against the Angel; my hands instinctively wrapped around the dog's throat, praying to keep its sharp teeth from my skin. Saliva streamed downward from its mouth; claws flailed trying to knock me to the ground.

I tried to yell for help, but I couldn't catch my breath. I was aware of snorting short involuntary fear noises, adrenaline-fueled; they weren't loud enough to bring aid.

I turned hard to my left, hoping to slam the animal against the statue, knock it off me. The dog had other ideas. Thrashing, it pushed off me, landed on all fours, crouched ready to leap again.

Steadying my back against the Angel, I raised both hands high and shook my palms, growled a guttural curse that didn't seem mine. The dog's eyes darted upward, making certain I had nothing in my hands. I took that opportunity to kick its head.

Not connecting as solidly as I would have liked, my boot caught the underside of the jaw. Enough to surprise the thing, it shifted backward, whining.

"Help!" My verbal skills returned.

The dog recovered.

It lowered, ready to pounce. I bent at the knees as well, a larger imitation of its dark posture. I unzipped my leather jacket as quickly as I could, tore at the arms, slung it around like a whip, snapped the dog's face.

It was taken aback—for perhaps a second. It snarled, readying to strike.

I pulled the jacket to me, held it open wide.

"Come on," I whispered hoarsely, staring the thing in the eye, flashing telepathic threats.

It leapt, flying the air, mouth snapping, teeth like white coffin nails.

The black bulk hit me hard. If I hadn't been backed by the Angel, I would have gone to the ground. As it happened, I was able to wrap my jacket around the dog's head so it couldn't see, lock my arms around it in an embrace so tight it couldn't breathe. I used every bit of fear and rage I could muster from the depths of my unconscious bestial heritage, squeezing, holding fast.

The animal flailed wildly, trying to loose itself. I was breathing like a broken pump organ, gasping, swallowing, barely able to stand.

Skid must have appeared about then, throwing himself at me, sandwiching the dog in between us. I heard something snap, and the dog gave out a muffled howl. I realized then that I might kill the thing and let go my hold.

The dog was barely moving. Skid took a step back and the dog tumbled to the ground, rolling out of my jacket onto its side, panting. Its tongue lay out one side of its mouth.

"Dev?" Skid's voice was panicky.

"Am I bleeding?" I said, dazed. "Did it get me?"

He make a quick check. "Seems okay." He looked down at the dog. "My God. Did it do this?"

"Do what?" I still couldn't catch my breath.

"The . . ." His eyes drifted to the corpse of the scarecrow.

"No," I told him quickly. "I think, in fact, that's why the dog attacked me. It was trying to protect . . ." but I was breathing so hard I couldn't finish the sentence.

Skid reached down and got my jacket off the ground. "Better put this on. You're hot now, but you could get cold again quick, shock."

"Did we kill the dog?" I asked shakily.

"Naw. I think I busted a rib when I flung myself on him, though."

"What the hell?" Andrews had appeared only to stop short.

Dead man in his own blood, wheezing dog at my feet, Skid and I gasping like maniacs—Andrews was right to stand back.

A brief explanation satisfied him for the moment when I made it clear to all that our task was not complete.

"The person responsible for this," I said, putting my jacket back on, "is still around."

"There *is* someone over by the grave," Andrews confirmed, his voice more animated than it had been all afternoon. "I saw something moving there before I heard all your commotion."

"We've scared him off by now," Skid said, sighing between clenched teeth.

"Not really," I said, zipping my jacket and heading toward the Deveroe plot. "He can't leave. He doesn't have anywhere else to go."

A dark figure in a light coat knelt on the grassy grave, cheek pressed against the stone, eyes a thousand lifetimes away, fingers absently twining a bit of rosy thread.

"She belonged to me once," he told us as we approached. "Threw her away. I wouldn't mind being dead."

"Come on, Rud." Skidmore's voice was gentle, but the pistol was still in his hand.

"I wondered when you'd finally come for me." He didn't move, but his eyes darted my way. "Knew when I saw you nosing around this grave the other night—when Able nearly got hung."

"What are we doing?" Andrews asked me uncertainly.

"I believe we're about to arrest Rudyard Pinhurst for the murder of his cousin," Skidmore said, his voice still soothing. "You are confessing, aren't you, Rud?"

Rud put the thread in the outside pocket of his coat, didn't stand.

"You saw Andrews and me up here that night," I went on. "You were watching. You didn't care if Able got killed."

"Not much."

"It wouldn't help," I told him. "She still wouldn't love you."

"I know." His voice was a gasp, the last air forced from a closing coffin lid.

"Rud did it?" Andrews jutted his chin, brow knit. "And you knew this?"

"Rud did a lot of things, I was pretty sure," I said. "He saw us up here the other night, for example, and thought we were already on to him. Is that right?"

"Guilt." Rud shrugged. "My perennial undoing."

"Rudyard killed Harding." Andrews took a step toward us, still trying to get his mind straight.

"The night you and I saw the Deveroe boys over there trying to hang Able," I said, eyes on Rud, "Rud saw us. After we left he spent time digging up my great-grandfather's grave. Still right?"

"I thought it was a particular stroke of genius," he answered, "yes."

"You mean he remembered the stories about Conner Devilin," Skid guessed. "Not a person in this town's been able to escape the Devilin family history."

"Rud thought I'd be thrown if the little community of vagrants he sheltered had something to do with me," I said, "so he took a chance, found the lily in my great-grandfather's grave, amazingly enough, set up that pile of rubbish in the corner of the crypt where everyone camped. My guess is he also scratched my great-grandmother's name in the rock, got the others to go along with him."

"They all helped build the monument," he said, smiling. "They had fun, especially May. She's good."

"That she is," I agreed.

"You weren't taken in?" Andrews asked.

"I was." I folded my arms; afternoon was turning to evening, and a chill rose from the stones. "Until I realized, much later, that the whole thing was held together by old shoelaces. That started me thinking."

"They'd all just got new sneakers." Andrews rolled his head. "And the sculpture thing was made out of old shoelaces. Christ, how did you figure that out?"

"May played for both sides," was all I would say to Rud.

He was past caring.

"Now get to the part where the caretaker kills the mortician," Andrews rolled out, enthusiasm growing with his ironic tone.

"I don't have a life," Rud said slowly, coming to his feet. "I have a shadow. I live between this world and the next. The reason for my state is that I betrayed a young girl who believed me. I deserve what I got. She's a simple girl, took me at my word. I took advantage of her, as I believe the novels of a previous century might say, and I married someone else. I didn't know she was a witch who would put a curse on me. It affected my mind, my face, my posture. Now I look like this."

Rud held his hands wide, a mockery of the crucifixion. He looked sixty, his face deep-ridged, his eyes dead, thin as a skeleton, stoop-shouldered, bent at the knee. Had I not seen a splinter of myself in him, he would not have been human.

"You invented the *Adele* community, like, two days ago," Andrews said, still stuck, "just to throw Dev off the track?"

"It almost worked." He let his arms fall to his sides.

"It might well have, of course," I informed him, "except for the fact that it wasn't necessary; it was only a distraction. I hadn't come for you at all. I was looking for Girlinda Needle's brother."

"Able," Rud growled, that name a curse.

"And you killed your own cousin," Andrews went on.

"It was dark," Rud snapped. "I didn't know who it was."

"That's not entirely true. You thought it was Able," I said. "You heard the argument at the church, lurking in the shadows as you always are, constantly following Truevine."

"Following Truevine?" Andrews echoed.

"It's my guess that Rud has been Truevine's unseen companion for several years," I explained.

"I prefer the word *guardian*," he said plainly. "My watchful eye increased recently, as a matter of fact."

"He follows her," I continued, "partly to protect her, if he says so, but mostly out of obsession. He stalks her, half-hoping for . . . what should we call it, Rud? Redemption?"

"Let's leave that to the court psychiatrist, why don't we?" he sneered.

"It's also my surmise that Truevine was aware of his presence in some way," I went on. "She told me she felt someone was watching over her, but she grew increasingly uncomfortable about it."

Rud's face lowered.

"At any rate, he saw someone attack Truevine on the path close to my house," I said.

"She was wearing one of Able's big old flannel shirts," Skid interjected. "She told me, told you too. *That's* how thread from Able's clothes got under Harding's fingernails: when Harding attacked her."

"The fiber evidence." Andrews struggled to remember.

"Without thinking about who it was, or caring," I went on, glaring at Rud, "you murdered her attacker."

"Hit him with a piece of gravestone," Rud said, lifting his head, a scratch of a smile at the corner of his mouth, "that's in the pile underneath your lily. A little poetry."

"Very nice," I responded coldly.

"And the folks who stay there," Skid began, "went along with you . . ."

". . . because I told them to!" Rud snarled. "They do what I say."

"Okay." Skid had raised his pistol a little.

"Did they know what you'd done?" Andrews whispered.

Rud hissed an exasperated sigh, shook his head.

"Look, Truevine was dazed; Able came running up." I rubbed the backs of my arms, shivering. The air was hard and the adrenaline of my dog fight was dissipating. "You hid, realizing you hadn't killed Able. They had their scene and left; you made it to the bottom of the ravine, found Harding dead."

"He was hurting Tru." Rud's voice wavered. "I saved her life."

"I doubt that," I disagreed. "He wouldn't have harmed her. He was angry, but that was all. He's not capable of anything serious. Harding Pinhurst is a coward."

"Was," Andrews corrected softly.

Skid eyed Rud. "And what were you doing with a chunk of tombstone in your hand that far away from the graveyard?"

"Comes in handy in these woods," Rud answered, calming, "something like that. Had to scare away that damned dog of hers— on occasion."

"You killed the scarecrow too?" Andrews suddenly asked. "Why?"

"Let's save some of it for the police station," Skidmore told us all, pistol raised, pointing in the general direction of Rud's heart. "I'm sorry, Rud; I've got to cuff you. Turn around, do you mind?"

" 'Come, all you young men,' " Rud said, his eyes boring into mine, " 'take a warning by me.' What's the next line, Dr. Devilin?"

" 'When courting the girls,' " I finished for him, " 'don't be easy and free.' "

"How many songs begin with those lines?" he asked.

"Ten thousand," I told him. "Or more."

"And I didn't listen to a single one. That's the problem with your discipline, you know." Rud turned around, hands behind his back, waiting for the cuffs. "No one pays attention to it anymore. It's useless."

Eighteen

By sundown Rud had officially confessed to the murders of Harding Pinhurst and an unknown vagrant. Skidmore had taken us by the mortuary to pick up my truck, allowed us to be present at his office for the show.

Rudyard Pinhurst turned out to be the most exhausted human being I'd ever heard, sitting at the table with us, picking at his fingernails, telling us the details of the week we'd all endured.

He had been shadowing Truevine Deveroe since his wife left him and he'd been forced into the caretaker's position by his uncle Jackson. With little to do but reflect, Rud had grown more bitter at his own bad choices. He knew about Truevine's love for Able; there was nothing he could do. He was dead to Blue Mountain.

Thursday night he heard the argument, followed the lovers, murdered his cousin, realized his mistake—all before the moon was up. Loathe to handle his relative any further, he went back to the cemetery, told the scarecrow to take care of the body. Instead the scarecrow chose to strip the body down to underwear so Billy could have more clothing—nice clothing, burial attire—and take Harding's wallet. He covered the body with dead leaves and left it. He'd been drinking.

Realizing Rud might eventually check the spot for the body or fearing it might otherwise be discovered, the scarecrow waited until late the next night. He went to the mortuary, where he knew from previous experience that three drunken boys would be waiting, ready for more work from Harding, digging, moving, covering dead bodies in the woods nearby. They were only moderately surprised to get instructions from a stranger. He told them where to find another body, that Harding himself would be there—he simply failed to mention these two entities would be one and the same. He shared a bounty of stolen alcohol with them until the night was almost gone.

They made such a commotion by the time they found Harding, were so amused by it all, that they woke me up. It turned out that they had been the ones to remove Harding's underwear. They thought it was funny—a final indignity for my childhood tormentor. Andrews and I came out, saw the body naked, called Skidmore, insisted that the boys stay put. They didn't care. They said they hadn't done anything wrong. They were too drunk to fully understand what was going on anyway.

When Rud discovered what had happened, he assumed that someone would uncover his crime, find him—a product of his own self-confessed phobia. He invented the *Adele* community, knowing from abundant town gossip how my family's ethos was often disturbing to me. The others in his little village went along out of fear or fun. Thank God May had played double agent, or at least dropped hints my way.

"You weren't taken in at all by the lily?" Skid asked while Rud gulped his fifth glass of water.

"Too fantastic," I told him. "Too far-fetched." But I avoided Andrews's expression. He'd been there when I'd seen the lily. He knew what seeing it had done to me.

Rud set down his water glass. "All right, there's more."

Skid sat back, glanced at the tape recorder to make sure it was still running.

"Uncle Jackson set me up in the cemetery," Rud began serenely, "and Harding at the mortuary. You see the connection. No questions about bodies. Jackson didn't want any more riffraff filling up our family graveyard because he didn't want to expand its boundaries. Harding was too stupid to do anything with them anyway. And Jackson had been working on his landfill scheme for years, setting things in place. I assume you know about that. Imagine if the state's garbage problem could be solved with one stroke. There it was: a single location between a mortuary and a cemetery where no business would locate or developer would ever build. Three hundred acres already owned by the state." He trailed off, reaching for his glass again.

"But why didn't Harding just dump the bodies into caskets, then?" Andrews asked, amazed at the story.

"Didn't you notice there was no embalming room at the mortuary?" Rud asked, as if Andrews were an idiot. "Harding pushed cremation. Imaginary, as it turns out. He didn't know a thing about that, just told everyone the crematorium was in the woods and no one was allowed, for health reasons, to visit. Inspectors and that sort of thing were all taken care of by Uncle Jackson. Anyone who wanted a casket and a funeral actually buried . . ."

". . . bags of red Georgia clay," I interrupted.

"Mainly useful for hiding the bodies in the woods." Rud saluted me with his glass, drank heartily. "But they were sometimes a substitute for the dearly departed, yes."

"But why?" Andrews whispered. "Wouldn't it have been just as easy—"

"Harding was a nimrod." Rud's turn to interrupt. He gulped water again. "That's not obvious?"

"If those woods turned into a landfill," Andrews said, slumping in his chair, "it would be even easier to dump the bodies there."

"You're beginning to see the beauty of the scheme," Rud agreed.

"But Jackson is insane," I insisted. "As much as Harding."

"Oh, completely," Rud said instantly. "In my opinion they're a product of the worst part of our family heritage. Bodies normal, dwarfish minds."

"And this Uncle Jackson is some sort of power broker or politician?" Andrews asked, confused.

"He's our congressman," Skid said, shaking his head.

"In the state house of representatives?" Andrews rubbed his forehead with both hands. "Of the state where I live?"

"Didn't we tell you that?" I asked.

"No!" Andrews fumed. "You think your own common knowledge extends to the world."

"It's a small-town foible," I agreed. "But Jackson Pinhurst is, indeed, our congressman. And the chief supporter of Skidmore's rival in the upcoming election."

"Cheer up." Skid patted Andrews once on the shoulder. "I'm pretty sure I can do something about that when it all comes out in the papers. Don't you think?"

"Georgia." Andrews had given up.

Neither of us wanted to point out to Skid how the events would help his campaign.

"Why did my skit fail to work on you, Dr. Devilin?" Rud's tone had grown mocking. "Too smart for the likes of me?"

"We first encountered the black dog," I said steadily, "sitting on my great-grandfather's grave. A nice coincidence. I later realized that the dog was sitting on freshly dug earth, not grass, not moss." I knew there was no explaining to anyone in the room that my great-grandmother had told me a ghost story that included a dead horse, tongue hanging out, lying on a freshly dug grave, and I put two and two together. Or had it been my own subconscious delivering me a message? Either way, there was no making sense of it in a police station.

"I covered it up better than that," Rud insisted, the arch edge gone from his voice.

"The dog, apparently, had other ideas," I suggested. "Or needs."

"Black dog piss on a fresh dug grave," Andrews chanted. "There's *got* to be some kind of folk crap about that."

"Or at least a verse of Vachel Lindsay," I suggested to Andrews.

"To conclude," Rud went on, the sneer returning to his words, "the person you call *Scarecrow* was concerned about his involvement with Harding's body, convinced you were visiting the crypt because of *him*. He wanted to return the wallet. Not the money, of course. He wanted to say he'd come across the body in his nightly scavenge, taken the clothes, knew nothing more. But I was certain he wouldn't be capable of withstanding any sort of interrogation. We argued, understandably. Things got out of hand. He called that damned dog on me and it made me mad. I didn't mean to hit the old man so hard. I did mean to kill the dog, though." His voice deepened. "Choked it with my bare hands. It was exhausting."

"You didn't kill that dog," Skid said, smiling. "Nothing can kill him, apparently. I called a vet to take care of him; he's fine."

Rud started to protest, but the light left his eyes; he let go a heavy sigh. "Is there anything else? I'd like to lie down."

That was that. Deputy Needle locked up Rudyard, let Able and Truevine go.

Papers were signed; small talk avoided larger issues. I was dying to ask Truevine a dozen questions, Skidmore only allowed me one while he finished up with Able.

"Why did you seal your house?" The glare of the fluorescent lights, bustle of office noise, made the question seem foolish even as it came out of my mouth.

"Sir?" She wrinkled her brow.

"You sealed your house recently," I insisted, "the stones under your porch."

"I don't know what you're talking about, Dr. Devilin," she stammered, a quick eye to Able. "Able's told me a dozen times that the dark shadow I seen following me these past weeks, it was just my imagination."

"You sealed your house against Rud," I whispered so no one else could hear.

"Didn't know it was Rud," she murmured, eyes down, "but I was scared."

"How did you know about the geothermal pockets?"

"What?"

"Who taught you to do that, with the stones?"

"Momma," she said, her face bright. "She done it several times to keep the boys in at night. Didn't work none too good, I reckon. They just went out the window."

Unfortunately, further investigation into Truevine Deveroe's craft was cut short. I still wanted to ask her how she'd gotten out of the

Carter crypt when Andrews and I had her cornered. All further questions would have to wait until my next visit to her home, tape recorder in hand.

Skid gathered us all together. An informal pact was made to keep mum about the homeless vagrants in our town cemetery. Skid promised to check in on May, but everyone was fairly certain she'd be gone. Only the dead would sleep up there that night.

When the deputy finally escorted Truevine to the door he spoke in no uncertain terms. "Ms. Deveroe, I want you to go round up your brothers. Tell them they didn't kill Dr. Devilin. I'm not too mad at them, but they got to come in so I can talk to them. You make them do it, right?"

"Yes, sir," she answered sweetly. "Thank you, Deputy. I didn't tell you what they said last night."

"About what?" Skid tensed.

"They're thinking of taking up mortuary," she said, amused herself. "Studying to be morticians, since the town needs one now."

We didn't laugh at her as much as with her, I'd like to believe. The thought of the Deveroe boys running our funeral parlor seemed the perfect, if hilarious, end to that particular saga.

Truevine offered us one final, enigmatic smile, slipped out the door, and was gone up the street, a warmer breeze in the cooling air.

"Now then, Able," Skid said, blocking his brother-in-law's egress, "you get home, wash up, come on over to dinner with your sister and me. Leave Truevine be for the evening." He stepped aside. "It's not a request."

"See you at seven," Able acquiesced.

"You'uns come too," Skid said to Andrews and me.

"No." Andrews had finally had enough. He scanned the western horizon. "I think I'll head back to Atlanta."

"What for?" Skid was genuinely surprised. "You ain't had your vacation."

"I think I've endured about as much *vacation* in this town," he replied, heavy-lidded, "as I can handle. I have to go home to rest."

"You don't want to drive at night," I argued as we stepped out the door. "Wait until morning."

He pulled the coat around his neck, headed for my truck. "Isn't Lucinda back by now?"

"She is," I said slowly. "Probably."

"Wouldn't you rather have dinner with her tonight—alone?"

"Ah."

"Exactly."

"Sorry about the vacation thing," I said, climbing in the cab.

"I ought to have learned by now," he said, slamming his door, "that a visit to your town is a trip to Salvador Dalí's amusement park: the rides are treacherous and make very little sense."

"Still." I cranked the engine. "You did use the word *amusement*."

There was no talking Andrews out of his departure. He'd be back in Atlanta for a late dinner. As we stood by his car in the failing light I considered telling him about the dream, or visit, from my great-grandmother, how she'd been the one to tell me, twice, that Rud was the murderer. Once she had mentioned *la belle dame sans merci* for Rud's motive, and several times her story told me that the blacksmith saved the girl from her ghostly suitor. It had taken me a while, but the message became clear.

"You seem healthier than the last time I visited," he said sincerely, hand on my upper arm. "I think being back in the mountains and having a steady girlfriend might be doing your mental state some good. Not that there's any hope for you, of course."

"Thanks." There was my decision. Best keep the dream to myself, and a nagging complicity with Truevine's ways.

"Call Lucinda right now," he said, climbing in behind the wheel of his Honda. "Let her know you're glad she's back."

I waved until his car disappeared around the bend. Night noise stirred, filling the stage. The sky turned more Parrish than robin's egg. A star blinked; its darker cousin starling drew across the sky; then a flock of them headed south. Tree frogs, still singing despite approaching winter, started up. The temperature dropped like a curtain.

I suddenly took the steps two at a time, bounded into the warm house, turned on every light downstairs, and grabbed the kitchen phone, jacket still on.

It rang three times, then: her voice.

"Hello?"

"Lucinda!"

"Fever!" She was happy to hear me on the other end.

"You're back."

"Just."

"You are not going to believe," I began, "what-all happened while you were gone."

"And you won't believe," she countered lightly, "what I learned about cholesterol at this conference. You need to think about a vegetarian diet. You know they call it *Mediterranean;* we need to discuss it. I'm not having you get a heart attack."

"Lucy," I tried again.

"And you can't imagine how Birmingham's grown. I took pictures."

Before I could interrupt her a third time with my news, I saw something moving out in the darkness barely beyond the porch light.

"Hold on, would you?" I said suddenly.

I turned off the kitchen lamps and stood to the side of the window, peering out, holding the phone to my chest. Someone was out there, walking slowly past my house. I thought at first to call out, but after a moment it was clear the figure was only passing by, a stranger on a stroll, and would be gone down the road in the direction of the ravine in short order. I let out a breath.

"Fever?" Lucinda asked, her voice tinny in the receiver.

I lifted it to my ear once more. "Sorry. Nothing."

"You said something happened while I was gone. Is everything all right?"

"I'd really like to have dinner with you," I said quickly. "Could we do that?"

"All right," she said, a little taken aback. "When?"

"Right now. I'll come over; we'll drive around to the Dillard House."

"You surely are," she said, more surprised, "what's the term? A *live wire* tonight."

"That I am," I assured her happily. "I'll be right over?"

"Well, good," she said haltingly.

"Really glad you're back. I missed you."

"I missed you too." She started to say something else, took in a breath, changed her mind, it seemed. "See you in a minute."

We hung up. I should have showered, changed, maybe shaved again, but I didn't want to take any more time than was essential in getting to her door. I was slowly realizing just how much I'd missed her, and it seemed I might pop a blood vessel if I didn't tell her soon.

I left the lights on, zipped my jacket tight, locked the door behind me, walked quickly to the truck.

The woods all around me, dark now, were full. High wind, black birds, clacking branches, musical frogs, bats, weeds whispering low—here and there, a possible footfall. The night was alive, a different world from the day. Creatures of all sorts were abroad.

Some life walks in the sun, certain of a path made clear by light. Other things thrive in darkness, afraid of scrutiny or too shy for noon.

Occasionally a door is opened between these two worlds: dark beings roam the morning; bright souls are plunged into night. But the door doesn't stay open long, at peril of those few who discover, too late, that they are trapped on the wrong side. Some who were meant to live in the sun turn stunted and pale by moonlight; nocturnal spirits likewise burn in the sun's harsh eye.

I hesitated, climbing into my truck, peering down the road where the stranger had walked, imagining it might be May headed south for warmer nights. I found myself hoping we would see her again when the year opened its door to the promise of spring, rebirth of growing things, new mornings. I would discover the next day that my grandfather's lily was gone from the group crypt and invent a scenario where May took it, pinned it to clasp the rag of June's old wedding dress, another talisman for her, proof that somewhere in the world people actually had loved each other.

The truck started up, headlights a silver dagger against the night. I turned the wheel south, toward Lucinda.

Names are important, I thought as I eased the truck onto the road. *Hers means "clear light."*

The moon had risen past the treetops by the time I pulled up to her door. It seemed to hover directly over her roof, plaiting silver everywhere—covering her house in white lilies.